André Caroff's
MADAME ATOMOS

The Terror of
Madame Atomos

André Caroff's
MADAME ATOMOS

The Terror of
Madame Atomos

Translated by
Brian Stableford

A Black Coat Press Book

Acknowledgements: Thanks to Françoise Carpouzis & Catherine Losserand.

Visit our website at www.blackcoatpress.com

Table of Contents

Introduction

André Caroff was the nom-de-plume of André Car-pouzis, born February 28, 1924, and who died on March 9, 2009.

Carpouzis was born in the 6th *arrondissement* of Paris to a Greek father, Thomas Carpouzis, and an Auvergnate mother, Lucienne Michel. He was christened after his paternal grandfather who had been a farmer in Smyrna. His father was a sailor who met André's mother in Lyon; the young couple eventually settled in Paris.

Young André spent a good part of his childhood with his maternal grandmother, Esther, in Saint-Raphael in the South of France, where his parents worked at the Hotel Continental. Later, they worked as exotic dancers—the *Ballets Russes* being, at the time, greatly popular. Lucienne's grandmother, on the Breton side of the family, was named "Caroff," so they adopted that Breton name, which sounded Russian, as their stage name.

In the 1930s, while André was being raised by his grandmother, the Caroffs became rich and famous and bought their own cabaret in the posh 16th *arrondissement* of Paris.

As World War II approached, however, they lost the cabaret and had to move to more modest lodgings in the 9th *arrondissement*. André then moved in permanently with his parents. His mother, who went by the stage name of "Josy," became a snake dancer and a lion tamer at the Cirque Medrano in Paris, while his father, more prosaically, went to work at the Renault car factory, before being drafted into the French army. André, who had begun an apprenticeship as a sign painter, became a messenger for the city. His grandmother Esther read tarot and made enough money to keep the family financially afloat.

During the German occupation of France, André's father was diagnosed with tuberculosis and died in 1941. Six months later, his grandmother also died. André was 17 and his mother 38. A year later, André married Raymonde Hudry, a friend of the family. The young couple (with André's mother in tow) moved to the 15th *arrondissement*. Soon after, André was arrested by the Germans for having tried to steal a truck carrying canned goods. He did time at the notorious prison of La Santé, where his forced cohabitation with all kinds of thieves and villains later proved very useful when he wrote crime novels.

The SS officers had organized a brothel using young male prisoners dressed as women. A few months later, when André was assigned to serve at the brothel, dressed in drag, he and another prisoner escaped while in transit.

In the meantime, André's mother had moved to Pigalle, where she earned money doing pseudo-Indian dances in cabarets. André and his wife moved to the countryside, where André worked on a dam construction in the Cantal region. Then, in 1943, André worked as a foreman for the German "Organization Todd" that built V2 rocket launchers in Normandy. At night, he worked in concert with the local resistance to sabotage the site. Meanwhile, his wife, under the stage name of Caroll, danced at the Casino de Paris.

In 1945, as the war was about to end, André was drafted into the French army, was wounded in a battle against the Germans, and ended up in a military hospital.

After the war, the couple worked at the Casino de Paris, then at the Theatre Modano, and later at the Folies-Bergères. André appeared as an extra in a number of films, then took a series of forgettable jobs, including selling encyclopedias door-to-door, but eventually preferred the freedom of being his own boss and became a taxi driver. That was when he began to write and publish short stories in the daily newspaper, *Le Parisien Libéré*.

In 1956, soon after the birth of their first daughter, Françoise, Publisher Fleuve Noir, founded in 1949 by Armand de Caro and Guy Krill for the purpose of publishing a great variety of popular literature (espionage, crime novels, science fiction, horror, etc.) moved its offices to Boulevard Saint-Marcel, across the street from where André lived. He began submitting novels to them and, after four years of effort, his first novel, *Névrose*, was published in the *Angoisse* horror imprint of Fleuve Noir under the non-de-plume of André Caroff.[1]

André Caroff quickly became one of Fleuve Noir's major authors, publishing novels in their *Spécial-Police*, *Espionnage* and *Angoisse* imprints. He wrote 17 *Angoisse* novels, of which the most famous were his series featuring the sinister Madame Atomos, which has since become a cult classic in France, and was recently reissued by Black Coat Press' sister imprint, Rivière Blanche. Prior to creating Madame Atomos, Caroff had

---

[1] More information about Editions Fleuve Noir and their *Angoisse* imprint can be found in our introduction to Kurt Steiner's *Ortog* (Black Coat Press, ISBN 9781935558286), also initially published by Fleuve Noir.

penned the adventures of François Petit, a sociopath *à la* Hannibal Lecter, visibly inspired by the real-life French serial killer, Doctor Petiot. (Petit appeared in three novels.)

When Fleuve Noir cancelled its *Angoisse* imprint, in 1974, Caroff moved to *Anticipation* for which he penned 34 novels until 1989. His series included the adventures of a futuristic space trooper named Rod (four novels) and the series Abel 6666 (eight novels), which took place in a computerized future. For the *Espionnage* imprint, he wrote a series of spy thrillers featuring the character of super agent Bonder; many of these often contained minor sci-fi or horror elements.

Two of Caroff's novels for the *Spécial-Police* crime thrillers imprint were eventually filmed, including one which starred Alain Delon.[2] Caroff also wrote 18 made-for-television movies, 45 radio plays, and, with Daniele, his second wife, over 500 romance novels under the pseudonyms of Daniel Aubry and Danièle Thomas.

Amusingly, his mother (Josy), when informed of André's success as a writer, decided that she, too, could write horror novels and ended up having six novels published by *Angoisse* under the pseudonym of José Michel.

At the time of his death André Carpouzis was again writing science fiction novels for Rivière Blanche, having embarked on a vast, post-cataclysmic saga.

The saga of Madame Atomos is comprised of 17 volumes published between 1964 and 1970, with a final novel, which had remained unpublished at the time, eventually coming out in 1979.

---

[2] Another of Caroff's thriller is being filmed in 2010.

André Caroff understood right from the start that, in order to be both credible and different, his mastermind villainess had to be different from Sax Rohmer's Doctor Fu Manchu or Ian Fleming's megalomaniacal Ernst Stavro Blofeld. He succeeded beyond his wildest hopes with Madame Atomos.

Madame Atomos does not seek to conquer the world or assert the supremacy of Oriental values like an old "Yellow Peril" villain. Her goals are simple: she seeks revenge upon the United States for the nuclear holocausts of Hiroshima and Nagasaki which cost her the lives of her loved ones. The morality of dropping the two atom bombs to speed up the end of the war has always been more debated outside of America. The irony is that Madame Atomos is just as much a creation of America as Osama bin Laden, because she is the evil embodiment of the consequences of our mistakes. Her fanatical hatred of America and obsessive desire for bloody revenge make her the first fictional terrorist with whom there are no possibilities of dialogue or compromise. In that, she is truly a ground-breaking character, more relevant today than ever.

Jean-Marc Lofficier

ANDRÉ CAROFF

LA SINISTRE MADAME ATOMOS

ANGOISSE

Editions
"FLEUVE NOIR"

THE SINISTER MADAME ATOMOS

Chapter I

Tac, tap...tac, tap...tac, tap....

It was as regular as the beat of a Diesel motor, and the road-sweeper ended up turning round to see what it was. The rain had been falling all morning, and the deserted streets were infinitely dismal. Sweeping miles of tarmac all one's life is not exactly enjoyable, but when it is necessary to do it in solitude, without saying a word, it is truly intolerable—so the road-sweeper leaned on his broom and pivoted on his heel.

The man coming along the street was limping on his right leg. He was bare-headed, with no overcoat, but—in spite of his white hair and livid complexion, and the cold and the rain—he stood up straight as he moved forward. He did not look at the edge of the sidewalk he was following, the bare trees, the lamp-posts or the pools of water.

The road-sweeper blew on his hands and smiled amiably. "Lousy weather!" he remarked.

The old man passed within three feet, stiff and icy.

Tac, tap...tac, tap...tac, tap....

The man's heels were steel-tipped and the loose lace of his left shoe was wriggling like a worm. His hands hung down by his sides, curiously motionless, without the slight swing that walking provokes, and his feet only seemed to part company with the ground at the cost of a fantastic effort. He was making rapid progress, however, in a jerky but effective fashion, seemingly insensible to his water-soaked garments and keeping his gaze fixed directly ahead.

The road-sweeper watched him cross the street, then turned his head as he heard the soft purring of the black car that was moving slowly, following the sidewalk. It was an enormous old Chevrolet with rusty chrome work, driven by a small yellow man in a felt hat, the rim of which hid half his face.

Further on, the old man turned in the direction of the town center, and the road-sweeper lost sight of him. Shortly afterwards, the Chevrolet changed direction in its turn and disappeared, releasing a puff of grey smoke from the corroded orifice of its exhaust-pipe.

The road-sweeper gazed at the cloud momentarily as the wind drew it out into a thread, then lit his cigarette-end and stoically resumed sweeping the greasy surface.

It as ten o'clock in the morning; the month of January was ending and people who had no reason to go out were staying indoors, by the fireside. It was very cold in Chinook, Montana.

Tac, tap…tac. tap….

The cashier darted a glance at the little old man who had just come in, saw that he was carrying a large suitcase and that he was completely soaked, and thought that a man of that age ought to take better care of himself.

The bank was almost empty. Apart from the cashier, there were five employees, all hunched over their work, and Mr. Linding, the manager, who could be seen behind his desk in a room whose door was ajar.

Harold, the cashier, resumed counting the wad of notes that Mr. Belegs of Belegs, Hunter & Co. had just given him. His lips were moving silently.

"Eight hundred, eight fifty, nine hundred, nine fifty...."

"Come on, Charlie!" said Mr. Belegs, impatiently. "You know full well it's all there!" He was speaking softly, complaining out of habit, but the felt slightly intoxicated in the warmth of the gas central heating and was in no hurry to get back to the cold air of his office. He lit a cigar, and looked at the old man with the suitcase through the flame of his match. The latter was standing still, mid-way between the door and the counter, and a large pool of water was beginning to form around his bizarrely joined feet. He was staring at the wall, where there was a poster advising subscription to a share-issue, but Mr. Belegs was quite sure that he could not see it.

Suddenly, the old man turned slowly, and his dull eyes settled on Mr. Belegs, then slid to the cashier's skull and fixed again on the wad of notes.

Mr. Belegs got such a bad feeling that he removed his cigar from his mouth, clenched his fist and wedged himself firmly on his feet, exactly as if the old man represented an immediate threat—imprecise, but certain.

Suddenly, Harold stopped counting and lifted his head, at the same time as the other employees. Mr. Linding appeared on the threshold of his office and removed his spectacles.

No one had said anything. Nothing had happened. The little old man had not budged. It seemed, though, that the atmosphere had suddenly thickened, to the point that the smoke that had been rising from Mr. Belegs' cigar in eddying spirals a second before now seemed to be extended like a cotton thread between the cigar and the ceiling.

"Well?" said Mr. Linding. "What's up?" He had intended to say something more, but shut up when he realized that no one was listening. Then, suddenly, he no longer had any desire to speak or move.

Everyone was as motionless as the old man with the suitcase. Mr. Belegs noticed that a fly that had been buzzing around a moment before must have settled, since he could no longer hear it. Then he reminded himself that it was January, and that the buzz could not have come from a fly. Then he no longer thought anything. Along with the employees, Harold and Mr. Linding, he watched the little old man go behind the counter, limp up to the safe and open the door. There, the old man lifted the lid of the suitcase and calmly started filling it with wads of bills.

When the suitcase was full, the old man closed it carefully, went back around the counter, and left without a backward glance. The batten of the door swung back after he had passed through, but nothing moved in the silent room.

Thirty seconds passed. Then, suddenly, Mr. Linding uttered a howl. "It's a hold-up! The siren, quick!"

Each employee's right foot stamped on the alarm pedal, and the siren linked to the police station howled lugubriously while Mr. Linding and Mr. Belegs rushed outside.

"There he is!" shouted Mr. Belegs.

The old man was, indeed, lying in the gutter—but the suitcase stuffed with cash had disappeared.

The police car turned the corner at a crazy speed, and braked in front of the bank. Six armed policemen leapt out.

"It's a hold-up!" Mr. Linding repeated, feebly—and collapsed, at the same time as Mr. Belegs, who was still beside him.

The policemen tried to reanimate them, but quickly discovered that they were dead. Then they went into the bank, and discovered the corpses of the five employees and Charlie Harold, the cashier. They were still warm.

"What's your name?"

"Harry Diamond."

"Occupation?"

"Road-sweeper."

The inspector let himself down into his armchair. "Well, Mr. Diamond," he said, wearily, "you claim to know this man?"

The road-sweeper leaned forward and looked at the picture of the old man with white hair. "It's definitely him," he said, "but I never said I knew him. I was just in the middle of sweeping when he passed by…."

"What time was this?" the inspector interjected.

"Ten o'clock in the morning."

"This morning?"

"Of course. It had been raining since first light, and this guy comes strolling through the flood without as much as a hat…."

"Where were you when you saw him?"

"Roosevelt Avenue."

"Where did he come from and which way was he going?"

"He was coming from the train station, heading for the town center."

"Had you ever seen him before?"

"No—nor the rust bucket that was following him."

The inspector started. "Are you certain of that?"

"And how! It was an old Chevy, driven by a little yellow chap with a felt hat pulled down over his mug."

"Yellow? Chinese? Japanese?"

"One of those. They all look the same to me. Then again, I say that, but maybe he was just suntanned."

The inspector made a sweeping gesture. "Let's get back to the Chevrolet, Mr. Diamond. What did it look like?"

"Black, with rusty hub-caps and a moth-eaten exhaust-pipe. I mean, it had done it's time! It was pumping smoke like all the devils in hell. It must have dated back to the War of Secession."

"You didn't notice its license plate?"

"No."

The inspector looked at the group of motionless detectives, and then returned his attention to the road-sweeper. "This man," he said, pointing to the picture the newspapers had published. "Did anything in particular strike you about him?"

Harry twisted his cap in his large hands. "Well, he said, "I thought it was peculiar...."

"What?"

"To begin with, he had a limp in his right leg; then again, when I spoke to him, he didn't even look at me."

"What did you say to him?"

"Oh, nothing special. It was raining, so I said 'Lousy weather', or something like that. There was no one about and I was bored. There's nothing odd...."

"So," the inspector cut in, "he didn't look at you and didn't answer you. Apart from that, Mr. Diamond?"

"Well, apart from that, he was as white as a sheet and as stiff as a broom-handle." He laughed briefly, rubbed his hands and added: "And I know my broom-handles!"

The inspector contrived a tight smile, and lit a cigarette. "That's fine, Mr. Diamond—I don't need you anymore."

The road-sweeper got up and left the room, feeling a certain sense of relief. The office had seemed a trifle airless.

As soon as the door had closed behind him, the inspector made a gesture. "Sit down, gentlemen."

The four men obeyed, the feet of chairs scraping the floor.

"Sullivan?" said the inspector.

The man consulted his notebook. "Black Chevrolet," he said, "1939 model, Ohio license-plate. We found it on Route 2 between Zurich and Harlem. The driver's seat had traces of mud and the back seat had the impression of an object that was probably metallic, about one foot by two, definitely heavy. No fingerprints." He closed his notebook and sat back, stretching out his legs.

"Detrick?" the inspector prompted.

The man removed a cigarette-end from his lips. "Nothing," he said. "No one saw the man. He wasn't carrying any identification and the labels had been removed from his clothes."

"How did he die?"

"I'm waiting for the medical examiner's report. I only know that he did have a limp—right leg. His prints have been sent to the FBI."

The inspector shook the ash from his cigarette and turned slightly to face the third detective. "Your turn, Lowey."

"I don't know the exact count," Lowey replied. "Only Linding and the cashier knew how much was in circulation at the critical moment. Belegs had brought $1500, and I think we can assume a total of something like $80,000. The tills hadn't been touched; they were content to take what was in the safe. There was no fuss; it all went off smoothly, and the people in the agency above the bank didn't hear a thing until the alarm went off. Only one young woman, who was coming back from college having felt ill, said that she noticed a black car. She wasn't able to say what make it was, but she remembered having seen it pull away from the sidewalk shortly before the alarm went off. In the meantime, she'd gone into the hallway of her building, and when she came out again after the alarm sounded the little old man was lying in the gutter, and Belegs and Linding were leaning over him. Then our car arrived. That's all."

The inspector stubbed out his cigarette in the ash-tray, violently. "Nine people dead for $80,000!" he roared. "It's beyond belief! Good God! Twain, do you at least know how they were killed?"

The fourth detective spread his hands in a gesture of helplessness. "Not yet, Chief. The medical examiner's reserving his judgment—he's asking the advice of two of his colleagues. Between two doors I vaguely heard talk of fulgurant coagulation of the blood, but that's hardly precise, is it? We'll have to wait for the medical examiner's report."

The inspector put his elbows on his desk, looked at his men, and said, unenthusiastically: "It's the first time in a long time that we've started an investigation without having the shadow of a lead! Sullivan, can't you get *anything* out of that Chevrolet?"

The detective shrugged his shoulders. "Tomorrow," he said, bleakly, "I'll know the name of its owner and the date when it was stolen—but that won't get us any further forward...."

The door opened violently, and the medical examiner came into the smoky room in a rush. He was red-faced, terribly overexcited. "I've got your report!" he snapped. "Hold on to your seats!"

A dull silence answered him. He took a step forward, into the light, and unfolded a sheet of manuscript with a trembling hand. "The examination I've carried out, with two of my colleagues, has revealed the following: Linding, Belegs, the cashier and the five employees have been literally atomized! Their blood is as dry as plaster, and we estimate that it has been subjected to a radioactive bombardment of at least 150 Roentgens."

He wiped sweat away from his forehead, darted a circular glance over his spectacles, and resumed, in a voice that was simultaneously vibrant and hollow: "As for the other one, the unidentified old man, we're absolutely certain that he's been dead for at least six months!"

He let himself fall into a chair, shook his head, and repeated, as if he were trying to persuade himself: "Six months! That's definite!"

Every eye in the office focused on the photograph of the old man with white hair.

Who was he?

Chapter II

His name was John Ferby. He had been seventy-one years old at the time of his death, following a massive cerebral hemorrhage, and he had been buried in a cemetery in Lexington, Kentucky, his home town.

Sam Forbes of the FBI was given the case, and set off for Lexington on the day after the hold-up. Sam was twenty-eight, with his feet set firmly on the ground, and the forty-page report that he was reading appeared to him to have been written by a particularly imaginative author. However, the report bore the signatures of three doctors and a district chief, and the photographs attached to it were quite authentic.

Sam lit a cigarette and turned a page.

...that it cannot have been the effect of an atomic explosion, however small, for if that had been the case, the furniture and the building would surely have suffered considerable damage. The specialists found no trace of radioactivity at the scene of the crime. On the evening following the inexplicable phenomenon, however, Detective Lowey observed that a cactus placed on a shelf in Mr. Linding's office was completely yellow. Inspector Lowey testified that during his preliminary enquiry, the plant had been bright green....

Sam turned another page, and set the picture of John Ferby down on his knee. The old man had been photographed bare-chested, and a deeply puzzling tattoo was discernible on his breast. The principal motif was the profile of a woman, Chinese or Japanese, not long out of adolescence, whose thick black hair was gathered in a chignon. To either side of the portrait were two names, reminiscent of a horrible tragedy: *Hiroshima* and *Nagasaki*; then, directly under the woman's face, the words: *Compliments of Madame Atomos*.

Sam laughed dryly. It was all so grotesque, probably lifted from the worst melodrama ever made. Someone was trying to pretend that this Madame Atomos was after vengeance, twenty years after the two atomic explosions—which seemed insane. John Ferby's cadaver had been conserved, one way or another, but Sam did not believe the road-sweeper's testimony. A guy six months dead couldn't walk....

By the end of the report, Sam Forbes was convinced that, even if the deaths were real, the presentation and the context of the pages transmitted by the Chinook authorities could only be the conclusion of the biggest hoax of the century.

He closed the file and slipped it into his briefcase, then crossed his legs and lit another cigarette. The train was making good time, and would pull into Lexington station in less than an hour....

Mrs. Ferby stood up very straight. She was only sixty, and managed a food store uptown.

"I'm quite certain that this man isn't my husband!" she affirmed, forcefully. "John died before my very eyes, and although he did have a limp, I can assure you that he didn't have any tattoo on his chest!"

Sam raised his eyes. "They're his fingerprints, Mrs. Ferby," he said, softly.

"It's a mistake!" the woman insisted. "John was buried in the south cemetery last August, and his grave is intact! I'm sure that you've made a mistake. This whole story is revolting!" She sat down abruptly and started weeping silently.

"I'm very sorry, Mrs. Ferby, but these are his prints...."

The woman sniffed and looked up at him mournfully. "But at the end of the day, Mister, John's dead! Dead! A doctor gave permission for the burial after having declared that my husband died of a cerebral hemorrhage, and I was there when he was put in his coffin. I accompanied him to his final resting-place with our family and a crowd of friends; everyone saw the coffin go down into the hole and the earth heaped on top of it...."

She fell silent, choked by her tears.

An employee darted a murderous glance at Sam Forbes and strode forward. "What Mrs. Ferby says is true, Mister," he said, aggressively. "I was there when Mr. Ferby had that attack, and I was the first to run to him. Now that I think back, I could swear that he was dead before he hit the ground."

Sam picked up his hat, excused himself and left. There was nothing left to do but obtain a warrant for the exhumation.

It took place in private, twenty-four hours after Sam Forbes' request.

A fine but penetrating drizzle was falling, and the men were skidding on the greasy earth while they maneuvered the lifting-tackle, whose chains were grating lugubriously. Same had the feeling that it really was a sacrilege that was taking place.

The coffin abruptly appeared, describing a curve at the end of the chains supporting it, and settled into the mud with a soft, repulsive splash.

Sam threw away his damp cigarette, watching the man who was plying the screwdriver, the water that was spattering the muddy coffin and the lid that was slowly coming off as the screws gave way. It was as if a hand was pushing it up from inside, and Sam sensed the malaise hanging over the little group gathered by the graveside. All the watchers had read the newspapers, and understood that the operation in progress might confirm or deny the craziest suppositions that the reporters had not hesitated to raise. There was talk of supernatural manifestations, and the nine corpses in Chinook, which retained the mystery of the death that had struck them down, leaving the door open to the most inane hypotheses.

The man slipped his screwdriver into his pocket, introduced a crowbar into the gap, and detached the lid with a dry crack. It fell to one side, and everyone leaned forward, to see that the coffin was empty.

An inscription was traced on the bottom, in white chalk:

Compliments of Madame Atomos.

Sam Forbes covered a lot of ground very rapidly in the days that followed. He went to visit the owner of the Chevrolet, learned that the car had been stolen a week before the hold-up in Chinook, and made it to the latter town in double-quick time.

He visited the bank, questioned the detectives and the doctors, and grilled Harry Diamond, the road-sweeper. He also examined the Chevrolet, but discovered nothing more than the report had already told him.

He was at the end of the trail, without a clue, privately regretting that bank robbery was a federal crime and that, by virtue of the fact, he had been put on the case. His regrets and ill-humor changed nothing, however; he had been given a job to do, and he had to see it through to the end.

"Pssh!" the Boss had said. "Sam, my lad, you can marry your Maggie after...."

After what?

That risked going too far.

To our dear child.

The crown that bore the inscription rolled a little way and settled; one of the men carrying the coffin was obliged to step over it in order not to trip. The dead woman was twenty-two years old. She had had heart trouble since infancy, and the operation that might have ameliorated her condition had put an end to her days.

The coffin went down; the hole was filled in, and while the weeping family turned way, the man who was to put the headstone in place the following day wrote in his notebook: *Mabel Wrist. Lane 60, plot 12. In perpetuity....*

Some distance away, a little yellow man inscribed almost identical words—except for the last....

It was three o'clock in the morning when the van stopped alongside the wall. The driver switched off the headlights. As one of his companions groaned, he pointed to the round pale moon, seemingly as cold as an ice-cream in its cone, but whose wan gleam illuminated the place sufficiently

The four men took a ladder out of the van, along with a flexible stretcher, a pick and a spade, and used the ladder to climb into the cemetery. They must have been experts in this sort of work, for the job was done in less than an hour. When they reappeared, nothing seemed to have been disturbed, but the body of Mavis Wrist was lying on the stretcher, and the young woman's long hair was sweeping the muddy ground.

In the dark sky, the moon seemed even colder.

On Tuesday February twelfth, a consignment of diamonds was eagerly awaited at Dubinsky Junior's store.

Junior was fifty-three years old, weighed two hundred pounds, and was no longer keeping his impatience in check. He was smoking a Havana cigar as thick as a girder, striding back and forth in the store at the pace of an Alpine hunter and squinting at the security men with the eye of a general inspecting his troops.

A million dollars....

In the back of the shop, the safe was agape, and so long as the diamonds were not secure in the shelter of the thick armor-plate, Junior knew that he would be unable to stop his feet marching, his arms waving and his cigar belching smoke like a factory chimney.

There was a mad whirl in the store. Clients were coming in and going out incessantly through the five doors opening in to Fifth Avenue—for them, everything was normal.

Junior went to the step of the first door. That was where the diamonds were to be delivered. The armored car would arrive any minute, stopping exactly in front of the door, in the spot reserved for that purpose by the police, and eight armed policemen would accompany the precious package to the safe. Good! Nothing could go wrong now! Everything was going like clockwork!"

His round eyes settled for a fraction of a second on a young woman with a pale face who passed between two display-units and headed back toward the street. Junior did not care at all about young women, pale or not; only diamonds interested him.

The young woman was a brunette, and her long hair gathered into a pony-tail, hung flexibly down over her fur wrap. She was carrying a large bag, advancing with a mechanical step, and not stopping for anything. Her gaze had an incredible fixity, her eyes slightly dilated, devoid of any gleam. An attentive observer might have thought the unblinking immobility of her eyelids abnormal.

A policeman in plain-clothes glanced at her, thought that she was probably sickening for something, and redirected his gaze to a guy with a furtive appearance. A moment went by, and then a soft purr became audible through the hubbub. Every client, every cop, and Junior himself had the sensation that a fly was buzzing in his ear—and that was all.

An order was barked outside, and an aged man, escorted by eight policemen armed with submachine-guns, made his entrance. He was carrying a black box and marching rapidly, his head sunk between his shoulders.

A young messenger-boy whistled admiringly, went out of the shop, climbed into his van and drew away at top speed. It saved his life, although he did not find that out until later.

In the meantime, inside the shop, the buzzing was amplified, and the hundred and fifty people present suddenly felt a need to stand still and shut up.

The eight policemen and the man who was carrying the diamonds stopped between two display-units; the people going out remained in the doorways, petrified in front of the people trying to get in.

Outside, gawkers gathered in front of the windows, looking in amazement at all those motionless people, while the two guards on watch beside the armored car drew their weapons and ran into Dubinsky's. Their momentum carried them forward for four yards; then they stopped in their turn, pistols in hand, neither able nor wishing to take another step.

Then the pale young woman walked calmly forward, crossing the shop floor, and reached the man who was carrying the diamonds. Slowly, she took the black box from his fingers, slid it into her bag, and headed at a modest pace toward door number five, while the buzzing sound followed her. The people who had been watching the scene though the windows tried to stop her on the threshold, but they could not get close to her. Later, those who had not died affirmed that they had run into an invisible wall.

Protected by that strange barrier, the young woman went along the sidewalk, and held out her bag horizontally. A large grey car came along, slowing down, and a yellow hand grabbed the bag. The car accelerated again, and turned the next corner.

At that moment, the young woman collapsed between two stationary vehicles, and people rushed toward her. The people who were inside the shop were seized by a great agitation.

The plain-clothes policemen tried to get out, but the maddened clients were blocking the exits. Junior uttered harrowing howls. Some people fell down between the display-units and were trampled by the terrified crowd. Women were screaming and men were shoving one another in order to get to the nearest exit, and the confusion was at its height when the ululation of police sirens burst out in the distance.

Suddenly, with frightful completeness, silence fell within the shop, and the people outside saw through the windows that dozens of corpses were strewn on the floor.

For the sake of a million dollars, there were nearly two hundred dead....

Chapter III

Sam Forbes, transformed into a carrier pigeon, disembarked at La Guardia Airport on the afternoon of February twelfth. He leapt into a waiting car and was immediately taken to Dubinsky's.

The shop was protected by a metal barrier and a police cordon, and technicians with Geiger counters were moving between the deserted display-units. An enormous crowd was standing silently outside, but the usually-noisy newspaper vendors had fallen silent, abandoning that section of Fifth Avenue.

Sam sensed that a muffled anguish was gripping the city's inhabitants. It was already common knowledge that the young woman's name was Mabel Wrist, and that she had been dead for four days. It was also common knowledge that two hundred people had been atomized and that Mabel's breast bore the terrible tattoo: *Hiroshima, Nagasaki, Compliments of Madame Atomos*. Madame Atomos' profile was on the first page of every newspaper in the USA, underlined by the caption: *Public Enemy no. 1*.

The entire FBI had been mobilized on the case, and J. Edgar Hoover, with the President's approval, had appeared on TV to make a sensational statement: a veritable declaration of war, in which he demanded the help of every American citizen. Madame Atomos had to be rendered harmless, no matter what the cost.

Hundreds of women of Chinese or Japanese origin were summoned to police stations and interrogated. Their identities and employments were checked and their fingerprints taken.

Sam Forbes got out of the car, and flashbulbs crackled. A man approached him, holding out a microphone, speaking all the while: "And this is the man the FBI have put in charge of the Atomos affair. His name is Sam Forbes; he's five foot ten, brown-haired and twenty-eight years old. His manner is energetic. I'll try, listeners, to get a few words from him...."

Sam saw the television cameras aimed at him and took a step back, but the man with the microphone followed him, tugging on his cable. "Sam," he said, jovially, "Have you any leads? Can you tell us...."

Two policemen hauled the radio reporter away unceremoniously, and he said into his microphone. "Sam Forbes can't say anything, which is understandable, but the wink he just gave me undoubtedly signifies a great deal...."

Disconcerted, Sam went into the shop, where he immediately found himself the center of attention. The Boss was there, and beckoned his agent to approach. "Shhh!" he hissed, chewing an extinct cigar. "Sam, my lad, I have an idea that you're carrying a crushing responsibility...." He drew Sam to one side and jabbed a thumb at a group of seven people that were waiting a short distance away. "It's not like Chinook this time," he said. "We've got a hundred witnesses, but I kept those fresh for you. How much do you know?"

"Everything the press has revealed. It happened exactly as in Chinook, didn't it?"

The Boss lit his cigar and furrowed his brow. "Shhh! I'd rather be in my shoes than yours. The witnesses agree, but haven't told us anything. The dead woman came in, then stole the diamonds without anyone being able to lift a finger. She went out the same way, handed the bag to a Chink driving a grey rattletrap, and then collapsed. Thirty seconds later there were a hundred and fifty-eight corpses inside the shop and about thirty more on the sidewalk."

"The car?"

The Boss shrugged. "It got away without any difficulty. There was panic, and none of the witnesses thought to follow it, or even of getting its plate number." He threw away his cigar, crushing it angrily underfoot. "You'll take it from here, of course. Unlimited funds. A free hand. Okay?"

"Okay."

The Boss turned on his heel, left the shop and disappeared into his car.

Sam pivoted and walked over to the group that was waiting for him. It included several FBI men familiar to Sam and a puny little man with grey hair wearing steel-rimmed spectacles, who introduced himself as soon as Sam arrived: "Dr. Alan Soblen."

Sam shook his hand. Soblen had been a member of the Atomic Energy Commission set up in 1951, and was a leader in his field.

Smith Beffort of the FBI gave Sam the necessary explanations. "Dr. Soblen will assist in the investigation. He'll be entirely concerned with the scientific aspects of the problem, but might now be able to give you his opinion as to what's happened here...."

"No," Soblen interjected, in a soft voice. "I can't tell you anything you don't already know. Nearly two hundred people have been subjected to about 150 Roentgens of radiation, but the extraordinary thing is that we haven't found any trace of Strontium-90 here."

Sam scratched his head. "Could you translate that, doctor?"

The scientist peered at him over his spectacles. "Strontium-90," he said, "is a radioactive isotope projected into the atmosphere by atomic explosions, which, when it falls to earth, contaminates water, soil, vegetation and crops. It is, in consequence, absorbed by living organisms and always settles in the most dangerous place—which is to say, the bones and the bone-marrow. It was, therefore, very important to find out whether that deadly isotope had been released into the atmosphere of New York." He adjusted his spectacles on his pointed nose and added: "Having found no pollution, I deduce that there has been no explosion—in which case, it's necessary to admit that this…Madame Atomos has succeeded in domesticating atoms."

A shudder ran through the group, and Smith Beffort forgot to light the cigarette that he had just raised to his lips.

"Domesticating atoms?" Sam queried. "What do you mean by that?"

Dr. Soblen took off his spectacles. "Imagine," he said, "that you possess a weapon capable of shooting a bullet at a target, which it destroys, and that the same bullet then returns to the barrel of your weapon….."

"That's insane!" groaned Beffort.

Soblen looked at him mildly. "Isn't it insane, in your view, to make dead people walk?"

Beffort grimaced, and lit his cigarette. It was beyond him.

"As for the mysterious wall with which several people collided," the doctor continued, "and which no longer offered any resistance after Mabel Wrist's second demise, I think one might classify it in the category of radiations provoked, and in some way solidified, by a revolutionary technique." He put his spectacles on again,

33

and pointed his nose at Sam Forbes. "That," he said, in an apologetic tone, "is all I can tell you for the moment. It's not much, and rests entirely on suppositions."

Sam frowned. "You made allusion just now to a weapon capable of recovering a projectile after firing," he said. "Is it logical to assume that the weapon would have to be installed not far from its intended target."

"I don't know," Soblen replied, thoughtfully. "What are you thinking?"

Sam lit a cigarette, having offered one to Soblen, who refused. "At Chinook," he said, "a witness said that there was a car following John Ferby. When that car was found, the back seat bore the imprint of a metal object, about one foot by two, probably very heavy. Couldn't that be an apparatus—what you call a weapon—designed to control...dead people at a distance?"

Dr. Soblen squinted. "I was unaware of that detail," he said. "Your hypothesis isn't implausible, Mr. Forbes. All the more so because of the buzzing...."

"What buzzing?" Sam queried.

Smith Beffort interrupted, pointing a finger. "Over there, that young fellow on the right is the sole survivor of those who were inside the shop. I think it might be useful for you to interrogate him personally. He has a head on his shoulders and seems sure of himself."

"Let's go," Sam agreed.

They crossed the room. Beffort took out his notebook and consulted it before calling out: "Jack Urey!"

The young man got up and came toward the two men with a firm stride. He was wearing a leather jacket, and a stray curl of hair fell over his forehead. "That's me," he said, unceremoniously. "Tell me, are you going to keep me kicking my heels much longer?"

"No," Sam assured him. "Tell me what you saw, and you can be on your way."

Jack Urey put his index-finger to his nose. "To tell the truth," he said, "I didn't see anything much. I just heard that hum, and...."

"Just a minute," Beffort put in. "Tell Mr. Forbes about the girl."

"Oh, I barely noticed her. If the rags hadn't published her paper, I wouldn't have remembered...."

"Repeat what you told me," Beffort interjected again. "We're not asking for any more."

Jack Urey gave him a dirty look, then started again, ostensibly addressing himself to Sam. "Well, I was in that corner, on the second step, and I was watching the cops protecting the guy carrying the gems when the girl stuck herself in the middle...."

"In the middle of what?"

"Between them and me, of course." He turned to the door, pointing at the deserted display-units with his extended forefinger. "It was very impressive—all those cops with submachine-guns. It was like being at the flicks. In short, I think the guts were still outside when I first heard the humming in my ears."

"What was it like?"

"The noise made by one of those big flies that...."

"Yes," Beffort cut in, "We get the picture. What did you do then?"

"I went out! I had my deliveries to make." He pinched his lips and said: "I had a bit of luck, eh? A little longer, and I'd have been good for the morgue too! Can I go now?"

Sam noticed that the boy was looking round anxiously. He was afraid. "The girl," he said. "What was she like?"

"As white as her blouse and as stiff as a statue, Can I go?"

Sam agreed, and Jack Urey set off like a hare.

"He's got the wind up," Beffort observed, "and he's not alone. Look at the others…."

Sam looked at the other witnesses. There were four women and three men, all very pale, visibly intimidated. One of the women was almost lying down in her chair. She was sitting to one side and was obviously drowsy, for her chin was resting on her chest and her eyes were shut,

"They happened to be outside when the big drama unfolded," said Beffort, "and they bumped into the famous invisible wall. It's quite a trick…."

He continued talking, but Sam was no longer listening. He was looking at the sleeping woman. Her left hand was hanging down with a strange limpness, and her knees were wide apart. "Smith!" he snapped. "Fetch the doc—that woman's dead!"

Smith Beffort needed no further instruction. He headed for the exit, after having murmured a few words in Dr. Soblen's ear in passing. The latter came over to Sam, who was leaning over the young woman. "If she isn't dead," he warned, "don't touch her!"

Sam straightened up. "There's no doubt about it," he said. His gaze strayed over the other witnesses, which were still motionless. "Damn it!" he swore. "Look at that, Soblen!"

The scientist turned, and saw three men lie down on the bench they had been sitting on, while the three women collapsed limply in their chairs.

There was a commotion in the street outside, and Smith Beffort came back into the shop. A doctor and two orderlies carrying a stretcher were following him.

The doctor looked at the woman, slipped on rubber gloves, took her pulse and raised his eyes again. "Good day, Dr. Soblen," he said. "I'm sure you know what killed her, don't you?"

"Coagulation of the blood."

"Exactly. And them?"

"Same symptoms, obviously," the scientist retorted. "It's necessary to evacuate this place immediately, Mr. Forbes. Our Geiger counters aren't registering any radioactivity, but there must be something else we can't detect."

Sam made a gesture of denial. "It's not that. All these people bumped into the invisible wall—and they're dying of it six hours later...."

Smith Beffort started. "Good God!" he cried. "There are dozens in that situation—we let them go."

A profound silence fell inside the shop. It was Dr. Soblen who broke it. "At present," he said, coldly, "there must be dozens more corpses all over the city. That's frightful!"

In the hour that followed, that bad news flowed from headquarters to Sam. Eight corpses were found in the subway, ten had collapsed in the street, seven on the stairs of their buildings, and thirty-two had died at home after putting on their slippers. In spite of appearances, they had all succumbed at the same moment, and only the different paths they had travelled in going home had given the impression of a time lag. The bill for the Dubinsky operation was thus made up in the following fashion, to the account of Madame Atomos: one million dollars, 252 deaths.

Jack Urey was found and taken to hospital. He was submitted to a serious of examinations and obliged to go to bed, but the boy defied all prognoses and remained alive. With a cigarette in his mouth and his hands linked behind the nape of his neck, he scolded the doctor who was listening to his chest for the tenth time. "Come on, come on! This is getting tedious, Doc! Mother Atomos has missed me, and tomorrow night I'll be going to the ball!"

And he went—the Ureys, it seemed were hard to kill.

Chapter IV

At nine o'clock in the morning on the day after the Dubinsky affair, which was Wednesday February thirteenth, a man emerged from Penn Station and took the subway to Washington Heights in the Bronx. He stationed himself at the corner of Broadway and 193rd Street and, after waiting five minutes, was met by a woman of medium height, elegantly dressed in a brown skunk-fur coat, with very marked Oriental features.

The couple went into an expensive restaurant at 143 Dyckman Street and installed themselves in a booth in order to eat a lavish breakfast.

After a brief interval, a little yellow man wearing a soft hat drawn down over his eyes came into the restaurant and played a few records on the juke-box. He smoked a cigarette, drank a cup of coffee, and left the establishment whistling. At that moment, the companion of the woman in the fur coat got up and exited in her turn.

The two men seemed not to know one another, but they got on the same subway train and got out at 125th Street just as the doors were closing again, thus escaping any potential surveillance. They both went along 125th Street, then separated and continued on their way on different sidewalks. Ten minutes later, the man with the soft hat stopped in front of a rather shabby green Chevrolet, whose door was unlocked and which had an ignition-key in the dashboard.

His companion stopped, standing on his own sidewalk, surveying the street intently. The little man then got into the Chevrolet, started the motor, and was about to put it into first gear when a forceful hand pulled him out of the car.

"FBI! Hands up, slowly."

The Oriental saw that two other policemen in plain clothes were ready to intervene and, thinking himself lost, made a desperate move. He ducked down sharply, dived between two cars, and pulled his Colt Cobra out of its holster.

The fourth policeman, whom he had not spotted, bludgeoned him and laid him out for the count.

Thirty seconds later, still unconscious, the little man was rolling towards Sam Forbes' headquarters. An FBI agent consulted the papers that he had just extracted from the Oriental's pocket, tilted his head and read aloud: "Hisato Keichu, thirty-five years old. Naturalized American. Born in Nagasaki, Japan...."

Mechanically, the driver stepped on the gas and switched on his siren.

Hisato Keichu's companion remained rooted to his sidewalk momentarily, and when the police car had disappeared he ran to the glass-sided telephone booth that he had perceived on the street corner. Feverishly, he dialed a number, and when the receiver was picked up he asked, gaily: "Is that you, Lou?"

"No," replied a masculine voice. "This is twelve fifty-eight thirty-four."

The man hung up, left the booth and rifled through his notebook while walking. Thirty-two signified Allison Park, thirty-three North Hudson Park and thirty-four Sound View Park.

The man hailed a taxi, had himself taken to the southern extremity of Sound View Park, settled up and continued on foot as far as the bank of the East River. A car drew up alongside him and the woman in the fur coat opened the door. The man got in swiftly and the car set off in the direction of Yankee Stadium.

"Well?" the woman asked.

"Hisato's just been arrested."

"Was it chance, or was he being followed?"

"Chance. Probably FBI men."

The woman pursed her lips. "I knew that we shouldn't use Hisato again. Madame Atomos foresaw this."

"Good. What should we do?"

The woman stopped at a red light and tuned her cold gaze on her passenger. "Sam Forbes has a fiancée," she said. "Her name is Maggie Fairbanks. Her address is in the glove compartment."

The man rummaged in the compartment and read the address. "When?" he said, simply.

"This evening."

To keep watch on all the cemeteries in the USA was too gigantic a task, and Sam Forbes had preferred to mobilize his G-men in the direction of men of Oriental extraction driving cars. At Chinook, and during the robbery of the Dubinsky jewelry store, a little yellow man had been at the steering-wheel of both vehicles, and it seemed reasonable to direct the initial search in that direction.

Sam had not, however, expected such a rapid result.

When Hisato Keichu was brought into his office, the federal agent immediately sensed that he had got his man. That intuition might have originated in the violent desire that he had to seize the first link in a chain that might be interminable, but that ambition had pushed him to help himself, and now heaven had come to his aid.

At first, Hisato refused to answer any questions. The bludgeon had struck him a ranging blow, and his hand often went to the nape of his neck. That was, however, his only manifestation of emotion. The fact of being accused of carrying an illicit weapon and the theft of the car left him visibly indifference.

Hisato was playing for time, waiting.

Confronted by his silence, Sam sent two men to collect three witnesses who had declared themselves able, if the opportunity arose, to recognize the driver of the grey car to which Mabel Wrist had handed the bag containing the diamonds, and waited in his turn.

The Japanese man had been standing up for two hours. His pockets had been emptied; his tie and shoelaces removed. The window was wide open in spite of the intense cold, and Sam had cut off the heating. Sam and his men went back to the office, but Hisato Keichu stayed where he was, turning white and unable to prevent his teeth from chattering.

At midday, the three witnesses were put in the presence of the Japanese man. Two of them formally identified him; the third remained hesitant. He had been poorly placed in relation to the grey car, and had only seen the man from an oblique angle, his view also being hindered by some luggage that was on the rear seat.

Sam had the room cleared, keeping only one G-man, charged with preventing the Oriental from reaching the window. Hisato's silence and his resistance to the cold demonstrated that the man had nerves of steel, and that if the situation became desperate, he probably would not hesitate to commit suicide. Sam's office was on the fifth floor.

"Admit that you were driving the grey car," said Sam, not hopeful of obtaining an answer, "and that you work for Madame Atomos,"

"Yes," said the Oriental, dryly.

Sam and the G-man exchanged a surprised glance. Hisato's sudden capitulation, which had been quite unforeseen, seemed distinctly suspicious. Sam closed the window, pushed a chair over to the Japanese man, and offered him a cigarette.

"Who is Madame Atomos?"

Hisato Keichu took a long puff and crossed his legs. He seemed less tense, and Sam had the feeling that he had been biding his time before talking.

"I don't know," Hisato replied. "I only know that she was living in Nagasaki in 1945, and that her husband and children were killed by the atomic bomb." His slanted eyes flashed briefly, and he added, without his impassive face changing expression: "I was at Nagasaki, but I was only a child when your second bomb exploded. My parents, my brothers, my sisters and my friends were transformed into ash in less than a minute. All those who assist Madame Atomos were in Nagasaki or Hiroshima. America has only known Pearl Harbor, but the territory of the USA will soon be an immense cemetery." He looked directly into Sam Forbes' eyes and said: "You can do nothing against Madame Atomos. It has taken her twenty years to put her vengeance into execution, but now nothing can oppose her plans."

Sam restrained an impulse to lash out. "You live in a hotel," he said, in a voice vibrant with anger, "and you don't have a job. Your personal effects are limited to two worn suits, underwear, a few bathroom items and a Colt Cobra! We found fifty dollars and some small change on you. I don't believe that a man working for Madame Atomos could be in such a sorry situation."

The Japanese man smiled. "You won't get me that way," he said. "You think that men of my race are primarily concerned with not losing face, but that's a typically Occidental notion. The next few hours will show you that I'm only a pawn on a vast chessboard, and pride won't choke me to the point of trying to appear more important than I am. I drove the car in Chinook, and yesterday, and I don't know any more...."

"What about the apparatus that was on the back seat?"

"I steal a car and am contacted."

"Where?"

"At home. I'm given a rendezvous outside the city, and the apparatus is loaded into the car. I don't have to touch it. The apparatus is already working, remotely guiding a walking corpse somewhere in the city, and two dots move closer to one another on a screen. One is the corpse, the other my car."

Sam leapt to his feet. "That's a lie! In Chinook, you were following John Ferby."

Hisato Keichu shrugged his shoulders. "Hazard dictated that we were following the same route, but I didn't know that the old man was my subject. I only realized that when he went into the bank and the humming started. That sound warns me that the operation is imminent, and I get ready to act. Then I take what's held out to me and go back to the rendezvous. There I abandon the car and I get home by my own means. That's all."

Sam and his men interrogated Hisato Keichu until nightfall, but could not get any more out of him. The man was only an agent, an isolated link, and Sam anticipated that the other end of the chain would not be easy to grasp.

The doorbell rang and Mr. Fairbanks went to open it. He found himself face to face with a man armed with a pistol fitted with a silencer, and did not have time to say a single word before receiving a bullet in the head.

The man caught him as he fell, and gave a signal to two shadows, who joined him on the steps. Silently, the three men went into the house, and burst into the dining-room. Mrs. Fairbanks stood up, but a bullet between her eyes laid her out on the floor.

Maggie Fairbanks, who was watching television in the living-room, heard the faint noise of the shot and the muffled noise that her mother's body made as it fell, and got to her feet. She went through the bamboo partition that separated the two rooms, felt an atrocious pain in her skull, and plunged into a bottomless gulf.

At nine o'clock the telephone in Sam Forbes' office rang. One of the men present lifted the receiver and passed it to his chief. "It's for you," he said. "An outside line."

Sam immediately thought of Maggie. He had called her the day before, but had not seen her since the beginning of the Atomos affair. The young woman had told him in a letter how annoyed she was with him, and, with a very feminine sensibility, had concluded by saying that life apart from him was not worth living.

"Hello? Sam Forbes here."

"Have you heard from your fiancée, Mr. Forbes?" The voice was that of a woman, with a slight foreign accent that Sam could not identify.

"Who are you?" he snapped, abruptly alert.

"A colleague of Madame Atomos," the woman replied, phlegmatically. "I'm calling from a public booth, and there's no point in trying to trace the call. Here's what I have to sway: you've detained Hisato Keichu, but we've kidnapped Maggie Fairbanks. If you'd like to check, I'll call you back shortly...."

She hung up. Sam did likewise, and feverishly dialed a number, while issuing orders: "Warn the switchboard that my line will be activated shortly. Try to identify the call-booth, and have two radio-cars stay in touch with the switchboard. The usual system...."

A G-man hastily left the room and ran along the deserted corridor.

Sam listened to the telephone ringing interminably in the Fairbanks' home, and felt a horrible dread slowly increasing within him. At the fifteenth ring, he hung up and turned to his men, his features contorted. "Madame Atomos has just abducted my fiancée," he said, harshly. "In a moment, one of her acolytes will call back. It's absolutely necessary to trace the call. Warn the patrol cars to be ready to respond to any message from our offices. We have absolute priority. I'll try to keep the conversation going for as long as possible...."

Three men left the office. When the telephone rang, Smith Beffort grabbed a receiver. Sam snatched another. "Forbes," he said. "Talk."

The tense voice of the mysterious correspondent was heard: "Verification effected, Mr. Forbes?"

"Yes."

"Then here are our conditions. Free Hisato immediately—without trying to follow him, of course—and we'll release your fiancée."

"Where will the exchange take place?" the federal agent ventured.

"There won't be any exchange, Mr. Forbes. We have the advantage, and don't forget it. Free Hisato Kei-chu within the next ten minutes, or Maggie Fairbanks will be no more than a memory to you." There was a click.

"Hello?" shouted Sam, incredulously. "Listen to me!"

Smith Beffort gently replaced his own receiver. "Useless," he said. "She's hung up." He whistled mechanically through his teeth, and added, gravely: "You've got ten minutes to decide, old chap…."

Chapter V

It was nine-twenty. A message came from the switchboard to tell Sam Forbes that, because of the brevity of the previous communication, the place from which the mysterious correspondent had called could not be identified. The patrol cars were, however, remaining in a state of alert.

Crushed, Sam did not react.

Smith Beffort, who understood his state of mind quite well, posed the problem brutally, without attempting to minimize the consequences that an overly spontaneous decision might have. "You have full authority, but if you let Hisato return to the wild the press will shoot you down in flames tomorrow and the Boss will be obliged to fire you." He glanced at Sam and met his empty gaze. "I don't know what I'd do in your position," he went on, "but you have to act rapidly. Hisato Keichu has to be out of the building by half past, and it's nine twenty-four...."

Sam shrugged his shoulders. "I'll free the Jap, then write my letter of resignation." His hoarse voice seemed to be coming from a long way away.

Smith Beffort thumped the desk with his fist. "A nice solution! You surrender before having got into the fight. If everyone else does the same, Madame Atomos will set the country on fire without meeting any opposition!" He marched furiously across the room, looked at his watch, planted himself in front of Sam and said: "Release Hisato immediately—I'll take care of it personally."

There was a gleam in Sam's eye, but he did not budge. "The woman specified that he mustn't be followed," he said.

Beffort took the bull by the horns. "Listen," he spat, violently. "Even in broad daylight I can follow a guy while leaving my shadow in my desk drawer! Cut Hisato loose, let the patrol cars go their own way, and we'll play the game quietly. You stay here, and I'll call your hourly. I'll walk on tiptoe, of course, so long as Maggie Fairbanks hasn't been returned to you—but afterwards, the fireworks start! Go on, Sam—throw the Jap out. I'll wait for him outside."

Same gave the order to release Keichu, and Beffort left the office like a gust of wind, ran down the stairs and left the building by a door that let out into the parking lot. He climbed into his car, went around the block, found a spot fifty yards from the door through which Keichu would come, and started watching.

After thirty seconds, the Japanese man appeared, alone. He looked round, raised the collar of his overcoat and drew away from the building slowly. He came toward Beffort, and the latter crouched down in his seat, hiding in the shadows.

Hisato Keichu slid between two stationary cars and made a gesture. A taxi stopped beside him. The Japanese man climbed in beside the driver, and the vehicle moved off.

Surprised, Beffort began to trail him. He had expected his prey to flee like lightning, plunging into the subway, or a pick-up arranged by his accomplices, but here he was, calmly setting forth at a modest pace. It was worrying….

Sam Forbes sat in his armchair and smoked one cigarette after another. A call from the police in Tarrytown had just informed him of the death of Maggie's parents, and that news had plunged him into the deaths of depression.

At eleven o'clock the telephone rang. Sam picked it up nervously, sure that it would be Maggie, and experienced a terrible disappointment on recognizing Smith Beffort's voice.

"Hisato went back to his hotel and packed his bags," the agent told him. "We're now in Jersey City, not far from the Holland Tunnel. The Jap's in a bar; I'm in one across the road. Any news of Maggie?"

"Nothing."

There as a silence; then Smith Beffort said, in a voice he wanted to be reassuring: "That doesn't mean anything. Above all, don't torture yourself. Mother Atomos is doubtless waiting for her boy Hisato to be safe before releasing your fiancée. I'll call you as soon as possible."

He hung up, and Sam sat down again, his mind empty, completely demoralized.

At midnight the phone rang briefly, but it stopped before Sam could move. He got up, tugged on the wire, set the apparatus down on his knee, and resumed waiting.

Chilled to the bone, he woke up two hours later, with a strident ringing drilling into his ears. He grabbed the apparatus

It was Smith Beffort again. "I'm in a hurry," the agent said, rapidly. "I'm calling from Dunellen police station. Hisato was picked up by a Buick shortly after my last call and we took Route 22. The Jap's in an isolated cabin two miles from Dunellen and the Buick's gone. I'm going back. Anything new?"

"No," Sam murmured, "except that Maggie's parents have been murdered. I forgot that when I talked to you before. Don't let Hisato get away, Smith!"

"Don't worry. He's sleeping like a log in his hidey-hole, and he hasn't got a car at his disposal. I'll call again later. Bye...."

Sam hung up, and lit his last cigarette.

At four o'clock in the morning, the long wait finally produced a result. He immediately recognized the voice of the woman with the foreign accent in the receiver.

"That's perfect, Mr. Forbes—you've played it straight. Hisato's safe, and we know now that you couldn't make him talk...."

"Enough chit-chat!" Sam interjected, ferociously. "Where's my fiancée."

A ripple of laughter replied. "In our power, Mr. Forbes!"

Sam's fingers went white as he gripped the phone. "You promised to set her free!" he said, in a voice vibrant with hatred.

"We didn't say when, Mr. Forbes. First, we intend to make use of her. Madame Atomos invites you to attend the performance that will take place tomorrow morning, at nine o'clock sharp, opposite the Schwartz Bank. Goodnight, Mr. Forbes."

The click sounded lugubriously in Sam's ear, but two phrases were still vibrating in his skull: *make use of her* and *the performance*.

Sam foresaw, confusedly, that he would witness a particularly terrible scene, in which Maggie Fairbanks would doubtless play the leading role—and a murderous rage took hold of him. His mouth twisted into a mute insult and, to vent his anger, he smashed the telephone against the wall. It was childish, but it helped to make his impotence less intolerable.

The Schwartz Bank was situated in a quiet street of antiquated houses in the heart of the Bronx, and a thick mist rising from Eastchester Bay was swamping the police cars stationed under the NO PARKING notices.

In one of the vehicles, Sam Forbes and Dr. Alan Soblen kept their eyes firmly on the front of the bank.

"What's going to happen, do you think?" asked Soblen, wiping the lenses of his spectacles.

Forbes turned a face ravaged by a sleepless and anxious night toward him. "I don't know," he said, in a toneless voice. "We've been invited to a performance given by Madame Atomos, and I'm afraid that it might have a tragic ending. Ten armed men are inside the bank, and there are five more on the first floor of the building.

"If things happen the way they did at Dubinsky's," Soblen objected, "guns will be as useless as bicycle-pumps, and the men in the bank will die there."

Sam threw his cigarette-butt out of the car window. "If we find the same situation as at Dubinsky's," he said, wearily, "my men know what they have to do. Our aim is to avoid any casualties."

"How will you know that there's danger?"

"The corpses remotely controlled by Madame Atomos are easily recognizable. They can walk, doctor, but they still have a livid complexion, unblinking eyes and a mechanical gait. As soon as anyone with that appearance goes into the bank, it will be immediately evacuated via an emergency exit."

"What's your plan?"

Sam pushed his hat back over the nape of his neck and rubbed his swollen eyelids. "We'll let the corpse walk, since we have no way to stop it—but when the car comes to pick it up, or collect the loot, the road will be immediately blocked at both ends. Two trucks are ready to roll, and men hidden under the tarpaulins can open fire as soon as I give the signal. What I want, Dr. Soblen, is the remote control apparatus on the back seat of the car."

"I agree that, from our viewpoint, that's the most important thing at present," Soblen admitted. "What time is it, Forbes?"

The federal agent consulted his watch, and murmured: "Eight fifty-nine, doctor. In one minute, Mother Atomos's circus will begin its parade. Do you notice anything strange about the street?"

Soblen squinted. "Presumably you mean the fog," he said, pensively. "It's been a long time since I've seen one like it." He sniffed the air, and said: "Besides, it has an odor, doesn't it?"

Sam sniffed. "Hmm! It's coming from the docks. Sometimes, odors come out of the drains and invade the Bronx."

The radio-set crackled, and a voice emerged from the receiver. "Tom Six calling Tom One!"

Forbes flicked the switch with his thumb. "This is Tom One," he said "What is it?"

"The mist's getting thicker here," said the voice.

"So?"

"It has a funny taste, this mist. Have you taken a look at your windscreen?"

Sam saw that a thin oily sheen was spreading over the glass, but that wasn't infrequent in the city, and didn't seem unduly peculiar. "Well?" he growled.

"What's bizarre about that, Tom Six? The wind's blowing north-westerly, bringing all the pestilential factory-smoke down on the Bronx."

"It's not that!" croaked Tom Six. "Try your windscreen-wipers, and we'll talk again…."

Forbes pressed the switch, and the wipers began to beat madly over the greasy surface, redistributing the oily substance in long opaque streaks.

"Tom Three here," said the speaker. "I heard Tom Six and I just tried to move my car. It's impossible. The motor's running, but the wheels are spinning as if on black ice. My partner got out, and he's now face-down on the ground. It's impossible to stay upright!"

One by one, the other cars confirmed that they were in the same situation. It was impossible to move off or to set foot on the ground. The neighborhood was suddenly impassable. The pedestrians took refuge in doorway if they were already on the sidewalk; the majority found themselves immobilized in the roadway, between vehicles that were equally becalmed, and all those people flat on the ground offered a spectacle that was both grotesque and frightful at the same time.

Dr. Soblen passed his finger over the windscreen, brought back a sample of the oily substance, sniffed it and pulled a face. "I don't know what it is," he confessed, finally.

Sam laughed. "It's nine-oh-three," he said, "and Madame Atomos has kept her word. The performance has begun." He opened the door abruptly and set his feet on the slippery ground. Before releasing his grip, he said: "At university, I wasn't bad at ice hockey…."

He let go, and immediately collapsed, departing on his back with his arms and legs spread, and slid in this fashion into the middle of the road. Immediately, he attempted to pivot, but his fingers could find no purchase, and he had the strange sensation of being separated from the asphalt by a cushion of air. He twisted his neck, and saw that Dr. Soblen was about to get out of the car. "Don't move!" he shouted. "Instead, throw me the rope that's under the seat."

Alan Soblen bent down and fetched out a tow-rope fitted with metal hooks. He fixed one end to the door-frame, uncoiled the rest and threw it to Sam, who caught the hook in mid-air, tugged gently, and pulled himself back to the car.

"Good God!" he said, when he was back behind the steering-wheel, "this is crazy. We're stuck here like flies on fly-paper.

Soblen, who had turned toward the bank, grabbed him by the arm in sudden anxiety. "Look, Forbes! The lights have just been switched off. In weather this dark, that's abnormal….."

The fog was now so thick that visibility was reduced to ten yards.

"Something's happening in the bank," Sam growled. "Did you see anyone go in while I was doing my little turn?"

"No. Besides, it's practically impossible to move around….." He interrupted himself, his eyes widening, and he pointed to the radio. "Why can't we hear anything anymore?"

Sam verified that the equipment was working and put his lips to the microphone. "Tom One calling…Tom One calling…."

The speaker remained silent, and Sam put his hand on the apparatus. "It's cold," he observed, grimly. He turned the ignition-key without any result, and turned a stony face toward the scientist. "No more juice in the battery, no more light in the bank. What does it mean, Doctor?"

Soblen blinked. His face expressed nothing but amazement. "I don't know," he whispered. His gaze fell upon Sam's wrist and looked up again immediately. "Your watch has stopped," he said. "Time has passed, but the hands are still indicating nine-oh-three!"

Sam jabbed his chin in the direction of the fog that was now extending in thick sheets, blurring the contours of the hood and pressing against the windows in large fleecy stripes. "We can't see further than three feet anymore," he said, "and we can neither move nor communicate with the other cars. In the heart of New York, we're as isolated as in a desert. If the entire city is paralyzed, Madame Atomos can kill us, set fire to the buildings, crush us or disintegrate us!"

Mechanically, Soblen took off his spectacles, and for the first time, Sam noticed that without the lenses the scientist's eyes were glaucous, empty and cold, like a serpent's.

"We're in the hands of a madwoman," Soblen said, slowly, "and we can't do anything about it." His lack of emotion was stupefying.

Chapter VI

Smith Beffort was on watch between the side road and the house, in a sunken lane furrowed by ruts that the frost had hardened, but which must be transformed into a veritable mud-bath when it rained.

In the nascent dawn, Beffort could see the house at a thirty degree angle and a long stretch of Route 22, and beyond a curtain of bare skeletal trees he could just make out the squat mass of a large barn topped by a curious concrete tower. Apart from the barn, the region was quite deserted. During his brief round trip to Dunellen Police Station, Beffort had made a mental note of the fact that there were no other buildings on the roadside in the two miles that separated the barn from Dunellen.

The federal agent stretched himself out on the seat, lit a cigarette and, having switched on the engine, activated the heating. It was eight o'clock in the morning, but the leaden sky only gave off a parsimonious light. The cold was intense and dry, and both the ground and the leafless branches were covered by a thin layer of frost.

At eight forty-five the purr of a motor roused Beffort from his torpor. He craned his neck and saw that a Buick was drawing up outside the house. A man and a woman got out. The couple cross the narrow strip of bare ground separating the road from the house and went inside.

Beffort slid down behind the steering-wheel and stopped the engine. He was about two hundred yards from the house and it was scarcely probable that the muffled sound of the engine could be audible at that distance, but the G-man did not want to run any risk.

A few moments went by, and then the couple reappeared, accompanied by Hisato Keichu. The trio got into the Buick. Beffort reached for the ignition-key again, but the Buick turned into the lane that led to the barn and disappeared around the corner of the building.

Beffort looked hard, and after a brief lapse of time caught sight of several silhouettes at the top of the tower. Then a window opened and a strange metal object emerged slowly from the concrete block. It bore a vague resemblance to a television camera, but Beffort was too far away to make out any details. He simply noted that the object was pointing north-eastwards, and that it was exactly nine o'clock.

Time went by without anything else happening. At about nine twenty Beffort turned on his radio and happened upon a special news bulletin.

…that a thick fog has submerged an entire district in the Bronx, and the ground is covered by an oily substance that prevents all movement. In addition, the electricity and the telephone have been cut off within the perimeter. Since nine o'clock, nothing in the district has moved. We have informed you that Madame Atomos has threatened to attack the Schwartz bank, and we remind you, without drawing any hasty conclusions, that the establishment in question is situated in the heart of the Bronx….

There was a slight commotion, and then the speaker went on: *Some last-minute information informs us that Sam Forbes and several of his men are in the affected zone, and that the FBI directorate cannot make contact with them. This last point is extremely alarming, and questions are being asked in high places as to how the*

radio equipment in all the G-men's cars could have bro-
ken down at the same time. Dick Slatt, our specialist in
scientific questions, is going to tell you why he thinks
that Madame Atomos is using an electromagnetic ray of
fantastic power...

The precise voice of Dick Slatt filled the silence, but Beffort was no longer listening. He was looking at the camera-like object whose barrel was poking out of the tower, and had abruptly realized that it was pointing directly at New York. "Good God!" he swore. "That's the explanation of the presence of the concrete tower! That barn is probably one of Madame Atomos's laboratories. The Bronx paralyzed! Shit!"

He got out of the car, took his thirty-eight from its holster and ran along the sunken lane. With a great deal of skill and a little luck, he ought to be able to reach the barn without being spotted.

Cutting through the fog, the face and then the body of Maggie Fairbanks suddenly materialized in front of the car's hood. The young woman was livid, and clad in a fur wrap that Sam did not recognize. When he met her dead gaze he felt as if his heart was going to explode. He howled and seized the door-handle, but Alan Soblen took hold of him with all his strength.

"Don't be an imbecile, Forbes! You can see perfectly well that she's been atomized!"

"In the name of God, Soblen, let me go! That's my fiancée!" He struggled savagely, but the little doctor would not let go.

"Calm down, Forbes!" he pleaded, in his cold voice. "You can't do anything, except lose your own life. Remember all those dead people at Dubinsky's...."

Maggie Fairbanks had already disappeared into the mist, and the last thing Sam noticed was the green suitcase dangling from the end of her rigid right arm.

"She's evidently just stolen the money from the Schwartz Bank," said Dr. Soblen, without any apparent emotion.

Mutely, Sam Forbes directed his hallucinated gaze straight ahead. Paralyzed by his pain, he was momentarily incapable of any reaction, and only a residue of self-respect prevented him from giving way to despair.

Soblen respected his silence, unaware of the fury that was building in his companion—which swept away his enfeeblement as a gust of wind snuffs out a candle. The doctor started when Sam exploded: "Soblen! I swear to you that from this moment on, I shall not rest until I have the hide of Madame Atomos!"

Soblen heard a crack, and saw that the steering wheel had just come apart in Sam Forbes' hands. Privately, he thought that Madame Atomos would certainly come to grief is she should ever fall into those hands....

At the southern limit of the impenetrable zone, Maggie Fairbanks emerged from the thick fog, and slid rather than walked into the middle of the roadway, where she stood still.

A murmur ran through the crowd that was gathered on the opposite sidewalk, and two cops ran forward, swinging their nightsticks. One of them had witnessed the hold-up at Dubinsky's jewelry shop, only a few yards away from Mabel Wrist, and he instantly recognized the symptoms of the terrible atomic contamination on Maggie Fairbanks' face. He caught his colleague's arm, forcing him to take a step back. "Look out, Joe!" he grated, in a voice that was suddenly hoarse. "This broad is one of Madame Atomos's corpses. Go warn headquarters—I'll keep the gawkers back."

Joe drew away in the direction of the call-box on Tremont Avenue, elbows pumping. The other cop set about herding the crowd into an adjacent side-street.

At that moment, Maggie Fairbanks came forward, leaving the part of the roadway that was covered with the oily substance, and was in an excellent position when a black Mercury hurtled up at top speed. The car braked, level with the young woman, and Maggie leapt into the back seat, with her suitcase.

The cop drew his pistol and opened fire, but the Mercury swerved into Tremont Avenue and the bullets hit the wall of a neighboring building.

For the first time, Madame Atomos had collected one of her corpses….

Smith Beffort stopped, having gone a hundred yards in the cover of the embankment, and threw himself to the ground as a bullet whined past his ear. He rolled in the ditch and raised his head. He saw a shadow move behind the barn and immediately heard the roar of an engine.

He understood that the three were about to escape, and hurriedly covered twenty yards, hugging the ground. His movement had been too rapid for the invisible shooter to have had time to adjust his aim, but Beffort knew that the other would not take his eyes off the place where he had disappeared. He crept forward in the ditch, stood up cautiously in the shadow of a tree, and darted a glance between two low branches at the barn.

He saw that the Buick was moving slowly along the pathway, and that the camera-shaped object was no longer projecting from the window in the tower. There was a whistling sound above his head. He looked up, and watched in amazement as the tree was completely consumed, already crumbling into ashes under the effect of some terrible radiation.

Breathlessly, Beffort threw himself flat in the ditch and began crawling backwards. Behind him, he heard the howl of an engine driven at full power, and a thorn-bush three feet away from him suddenly burst into flames, burning like a torch. It was reduced to ash in the blink of an eye.

With sweat on his brow, Beffort glanced back over his shoulder. He saw the Buick bearing down on him like a tornado, and the yellow face of Hisato Keichu grimacing behind the slim barrel of an unfamiliar weapon. In spite of his terror, the G-man's reflexes came into play. The thirty-eight barked three times, and Hisato swayed back in his seat as the Buick went past, groaning. Beffort followed it automatically, emptying his clip, but only had the feeble satisfaction of seeing the tail-light shatter.

A moment later, the Buick had disappeared.

Weak at the knees, the federal agent raced to his car, hit the clutch savagely while turning the radio-switch, and caught another newsflash as he moved off.

...surprising, that the Bronx has now recovered its customary animation. The mysterious fog is evaporating slowly, but the oil covering the sidewalks and the roadway is no more than an inexplicable bad memory....

Smith Beffort slid a new ammunition-clip into his thirty-eight, and cornered on two wheels. He did not expect to catch up with the Buick, only desirous of reaching Dunellen in time to launch a general alert over the radio-waves.

...if Madame Atomos has not caused a massacre this time, she has nevertheless kept her promise, and the Schwartz Bank has just lost a hundred thousand dollars. The sinister Madame Atomos used young Maggie Fairbanks to carry out the hold-up. We remind you that Maggie Fairbanks was Sam Forbes' fiancée. The latter has just resigned from the FBI....

Beffort swore dully, took a final turn and braked hard in front of Dunellen Police Station. He leapt out, climbed the steps furiously and went into the squad room like a shell. Badge in hand, Beffort identified himself and sent a message to the FBI himself, while the radio-operator beside him alerted the Highway Patrol: "A light-colored Buick carrying a woman and two men, one of whom may be wounded...."

Smith Beffort made an unprecedented effort to keep his eyes open, but slumped unconscious on the corner of the table. He had, after all, done his share of the work.

Two motorcycle cops caught sight of the Buick on Route 22, just short of Scotch Plains. They switched on their sirens and launched themselves in pursuit of the car. They caught up with it three miles beyond Scotch Plains.

The senior patrolman was named Alex Witter. He stepped on the gas and drew level with the Buick, flagging it down with his gloved hand. The driver leaned forward, revealing a woman holding a strange apparatus—similar, his colleague later said, to a short glass-fiber fishing rod—and there was a brief flash.

Alex Witter caught fire like a bale of hay, and his body fell from the motor-cycle, which went on its way alone. The other motor-cyclist cleverly avoided the fire-ball that Witter had become, braked and turned sideways without hesitation, giving no further thought to the Buick. He had known Alex for ten years. When his eyes came to rest on the asphalt strip again, he saw nothing but a heap of ashes, still smoking.

In his report, which he wrote that same evening, he recorded with a trembling hand that even metal objects, including the buttons of Witter's uniform, his belt buckle, pistol and helmet had been reduced to ash.

It was getting dark in the Boss's office, but no one thought of putting on the light. Sam Forbes, Alan Soblen and Smith Beffort were standing in front of the Boss.

"I understand your reasons, Sam, but they don't seem to me to be sufficient to warrant your resignation. I told you yesterday that I've given you a free hand as well as unlimited credit. What more do you want?"

Sam walked nervously to the window. "I need freedom of action," he said, looking back. "Madame Atomos merits the mobilization of every last resource I have. At the FBI, I'll be constrained by your sacrosanct regulations not to employ the illicit means that will be necessary for me to attain my objectives."

The Boss took time out to light a cigar, blinking in the fleeting light that the match gave off. "It's just," he said, finally, "that I fear you'll be very vulnerable, Sam. Besides, you're placing me in a nasty situation. Public opinion wants the hide of this damnable devil-woman as much as you do. At present, the whole world has its eyes on us—and on you, who represent the FBI. The Japanese feel involved to the extent they're sending the famous Yosho Akamatsu of the Tokkoka by plane. He'll be here tonight, and I can tell you that with a man of his stripe on the case, Mother What's-her-name is going to get her ass spanked!"

Red with fury, the Boss shot out of his armchair like a rocket and strode back and forth so energetically that the floor shook. Anger had restored the Brooklyn vocabulary of his youth, and he used it immoderately and without hindrance. "If the Jap grabs the prize before us, all the rags in the States will be on our case. I need you more than ever, and this is the moment you pick to set sail!" He spat out his cigar, ground it underfoot, and went back to slump heavily into his pivoting armchair. "Well," he said, in a tone that was suddenly soft, "I refuse your resignation, Sam Forbes. You're going to go on working for us under cover, which will allow you to strike all the low blows you need to use. Draw on FBI funds, call on my men—but rip the bandages off Mother Atomos. No need for reports—do whatever you want. Who do you want for immediate collaborators?"

Forbes thought for a moment, with his head lowered, than raised his eyes again, with his jaw set. "Smith Beffort," he said, "and Dr. Soblen. I know they'll agree."

The two men confirmed that with a gesture.

"OK, Sam," said the Boss. "Anyone else?"

Sam Forbes smiled joylessly. "Ask this Yosho Akamatsu if he wouldn't like a partner. In view of the importance of the game, that would be better than our dogging his heels."

Chapter VII

Subconsciously, they had imagined that he would be short, thin and more or less ugly, but Yosho Akamatsu was five nine, a hundred and sixty pounds, square in the shoulders and thin in the hips. He was dark-haired, and his elongated face with prominent cheek-bones had an undeniable virile charm.

The Boss made the introductions briskly, and rapidly passed on to the nub of the matter. "Sam, as you hoped, Mr. Akamatsu is in favor of a tight collaboration. Besides, before leaving Tokyo he had the same idea and hasn't arrived empty-handed. Armed with cuttings from the America press, he's ferreted through his files and discovered the true identity of the person who calls herself Madame Atomos. If you would, Mr. Akamatsu?"

The Tokkoka's special agent spoke the language of Uncle Sam with hardly any accent, and his rapid speech never stumbled over a current expression. Yosho spoke as a stream runs, with brief changes of intonation and a mobility of gesture surprising in a man of his race. Forbes sensed that he was possessed of a high-powered dynamism, a morality as straight as an arrow and a boundless enthusiasm. The man was captivating.

"First, one slight correction," Yosho Akamatsu began. "I'm not absolutely certain that Madame Atomos is really the woman in question, but let's say that I'd lay odds of ten to one. Two years ago, the Sasebo police were informed by a peasant named Masashi Shimuara that strange things were happening in the vicinity of her fields. Shimuara grows tea on the side of a hill. His house is at the bottom of the slope, and of the far side, beyond the tea-trees, there were three enormous rocks...." He paused to offer round his packet of Shinsei. "They're quite ordinary," he said, apologetically, "but I never smoke anything else...."

Sam gave him a light, and the Tokkoka agent continued: "Shimuara had tried to get rid of the three rocks cutting off his plantation himself, and then to get someone else to shift them, but their weight defied all efforts. They could have been blown up, but our peasant feared that the blast might ruin his trees, so he left them where they were. As you know, a tea-tree is a little round bush no more than three feet high, so Shimuara had a clear view of the rocks.

"One morning, the man observed that they had disappeared. He ran to the end of his field, and found nothing but an enormous heap of ash where the granite blocks had been. He thanked heaven for having accomplished this miracle, worked all day, and went to bed. The next day, two hundred tea-trees had been volatilized! Shimuara did not thank heaven for that, but went to inform the Sasebo police. They undertook an investigation, and quickly discovered an abandoned concrete building at the top of the mountain.

"The building had been recently constructed, and offered certain peculiarities that left the police perplexed. They informed Tokyo, and I was there that same evening. I figured out immediately that the building was a laboratory, and spotted the tracks left by a heavy truck—doubtless when the contents were removed—on the only trail leading down to the valley. Around the laboratory, within a radius of a hundred yards, there was not a single tree or pebble—nothing but earth covered with ash."

Smith Beffort scowled. "I know that tune," he said. "Out near Dunellen I was nearly burned like a matchstick! Go on, continue—I'm sure that you're on the right track."

Yosho stubbed out his cigarette-end and crossed his legs. "From the agency that sold the land, I learned that the purchaser was a woman named Kanoto Yoshimuta, and that she lived in Nagasaki. In that city, I was told that the woman had left her apartment ten year before, having resigned from the university, where she was a professor. The trail stopped there, but I found out nevertheless that Kanoto Yoshimuta was fifty years old that she had specialized in atomic research, that she had lost her family in the explosion of the second atom bomb, and that her hatred for Americans was limitless. I remind you that this took place two years ago.

"At that time, I had nothing much for which to reproach the woman, and I abandoned the case, forgetting it completely. Time passed—a year exactly—and the mystery of the *Mororan* burst forth. The *Mororan* was an old cargo ship only good for scrapping when it ran aground on a reef in the Bungo Strait. As it was sailing without a cargo at the moment of the wreck, and had little value, it was left where it was for the time being. The inhabitants of a nearby village, living entirely on the produce of their fishing, went to steal all its ropes, strip out all the woodwork and, in brief, to finish the job of making the old tub into a veritable wreck.

"One fine morning in June, however, the *Mororan* and the reef that had caused its ruin disappeared. The boat couldn't have floated away, since it lacked a bottom, and couldn't have been dragged out to sea since there hadn't been a storm. As for the reef, that was even more inexplicable! I received the information by radio, suddenly remembered the Sasebo affair, and telephoned to have all the roads giving access to the place blocked.

"We discovered a new concrete laboratory on the hill overlooking the village, and the inhabitants recognized a photograph of Kanoto Yoshimuta, but it was impossible to find any trace of her."

"Damn it!" interjected Beffort. "It seems to me, though, that you'd moved quickly enough!"

Yosho smiled amiably. "I had had the roads watched, Mr. Beffort, but not the sea! And I mention, in passing, that no point in Japan is more than six hundred miles from the coast…."

"What's your opinion regarding the disappearance of the Sasebo rocks and the *Mororan*?" Sam asked.

"One of my friends, Professor Omiya, thought that an extremely powerful thermal lance had been used."

"I think so too," said Dr. Soblen.

The Boss brandished his cigar. "So far as I'm concerned," he said, "there's no doubt about it: Kanoto Yoshimuta and Madame Atomos are one and the same. But how much further does that certainty get us?"

Yosho threw a file on to the desk. "This far," he murmured. "The fingerprints and photograph of Madame Atomos! The photo comes from the University of Nagasaki and is twelve years old, but fingerprints don't change, do they?"

Sam Forbes clapped the Japanese policeman on the shoulder, amicably. "Yosho," he said, "I think we're going to make a damn good team!"

"*Hai*," said the Tokkoka man. "I think so too."

Yosho Akamatsu expressed a desire to see the barn, so Sam and Beffort accompanied him, while Dr. Soblen followed them in his own car. The four men made a preliminary stop to examine the charred trees and bushes, and Yosho declared that the remains were similar in every respect to those he had seen in Japan.

In the concrete tower the Japanese policeman noticed hooks set next to the window and said: "This place has obviously never been used as a laboratory. Let's say, rather, that Madame Atomos made use of this tower to aim her electromagnetic ray at New York.

"Always inside concrete buildings," said Sam. "It's obvious that concrete plays a considerable role in the realization of our enemy's criminal projects. That might be a necessity for her, Soblen?"

The scientist pulled a face. "The material is efficacious against atomic radiations," he said, "but the thickness here doesn't seem to me to be adequate."

"It doesn't matter how it protects the operators—the important thing, so far as we're concerned, is that it's necessary. In that case, we have a radical means of preventing Madame Atomos from doing any harm."

"Yes," Yosho approved. "It's sufficient to identify all the concrete buildings in the region that aren't absolutely necessary."

"That's right."

Beffort clapped his hands. "Good idea! But we have to put it into application immediately."

They went back to the cars, and Sam's radio message triggered the biggest police operation in the history of the USA. The newspapers published special editions in the form of a tract, television and radio stations joined the dance, and within an hour of Sam's first call, all the concrete buildings in the region had been visited by the police or the civil authorities.

By midday, an impressive pile of reports had accumulated in the Boss's office, and the latter was wearing a smile that spoke volumes about his jubilation. "Fifty-three towers identical to the one in Dunellen have been identified in the vicinity of New York, Washington, Baltimore, Philadelphia and Boston. It's evident that Madame Atomos intends to attack those five cities first, and that the Chinook affair was merely a final trial, or a diversionary maneuver." Suddenly adopting a severe tone, he added: "Twenty towers surround Washington, and it's been noted that their principal windows are facing the White House. No need to draw you a picture, is there?" He opened a drawer and took out a sheet of paper. "These buildings," he said, "have been put up recently, always adjacent to farms, barns or houses rented by a certain Lydia Watanabe. The woman in question is a pretty young brunette—thirty at most, according to the witnesses She speaks our language perfectly, but he owner who've had dealings with her in declaring that, even if she isn't Chinese or Japanese, she's probably of Asiatic origin."

"A Eurasian," suggested Yosho Akamatsu

Smith Beffort started. "I know her!" he exclaimed. "She was in the Buick with Hisato Keichu!"

The Boss brandished another sheet of paper. "This report is from a motor-cycle policeman. He was partnered with Alex Witter and he also mentions a pretty brunette woman. She's obviously the same one you saw, Beffort, since she was still in the Buick. This Lydia Watanabe is, I'm convinced, one of Madame Atomos's closest collaborators. In twelve hours, I'll have a picture of her circulated. Until then, I don't suppose there's much we can do, eh?"

They agreed, save for Dr. Soblen, who was sitting on his own in a corner of the office. He was reading the *New York Herald*, seemingly utterly indifferent to the progress of the conversation. The Boss, who liked to be the center of attention, spoke to him directly: "What do you think, Doctor?"

Soblen jumped and blinked. "Excuse me," he said, "but I didn't hear what you said." He looked at Sam Forbes, and said, softly. "I don't want to give you any false hope, Sam, but I'll cut off my head if Maggie Fairbanks is dead!"

Sam went pale. "What are you saying, Doc?"

"Events are unfolding too quickly for us to be able to examine everything in detail," Soblen went on, "but reading this article has made me think again, about Chinook and Dubinsky's, and the way that John Ferby and Mabel Wrist were abandoned after having done their work. In both cases, witnesses heard the famous buzzing sound, didn't they?"

"Yes," said Sam, colorlessly.

"When we saw her through the mist, Maggie Fairbanks was less than ten feet away from us. Did you hear the buzzing, Sam?"

"No, but that doesn't mean anything. Harry Diamond, the road-sweeper in Chinook, didn't hear it either."

"Because John Ferby was not yet in action—but Maggie was, since we've established that she came to our car *after* stealing the hundred thousand dollars."

Sam shook his head. "I don't believe it," he sighed.

The little man became suddenly animated. "You don't want to believe it, but it's logical to presume that Madame Atomos has kept your fiancée alive, in order to have a means of putting pressure on you at her disposal. Besides, Maggie wasn't remotely controlled by the customary car."

"How do you know?"

"The streets were impassable, remember, Sam? This newspaper has an interview with a policeman who saw the whole thing and even shot at the car. He affirms that the Mercury picked up Maggie Fairbanks outside the oily zone, and that the young woman was literally thrown into the back seat. Previously, that back seat has been occupied by the mysterious remote control apparatus...."

Uncertainly, Sam passed a trembling hand over his face. "In that case," he said, full of emotion, "how is it that Maggie obeyed Madame Atomos so passively?"

"Hypnotism," said Soblen.

At that moment, the telephone rang, and the Boss answered it. "Hello!" he said. "Yes, it's me...."

The receiver crackled for some time; then the Boss sat down slowly, and made a few notes on his blotter. "Can you repeat the time?" he asked. There was another brief crackle of sound, and then the Boss hung up and put his hands in his pockets. "Madame Atomos has just warned our central office that she intends to attack the Finnegan Bank at three thirty," he said. "She's told us not to intervene. If we make a move, she threatens to destroy the building containing the bank completely. He consulted his watch, and continued: "It's two o'clock. We've got about an hour to find a mean of preventing another hold-up. It's not much."

Sam Forbes got to his feet.

"Preventing the hold-up is nothing," he said. "For that, it's sufficient to evacuate the building and put the money in a safe place—but that's not what we're aiming for. This is what I propose: warn the directors to have the door watched, and empty the place as soon as Madame Atomos's minion appears. That way, we'll avoid a repetition of the dramas in Chinook and Dubinsky's je-

73

welry store, and can concentrate on watching out for and following the car transporting the remote control apparatus."

Yosho Akamatsu raised his eyebrows. "Your plan is reasonable and logical, provided that Madame Atomos follows her usual procedure—but suppose she modifies her technique?"

"In that case," Sam replied, "We'll modify ours."

None of them really expected to be able to counter the action of the diabolical Madame Atomos, especially with a frontal attack, but they all thought that if an adversary telephones to advertise her next strike, she runs a considerable risk of falling prey to a poisoned arrow as she flees....

Chapter VIII

The Finnegan Bank occupied the entire ground floor of a projecting block, opening by virtue of that fact on to three very busy streets, with five doors piercing each of the three façades. At three fifteen p.m. the sidewalks were swarming and the roadway invisible beneath lines of vehicles. The intersection was a huge bottleneck, and every time a red light came on, a crowd of pedestrians invaded the void left by the cars, rushed into the large stores and created an indescribable confusion.

Shouting vendors were waving newspapers relating the discovery of the concrete towers, but the crowd remained indifferent. Madame Atomos remained a being native to an abstract realm, whose criminal acts belonged to the domain of anticipation, and the man in the street did not really believe in her. To be sure, there had been Chinook, Dubinsky and the mysterious paralysis in the Bronx, but humankind needs to see in order to believe, and only admits that reality surpasses fiction on rare occasions.

Lost among that swarming mass, Sam Forbes, Soblen, Beffort and Yosho Akamatsu anticipated that a fantastic catastrophe might leave hundreds dead in a matter of seconds.

Madame Atomos had chosen her terrain with a remarkable subtlety. That gigantic crossroads of New Yorker activity was practically indefensible; on the contrary, it presented an ill-omened vulnerability. The directors of the Finnegan Bank had refused to interrupt its activities, and the establishment's fifteen doors were allowing waves of clients in and out. If such conditions made the task of Forbes and his companions seem impossible, the density of the crowd at least established one certainty: no car, whether it were piloted by the Devil himself, could either approach or draw away faster than a man on foot.

At three twenty-eight Sam Forbes was lying in wait on the other side of the intersection opposite the main entrance of the bank. Dr. Soblen was fifty yards away, while Beffort and Akamatsu were watching the two roads along the sides of the building. Four cars equipped with radio transmitters and receivers were stationed in the adjacent streets, and it had been agreed that whoever spotted the car transporting the remote control apparatus would follow it, then immediately establish contact with the FBI switchboard. The latter was responsible for centralizing information and disseminating it to the other three vehicles.

At three thirty exactly, as she had promised, Madame Atomos attacked. It went unnoticed by the mass, but Sam, Soblen, Beffort and Akamatsu understood immediately that hostilities had been opened, and were attentive.

Three cars came to an abrupt halt while crossing the intersection, with the result that the circulation of traffic, already slow, was decisively interrupted. A jam resulted, while people tried in vain to push the vehicles that had broken down toward the sidewalk; their tires seemed to be stuck at the ground. At first, discussion was drowned out by an infernal cacophony of horns; then, all of a sudden, the engines stopped turning and the klaxons stopped howling.

In a strange silence, some drivers dived under their hoods, while others contented themselves with stubbornly turning their mute ignition-keys. Meanwhile, on the sidewalks, sniggering groups of people accumulated—with the effect that the nascent disorder got even worse.

Suddenly, with no apparent reason, the traffic lights stopped working. Simultaneously, the lights in all the stores, the bank and the advertising displays went out. The people inside the buildings were plunged into a disagreeable gloom, and flooded toward the exits.

The intersection and the neighboring streets were quickly overflowing, and the human tide was further augmented when the people who had been on the subway platforms surged back into the open air. The subways and their moving staircases had stopped; telephones were no longer working; television and radio sets, and hairdressers' driers and helmets had also broken down. An enormous quantity of people found themselves brutally deprived of all activity, and clusters of gawkers accumulated at the windows.

With a dull tramping sound, the crowd started milling around like a furious herd of cattle, with violent reactions whenever two waves headed in directly opposite directions encountered one another. Everybody wanted to get out of the whirlpool, but as no one would let anyone pass, they all remained in place, struggling, jostling and bumping into one another violently—and very soon came to blows.

A riot broke out in the middle of the intersection. Women and children were trampled underfoot, and cars turned over. A gas tank emptied out its contents and the dangerous liquid spread out over the roadway. There was a spark, and the gasoline caught fire, drawing the flames toward other tanks, which exploded in their turn with sprays of flaming gas that fell upon the panicked crowd.

A woman transformed into a living torch ran into a shop and communicated the fire to a display-unit loaded with net curtains. Within ten seconds, the entire unit was in flames, while the shop assistants, prisoners of their enclosures, disappeared in the conflagration.

Outside, it was frightful. The intersection was literally ablaze. All the cars were being grilled on the spot, and the ground was nothing but a sheet of flame. The streets by means of which the crowd might have been able to flee were blocked by curiosity-seekers arriving from neighboring districts, and vehicles were mounting the sidewalks, trying to turn around in order to escape the disaster, crushing those who could not help getting in their way. Black stinking smoke enveloped everything, and a horrible odor of charred flesh spread through the hot air.

Sam Forbes struck out hard at someone who grabbed hold of him, and ran to the sidewalk of the bank; his clothes were in tatters and a steel shard had traced a bloody gash on his cheek. He was bundled away by a howling group and slammed against a display-window, which gave way under his weight. At the same moment, a gas tank exploded, hurling its petrol on to the sidewalk he had just been obliged to quit, and the howling group disappeared within the crackling flames.

Sam leapt inside the store, fought his way through to the back of the shop and emerged into a courtyard stuffed with cadavers. The federal agent suppressed a surge of horror and forced himself to take a closer look at the corpses, which no flame had touched.

"Get out!" howled a voice. "Get out!"

Sam raised his eyes and saw a head leaning out toward him from a fourth-floor window. "What happened?" he shouted.

The man leaned forward, his finger pointing at an archway piercing the building on the far side of the courtyard. "These people had taken refuge here," he shouted. "Then a woman carrying a suitcase came out of the service entrance…."

Sam glanced to his left and saw a little door bearing a metal plate, bearing the legend FINNEGAN BANK SERVICE ENTRANCE in black letters.

"She went across the yard," the man continued, "and the people dropped like flies as she passed. Get out! Get out! She went out that way, but she might come back…."

Forbes ran in the direction of the archway and went through it, emerging into a passageway blocked by two bodies. He leapt over them, continued straight on, and abruptly emerged into one of the streets running alongside the bank. It was the one that Yosho Akamatsu had been watching, but Sam could not see him. In any case, crazed groups were running toward the far end of the street, and Sam was hustled in that direction.

An intact corpse lying on the sidewalk showed him which way to go; he knew that the woman had crossed over when he saw the corpses lying in the roadway. In the midst of the almighty confusion Sam accelerated his pace and reached the main road. He leapt on to the roof of a car while the crowd flowed around him, and finally spotted the person he was chasing. She was walking rapidly but unhurriedly, with the mechanical gait that was peculiar to Madam Atomos's dead people; a large cardboard-pulp suitcase was dangling from the end of her rigid arm.

Sam examined the street. It was extremely crowded, and it was obvious that the remote control vehicle must be parked further away, in the avenue where the sirens of fire-trucks were blaring. The woman would take at least seven minutes to reach the avenue. That left an appreciable margin.

Sam leapt down from the roof, ran off at top speed and reached the side-street where his car was parked. As he went, he observed that Madame Atomos's electro-magnetic ray had only paralyzed the intersection, and was not surprised when his engine turned over immediately.

He pulled out brutally, tearing the wing from a vehicle traveling in the opposite direction, and roared away. Twenty yards further on he was brought to a halt by the terrified crowd, and thought that his car was going o be overturned by the frantic assault, but then found himself suddenly in the clear. He floored the accelerator and the Chevrolet bounded forwards, narrowly avoiding a second human wave.

Sam turned into the avenue, rolled as far as the next intersection, and perceived Madam Atomos's dead woman moving placidly along the sidewalk at her automaton pace. A woman who had just brushed past her collapsed, thunderstruck, but no one paid any attention to her. At that moment, her life no longer counted for much, especially when there were others to think about.

Madame Atomos's instrument crossed a broad avenue, stepped up on to the sidewalk, and came to a halt. Almost immediately, a blue Chrysler stopped beside her, and the front passenger door opened. The driver grabbed the suitcase that the woman held out to him, closed the door again, and moved off.

The woman collapsed gently, rolled into the gutter and did not move again.

Sam Forbes executed a swift half-turn, spotted the Chrysler heading in the direction of Manhattan, caught up with it in less than a mile and maintained himself at a respectful distance. With his index finger he activated his radio, waited for the tone and unhooked the mike. "Tom One calling Central," he said.

The switchboard-operator was on the alert, for the response came back immediately: "Central here!"

"I'm on the track. It's a blue Chrysler and we're heading for Manhattan, presently on the point of going over the East River at Williamsburg. Over and out."

He replaced the mike, vaguely hearing the speaker repeat his position; and then, after a pause, the return call came in. Akamatsu and Beffort were already following, but there was no news of Dr. Soblen.

Level with Central Park, Sam gave his position again, and did likewise after having crossed the Hudson heading for Leonia. Via the intermediary of the switch-board, Smith Beffort let him know that he was getting closer rapidly, but Yosho Akamatsu declared that he had taken a wrong turn, and that they could not count on him in the immediate future.

Sam groaned. The Japanese man should have been able to follow the Chrysler with ease, but being alone, and not being sufficiently familiar with the city, he had become as ineffective as a new-born puppy.

Ahead of him, the Chrysler was heading west at top speed, and Sam sometimes had difficulty not losing sight of it. Once he got too close and had seen the driver's eyes looking at him through his rear-view mirror. Now he was keeping his distance, but that complicated matters.

The Chrysler took Route 56, turned on to 39 and finally turned on to 4. Sam picked up his mike. "We're on 4," he said. "Still heading west."

The speaker repeated the information, paused, then gave the position to Tom Two and Tom Three—Beffort and Akamatsu respectively. Smith Beffort was getting closer, with his foot down, having just past Leonia and joining 4 at 93. Akamatsu was a long way behind, but following nevertheless.

Dr. Soblen abruptly materialized. He had been caught up in the crowds and had only just reached Manhattan. He said that the large store had been half-destroyed, that there were hundreds dead and that it would take at least two days to clear the intersection of the burned-out cars that were blocking it.

The operator that had transmitted Soblen's message said no more, and there was silence in the car. Sam groped for a packet of cigarettes, took one out and lit it with a nervous hand, then returned his attention to the Chrysler, which had suddenly begun to slow down. Sam did likewise, leaving three cars between himself and his prey. The Chrysler suddenly swerved, passing through a side-tunnel, and Sam saw it take a dirt road that seemed to be heading toward Paramus. He turned too, went through the tunnel and grabbed his mike as he emerged in the vicinity of the dirt road.

"Tom One calling Central…."

The radio remained mute. Sam repeated himself without result. He went some way along the road before making another call, but the only response was a vague hiss. He gave his approximate position anyway, just in case, and replaced the mike because the road as gradually transforming into a sleigh-run and he required all his skill to negotiate it.

He accelerated, saw the Chrysler stopped at the bottom of the hill, and continued straight ahead, along a track that was scarcely visible but had the advantage of taking him down to a lower level, hiding him from the gaze of the Chrysler's driver.

Swiftly, the federal agent quit the Chevrolet, went back up the track at a run, and lay down behind the embankment.

A Lincoln station-wagon had just stopped in front of the Chrysler, and two men were transferring a square metal apparatus that appeared to be very heavy. The apparatus having been placed in the back seat of the station-wagon, the driver of the Chrysler took hold of the cardboard-pulp suitcase containing the money from the Finnegan Bank and climbed in beside is companion. Then the station-wagon moved off, passed in front of Sam and drew away toward 4.

Sam went back to his car, made a three-point turn, and launched the Chevrolet on the track of the Lincoln. Immediately, he tried his radio again, but he did not have time to find out whether it was still working.

Immediately after the first turn, the station-wagon had stopped, blocking the path, and one of the two men was standing in front of the car, aiming a bizarre weapon at Sam. Its slender barrel bore some resemblance to a short fiberglass fishing-rod. In a flash, the federal agent remembered the motor-cycle cop's report, thrust his door open and hurled himself into the ditch with a desperate leap.

At the same moment there was a brief crepitation, and Sam Forbes saw his Chevrolet burst into flames, melt and disintegrate. The gas tank suddenly exploded, producing a cloud of acrid black smoke, which spread spontaneously over the road, and probably saved the G-man's life.

In spite of the curtain of smoke, Sam emptied his thirty-eight in the direction of the station-wagon, firing blindly. So great was his rage that he continued pressing the trigger long after the last bullet had gone.

The roar of an engine restored the integrity of his self-composure, and he did not have time for self-criticism. For want of prudence he had nearly lost his life, but all was not yet lost.

He ran back along the road to the abandoned Chrysler, turned it around and followed the road, his jaws clenched in violent irritation, mingled with the intense fright he had experienced—but it gave way to an absolute emptiness when he passed what had once been a car. Nothing remained of it now but a miserable heap of ash, which gusts of wind were already dispersing.

Chapter IX

The Lincoln station-wagon was no longer visible when Sam reached the junction, and four routes offered themselves to his choice. The first two were formed by Route 61, and Sam eliminated them straight away. There remained the two branches of 4. One of them headed toward New York, the other continued westwards. Sam opted for the section of 4 that continued toward Paterson.

He put his foot down, passed under 62 and over the Saddle River, and continued flat out, without taking any notice of speed-limits. He was playing his last card, not unaware that if he lost track of Madame Atomos's fanatics, more crimes would be committed in the hours to come, and that the disasters would only increase in magnitude.

Sam thought momentarily about Maggie Fairbanks, but set it resolutely aside. Action alone could settle this, and any mental softness, however fleeting, could only have a deleterious effect. There are times when a man has to be able to forget the impulses of the heart, and Sam was firmly convinced that this was one of them.

He overtook twenty vehicles, went through Paterson, and continued along 504. He went past the golf courses at top speed, reached Pompton and uttered a howl of joy. Less than three hundred yards away, he had just recognized the square rear end of the Lincoln station-wagon. With immense prudence, he resumed his pursuit.

The dashboard clock indicated four-fifty, and dusk was slowly falling. In fifteen minutes the light would be inadequate and he would have to switch on the head-lights.

With moist hands, Sam slid a new clip into his thir-ty-eight, checked the gas, and wiped away the blood that was running down his cheek with his sleeve. He did not know when the wound had opened up again, but ob-served in the mirror that the collar of his shirt was stained with dry blood. A downward glance reminded him that his clothes were in a lamentable state, and he reflected that the preceding hours had been singularly fortunate. He had escaped death, had just found the Lin-coln again, and no cop had tried to arrest him. That was luck with a capital L!

Up ahead, the station-wagon's headlights had just come on. It left Pompton, and turned on to 202, heading for Oakland and Darlington.

Further on, the station-wagon turned on to a narrow by-road, and disappeared behind an exceedingly high wall that seemed to have no end.

With all his lights off, Sam followed cautiously, keeping watch for the Lincoln's lights. The other car slowed down and veered left, hidden once again behind the wall. Sam cut off the engine, letting the Chrysler's momentum carry it forward, and reached the angle of the wall. His eyes widened in amazement at the bare ground that he saw before him, extending all the way to the dis-tant summit of the hill.

There was no visible breach in the wall. The razed ground was perfectly flat, but the station-wagon was no longer visible.

Sam thought about a trap, started his engine again and continued on his way, ducking down instinctively. He saw a somber mass, cut off the engine and parked the Chrysler off the road, beside a ragged hedge surrounding a low building that seemed abandoned, and went back to the road on foot.

In spite of the gloom, he could make out the long pale strip formed by the wall, and thought that if the station-wagon had stopped on the flat ground it would be darkly outlined against the wall or the horizon. There was something mysterious and incomprehensible here, and the federal agent was momentarily disconcerted. Then, as his head was set very firmly on his shoulders, he concluded that if the station-wagon had not taken off into the air, it could only be under the ground.

Slowly Sam moved over the ground, advancing step by step in the direction o the corner formed by the wall and the road, and spotted, as he had hoped, the double furrows left by the station-wagon's tires in the soft ground. He followed the tracks for about fifty yards, and then suddenly lost them on open ground, and stood there dazedly, his legs weak, incapable of taking another step and very ill at ease.

He felt a strange torpor overwhelm him, suddenly lost consciousness, and dropped like a stone.

The room was rectangular and had no windows. The concrete walls gave off a dull bluish light, and a steel door occupied one entire side of the rectangle. The ceiling was pierced by an air-vent about three feet in diameter, terminated by a metal grille.

Sam Forbes saw that he was lying on a mat set on the ground, and that he was entirely naked. He looked for his clothes, but quickly understood, on seeing the ground and the bare walls, that the mat was the only object that had been left within his reach.

Sam did not feel anything in particular. He could not explain the origin of his unconsciousness, any more than he could estimate its duration, and no longer knew where he was.

He stood up without difficulty, stuck his ear to the door and perceived a distant hum; save for that, the silence was complete.

At a loose end, and vaguely anxious, the federal agent made a tour of his cell. Five paces by six, the ceiling within reach of an extended hand, a temperature probably somewhere between twenty and twenty-five degrees Centigrade, solid walls without any hollow resonance suggestive of an exit....

A perfect trap, from which a human being could not escape.

The grille at the mouth of the ventilation-shaft was tempting, but Sam was immediately discouraged by its rigidity. The blast of a mine would not have been sufficient to tear it away.

He sat down on the mat and examined it. It was made of braided jute, and could not serve any other purpose than the one for which it was designed.

Suddenly, the light went out and Sam was plunged into darkness. A few moments went by, and the G-man began to breathe lightly, under the impression that the air was getting heavier. He got up, felt the ceiling with his fingertips, found the grille and realized brutally that the air-supply had been cut off.

"Listen to me, Mr. Forbes," said a female vice, suddenly, "for this is the first and last time that you will have the opportunity. I am Madame Atomos. You are twenty meters underground and have absolutely no chance of escaping. You are an American, and I hate you. You will die of asphyxiation, in the same manner as your fiancée, Maggie Fairbanks, and I shall then make use of you. Goodbye, Mr. Forbes, and *bon voyage*...."

There was a faint crackle, and silence fell again. Sam started searching feverishly for the loudspeaker. He knew that the sentence could not be appealed, and only wondered how much time he might have before the lack of air did its work.

He forced himself to remain calm, but I hands were trembling as they wandered over the walls. Maggie's death was no longer in doubt now, and all Dr. Soblen's deductions had been swept away.

Slowly, Sam made a tour of his narrow cell, but the continuity of the walls was flawless. His fingers soon made contact with the grille again, and he understood that he would never discover the loudspeaker. Breathlessly, he pulled at the grille with all his might, but it did not budge. It must have been embedded in the concrete.

Sam let himself fall to the ground, exhausted. He was having difficulty breathing now, and guessed that he only had a few minutes left. He got to his feet again, painfully, and resumed the search for the loudspeaker. He hoped to be able to detach its wires and perhaps contrive a short circuit on the grille. If the current were sufficiently powerful, the metal bars might melt like sticks of wax…or break, or not budge at all.

It was problematic, but it was the only solution.

He located the loudspeaker when he had almost given up hope of doing so, in the corner of the cell to the right of the steel door. Despairingly, he felt the smooth orifice pitted with imperceptible holes. He broke his fingernails on the unassailable surface, his hands rapidly becoming bloody. Abruptly lacking oxygen, he felt his legs give way beneath him. He collapsed, coming to a rest with his back to the wall, his hands clutching at his throat, trying furiously to fill his lungs, while multicolored lights danced before his eyes, performing a frenzied saraband.

At one point, he emerged from the fantastic vortex that was dragging him down, experienced the sensation that his body was being crushed beneath tons of stone, and fell unconscious again.

His agony continued for a long time, and was extremely painful, interrupted by fugitive moments of lucidity, in the course of which he understood that he was living his final seconds, Then there was the great dive, the last sigh.

Sam Forbes died at seven twenty p.m., while Madame Atomos was in her office, carefully examining a map of Washington and pointing a neatly-filed fingernail at the White House…

The switchboard was bathed in thick smoke, and the Boss was turning round and round like a squirrel in a cage.

Sitting down wearily, Beffort, Soblen and Akamatsu were smoking cigarette after cigarette. Dr. Soblen, who was not used to it, coughed periodically, and every time, the Boss shot him a murderous glance.

The operator was at the apparatus, having just come to the end of a five-minute break.

"Get on with it!" barked the Boss.

The operator pressed his switch. "Central calling Tom One…. Central calling Tom One…." He persisted a while longer, but had addressed a negative shake of the head to the Boss.

"It's incredible!" said the Boss. "Forbes isn't a man to have us without news for such a long time. He was on 4 when he sent his last message…"

"I was about five miles behind him," Beffort said. He leaned over, stubbed out his cigarette-butt in an ashtray that was full to the brim, and added: "I went as far as Paterson; then, as nothing came through from the switchboard, I slowly retraced my steps. My radio was working perfectly and the transmission was clear. Forbes must have got into trouble."

This was what everyone thought, but they were carefully avoiding expressing the thought.

Time passed, punctuated every five minutes by a call from the operator, but the latter's speakers remained ominously silent.

About eight o'clock, a G-Man telephoned asking for Smith Beffort, and the latter, alerted by an orderly, went back to his office. "Beffort," I said. "I'm listening."

"Davis here. I think I've got something for you. I was there when Sam Forbes started chasing the blue Chrysler...."

"Good God!" Beffort swore. "I thought the matter was top secret!"

The other laughed. "Not in the service, pal! Are you listening to me or bawling me out?"

"Go on," Beffort groaned, "but look lively."

"I know, I know! You're at the switchboard with the Boss waiting for a call from Forbes' aren't you?"

Beffort sighed. Nothing in this damned place passed unnoticed.

"Don't moan." Davis went on, "for if I hadn't been on the ball, I'd have missed the whisper with the city police chief."

"All right! Down, boy!"

"A bloke just came into see him. He'd tried to park his car in his usual spot, but it was already occupied. As the place was deserted he got his dander up and headed for the nearest police station. A beat cop went back with him to cast an eye over the car. It's a blue Chrysler, this year's model. It had been stolen this morning, but because there was blood on the seat the cop left it where it was...."

"Where is this car, Davis?" Beffort interjected, dryly. When he had that information Beffort hung up without even saying thank you and ran back to the switchboard. He brought the Boss up to date and the latter jumped.

"This might be it!" he said, delightedly. "It's the road that Sam was following. Get out there right away, Beffort. I'll give orders for no one to touch the Chrysler!"

Beffort opened the door violently, but felt a hand on his arm.

"Gently," said Yosho Akamatsu. "I'll go with you."

The Boss had acted quickly, for there were no cops prowling around when Beffort and Akamatsu reached the place.

Smith Beffort parked his service Chevrolet on the far side of the two cars that were standing on the open ground, and went to knock on the door of the small house, through which light was filtering. A tall man with a mistrustful expression opened it, and Beffort stuck his badge under his nose unhesitatingly. The other relaxed immediately and let the two men into an ill-furnished room.

"I haven't got much," he said, as if to excuse himself, "but I only come here occasionally, after work. I live in Darlington, and I'm repairing this cottage bit by bit...."

"You don't have any neighbors?"

"No, and that why I smelled a rat when I saw the Chrysler on my land. I also wondered how the guy had left again. There isn't a train station or bus-stop for miles, and the road only has the tracks of the Chrysler and my old crock."

"What's that high wall along the road?"

"Shhh! It's the Senator's estate. He only comes out in summer, and the nest is empty for the rest of the time."

Beffort asked him a few more questions; then, convinced that he knew no more, he went out with Akamatsu and went to examine the Chrysler. Traces of blood were visible on the back of the driver's seat, only noticeable because the leather was very pale. They did not give rise to any definite conclusion.

Doubt was filtering into the minds of the two men when Yosho found an empty ammunition-clip for a thirty-eight wedged between the seat and the back. They searched the vehicle more carefully, and Smith Beffort discovered a jacket-button. It was nothing special, resembling thousands of other buttons, but Beffort had a feeling that he had seen it before somewhere. It was only an impression, but Beffort added the button to the ammunition-clip and sniffed something suspicious.

"I wouldn't be surprised," he groaned, "if Sam had driven this vehicle. We'll need to lift the fingerprints from that steering wheel, and not go too far from this place…one never knows." Beffort always followed his nose.

Chapter X

It was nine thirty, and a legion of large clouds were hiding the moon behind their moving mass, so well that Beffort and Akamatsu could not see more than ten paces ahead.

Someone from the Oakland Laboratory had come out very quickly after Beffort's call. He had spent ten minutes inside the Chrysler and had set off again with a set of fresh and clear fingerprints. He would identify them and telephone the Boss; the latter would let Beffort know the result by means of the radio.

In the meantime, the inhabitant of the small house had gone home, and no vehicle or pedestrian had materialized since his disappearance. Beffort and Akamatsu were watching the Chrysler, with all their lights off, not even smoking—in consequence of which the time went by infinitely slowly.

At nine forty-five the radio crackled and the operator's voice came over the speaker: "Central calling Tom Two...."

Beffort seized the mike and reduced the volume slightly. "Tom Two here," he said.

"Sam Forbes' fingerprints were on the steering-wheel, handbrake and door of the Chrysler. There were also those of the car's owner, and a third set that can't be identified."

"Thanks," said Beffort, winking at Akamatsu.

"Don't sign off!" said the operator, swiftly. "Someone wants to talk to you."

There was a pause, and then the Boss's voice rang out: "Beffort?"

"Yes?"

"Don't do anything reckless, old man. I want you to call in every quarter of an hour. Where are you now?"

"The same place," the G-man replied, laconically.

"What for?" growled the Boss.

"I don't know what else to do! Forbes disappeared here, so I'm staying here. The guy who lives in the house claims that the road only carried traces of the Chrysler and his own car. The region is completely deserted, having no train station or bus stops. Where the Devil can Sam have gone?"

The Boss coughed—a whistling cough that sounded like a shell-burst over the radio. "Do what you want," he concluded, "but call me every fifteen minutes, okay? Until then…"

Beffort replaced the mike and turned to the Tokko-ka man. "What should we do?"

Akamatsu pointed at the radio. "Our hands are tied," he said. "Calling in at intervals necessitates one of us being constantly present."

"That's what I thought, "Beffort agreed. "Listen— I'd like to take a stroll as far as the wall of the Senator's property. I'm wondering whether that uninhabited house might reveal some curiosity that would have attracted Forbes's attention." He bit his lower lip and added: "It would undoubtedly have taken something extraordinary for Sam to abandon his Chevrolet. The guy we arrested, Hisato Keichu, told us that the car carrying the remote control apparatus—the Chrysler, in this case—went to an out-of-town rendezvous once its work was done. Forbes was following that car and must have witnessed the transfer if the apparatus into another vehicle. It's incomprehensible…."

He turned up the collar of his overcoat and put on his felt hat. Before quitting the vehicle, he removed the bulb from the ceiling-light that came on automatically when the door was opened.

"I'm going out," he murmured. "Just a little stroll. If I'm not back in thirty minutes, it's because I've run into trouble. Do you know how to use the radio?"

"Yes," Akamatsu reassured him. "Go on—I'll call the switchboard, as arranged."

Smith Beffort got out, closed the door softly, and moved away. He walked on the left-hand side of the road, placing his feet circumspectly, as silently as a cat. To the right there was an immense field bounded by the crest of a hill, the wall of the Senator's property and the narrow by-road that the G-men was following. To the left there was a barbed-wire fence protecting the land attached to the house.

Beffort had almost reached the wall when he heard the hum. It was a dull sound, like that produced by a dynamo. It was coming from the field, and the suspicious Beffort flattened himself against the wall, by the roadside.

A grating sound split the silence, and the purr of an engine replaced the hum. This time, Beffort was certain that a car was coming through the field, but could not make anything out in the darkness. It was coming forward slowly, with its lights out, but was indubitably heading for the road.

It suddenly emerged from the shadows, and Beffort threw himself to the ground.

In spite of the darkness, the federal agent recognized a Lincoln station-wagon and saw that the seats were occupied by a man and a woman. The latter was driving. As soon as the car was on the road the driver accelerated and the headlights came on. The Lincoln leapt forward and disappeared like a streak of lightning in the direction of 202. It turned toward Oakland.

Smith Beffort got up, ran back to the house and hurled himself into the Chrysler. Yosho Akamatsu was just getting ready to contact Central, and Beffort snatched the mike from him.

"Tom Two calling," he spat. "Tom Two calling."

"Go ahead," the operator replied.

"A Lincoln station-wagon is heading for Oakland right now. It's driven by a woman, with a man sitting beside her. Make the necessary arrangements for the car to be followed discreetly. Discretion above all."

"What is it?" said the voice of the Boss, abruptly.

"Perhaps lovers who were making out in a field," Beffort replied, "but that would amaze me! The Lincoln wasn't there when we arrived, and no vehicle's come along the road since. I have an idea that the Lincoln came from the Senator's property."

"Good," said the Boss. "I assume you're going to take a look at it at close range?"

"And how, Boss—with a diamond-lensed magnifying-glass!"

"Don't forget to call me, Beffort," the Boss warned. "I've blockaded the area. Our guys are piled up in Darlington, Oakland, Wanque and Midvale, waiting to take a hand. A troop of parachutists can land in your field three minutes after I give the order, and I've got six bombers standing by."

Beffort went pale. "Damn it!" he swore. "Go easy!"

The Boss sniggered ferociously. "Oh yes! Do you think the evil mother is going easy?"

"Good God!" Beffort exclaimed. "We're not sure of anything."

"I don't need certainty," the Boss growled in his turn. "Four hundred dead, a department store and two buildings burned! I'm ready to drop an H-bomb on that bitch Atomos's shadow, and if I get a sniff of where she is, I will. Understood?"

"Understood," said Beffort, in a hoarse voice.

"Listen," said the Boss, "And let's understand one another: if you're unable to call me at the agreed time, I'll be patient for another quarter of an hour, but no one will be able to get in or out of a quadrilateral of which your field is the center. If you're still mute after the second delay, lie low if you're not dead. Since Madame Atomos wants to raze the entire USA, I'll do as much myself to make sure that she comes unstuck!"

A click indicated that the Boss had just signed off, and Beffort remained standing there, mike in hand.

"He's coming on strong," Akamatsu commented, "but the game is worth the candle. If nothing stops Madame Atomos, she will indeed reduce your country to dust. Let's take a look at this wall, Beffort."

"Both of us? What about calling in?"

Akamatsu, who was in the driver's seat, started the car. "Let's take the car closer," he said. "If we go softly, we won't attract attention. The quietness of American vehicles has always had my admiration."

He moved quietly away from the open ground and went forward slowly, but, in spite of all his precautions, nothing could prevent the gravel crackling under the tires.

Akamatsu steered through the opening in the barbed-wire fence surrounding the enclosure, straightened the car up when the tires bit the earth of the narrow verge. The Chevrolet eventually reached the wall. The Japanese man maneuvered skillfully, lining up the car less than two inches from the ditch and switched off the engine. "There," he whispered. "Now we'll be spotted if Madame Atomos has her headquarters in the vicinity."

Beffort ground his teeth. "I hadn't thought of that," he admitted, "but it's obvious. A woman like her must have prodigious means of detection at her disposal."

"Let's assume the worst," Akamatsu proposed, "And that Madame Atomos will make use of her famous electromagnetic ray. We know its effects: cars and radios become useless...."

"In that case," it will be impossible for us to contact the Boss, and he'll unleash the offensive." He turned to face the Japanese man and said: "You knew that, didn't you?"

"Yes," Akamatsu replied, mildly, "but it's the only means of cutting things short. Either Madame Atomos isn't in the immediate vicinity, and nothing will happen; or she is, and the bombing will become indispensable."

"You've got some front!" said Beffort, admiringly.

The Japanese man bowed. "*Arogato gozaimas*," he said, meaning *thank you*. "Are we going?"

"Okay. As you say, let's get moving."

They got out, went into the field and began to move along the wall. After taking a few steps, Beffort came to a halt and leaned toward his companion's ear. "I think it would be better not to put all our eggs in one basket," he said. "I'll go first. Follow me fifty paces behind. If a dog barks and I attract attention, you can intervene. Agreed?"

"Agreed."

"I'll follow the tracks of the Lincoln station-wagon. Logically, they should lead me to the place we're searching for."

The Japanese man stayed by the wall, and Beffort bent down over the ground. He could not see very much, but nevertheless made out the furrows hollowed out by the heavy vehicle. He walked in one of the furrows, so as to be sure that he would not lose it. His progress was slow, and he had the impression that the consistency of the ground had changed. The soil was firmer and, while its surface was still tormented, it was no longer giving way beneath the weight of his body.

Beffort stepped back and felt his feet sinking once again. He crouched down and touched the ground, crumbling soil beneath his fingers and sniffing it. It was good corn-growing soil and its odor was reassuring. He advanced slowly on all fours, and set his hand on the other soil. He tried to pull up a clod, but could not do it and broke a fingernail. He pressed his nose to the bizarre ground but could not detect any odor, and realized at the same moment that this was where the double furrow vanished.

Prudently, he stepped back again, and the sudden freshness of the air startled him. He sat down and loosened his tie, greedily breathing in a few pints of oxygen.

On recovering his lucidity, Beffort understood that he had just been subject to the commencement of an intoxication, without being able to determine exactly when it had begun.

Yosho Akamatsu glided to his side, and swift and silent as a serpent. "What's happening?" he enquired, in a whisper.

"I don't know," said Beffort, in a similar tone. "I nearly fell into a trap without perceiving it. There must be an area in front of us that's not authentic—an odorless soil as solid as cement.

Akamatsu leaned over, put out a hand, and straightened up again. "Or concrete," he said.

"Son of a bitch! You think…?"

"Why not? The Lincoln had to come from somewhere, didn't it?" He rested his finger on the strange material and felt an almost-imperceptible suction. Without saying a word, he rummages in his pocket, and then placed his cigarette-case on the ground.

"What are you doing?" muttered Beffort.

"Wait," said the Japanese man. "It's an experiment."

A few seconds went by, and then a faint hum rose from below ground. The cigarette-case sank very slowly, and the ground re-closed around it. Soon, it was no longer visible, and the terrain was exactly as before.

Amazed, Beffort whistled through his teeth. "Experiment successful!" he belched.

Akamatsu grabbed his arm forcefully. "Come on!" he said.

Beffort followed him at a run without asking for explanations. The Tokkoka man reached the Chevrolet first, started the engine and set off at top speed as soon as Beffort was inside.

"Call Central," said Akamatsu, "and tell your boss to send the bombers!"

As Beffort hesitated, the Japanese man added: "Hurry up! In a very short time my suitcase will arrive down below, probably in the hands of a receptionist, and the alert will be sounded immediately."

Beffort, who had finally switched the apparatus on and grabbed the mike, and said: "Tom Two calling!"

"I'm listening," the Boss replied.

"Start the bombardment immediately, about fifty yards from the road and the property."

"Stay on the line!" the Boss said, rapidly.

The loudspeaker emitted a confused sound, and then the Boss spoke again: "The bombers are on their way," he said, coldly. "They were waiting at Lincoln Park Airport, and will be with you in a minute or two. Try to find a hole and pull in the battens!"

Lincoln Park Airport was ten miles from the objective, as the crow flies. The Boss had certainly made his preparations!

"We're on 202," said Beffort, inspecting the sky, "heading toward Oakland.

Akamatsu raced along the deserted rod, and the trees whistled like blackbirds.

"Can you see anything?" asked the Boss.

"Not yet...."

He had scarcely finished speaking when there was a blinding explosion far to the rear. Immediately, thunder was unleashed, so violent that the Boss sniggered into the radio. "You're deaf, Beffort," he joked. "I can hear the chestnuts roasting from here!" He was audibly jubilant, and his laughter filled the car.

Ten minutes later, they learned that not a single bomb had reached the ground. The six bombers and their munitions had exploded in mid-air!

Chapter XI

There was a moment of stunned amazement as the news spread. Abruptly, everyone began running around madly, like blind ants, and it required all the Boss's authority to restore calm. The police and army gave him a valuable helping hand by intervening energetically, with the result that eventually, everyone was at his post, content to remain within the limits that people ought not to cross.

Rumor had it that two FBI men were examining the interior of the quadrilateral, trying to figure out exactly what had happened.

In fact, Beffort and Akamatsu had turned back of their own accord as soon as the Boss—who had found out about it before anyone else, God knows how—had told them the news, and were heading at full throttle toward the scene of the drama.

Still far ahead of them, the last of the bombers was going up in flames, amid an immense red glow illuminating the horizon. Closer to them, the Senator's estate, reached by the flaming debris, was burning like a hayrick. The road was pitted with potholes for more than a mile; thanks to brief luminous explosions the two men were able to catch occasional glimpses of the field, which the planes and bombs had miraculously spared.

It was, however, one of Madame Atomos's miracles, and neither Beffort nor Akamatsu was impressed by it. They found themselves in a state of cold anger, which was scarcely conducive to reflection. Meanwhile, the Boss was shouting himself hoarse into his mike.

"Beffort!" he said, for the third time. "I order you to get out of the area!"

"No way! Akamatsu and I are going hotfoot to knock on Madame Atomos's door, and see whether we can poke a finger in her eye!"

"Get out of there as fast as you can! I'm sending in the paratroopers!"

"That's a good idea!" Beffort sneered. "Send them! They'll be transformed into dust before touching the ground, if their plane hasn't been wiped out beforehand. You might as well cut your losses! What do you want, a bloodbath?"

"Shut up, Beffort!" the Boss barked, ferociously. "May I remind you that it was you who called in the bombers! Can you hear me?"

"Oh yes," groaned the federal agent. "No need to twist the knife in the wound, My guilt complex is as big as a house. By the way, what's become of the Lincoln station-wagon?"

"The latest news is that it's left New York, It must be on 4 by now."

"Give the order to stop it."

"What?"

"I'm not giving you orders, Boss—but Akamatsu and me are going to try to pass ourselves off as Madame Atomos's men. No need to have them turning up immediately after us, is there?"

The Boss made a gargling sound. "Do you expect to pull it off?" he asked, incredulously.

"No." And Smith Beffort simply switched off.

"You shouldn't have done that," said Akamatsu, softly. "He'll think that we've had an accident and take measures that will risk hindering us further."

"Or helping us," Smith amended. "In a little while, this rattletrap will take the same route as your cigarette-case. How do we know what's waiting for us on the far side of that absorbent ground? If the guy in reception mistakes our Chevy for the station-wagon, we'll benefit from a significant element of surprise."

"*Hai!* I'm not denying it—but if he sees us for what we are, we risk getting fried on the spot. In that eventuality, it won't matter what measures your Boss decides to take. Hold on—we're there!"

Yosho Akamatsu swerved off the side-road, avoided the debris of the collapsed wall, and launched the Chevrolet into the field. He followed the tracks left by the station-wagon, stopped where they stopped, and switched off his engine.

Without a word, the two men checked that the windows were closed, and drew their weapons with a single movement. The Chevrolet remained motionless for a few seconds; then it began to sink into the ground as the humming sound burst forth, and rapidly disappeared.

The descent, effectuated in absolute darkness, lasted about ten minutes—but when the vehicle was immobilized again, it was still surrounded by the strange matter. Beffort tried to open the door, and then to lower a window, but his efforts were futile. Although the matter was apparently malleable in the vertical plane, it was as resistant as granite in the horizontal one.

"If we've been spotted," Beffort breathed, "they'll only have to leave us here to transform us into corpses. In a little while, we'll run out of air, and then...."

He shut up abruptly, for the wall was sliding slowly along the windows, freeing the lower sections like a rising theater curtain, revealing an oval room without any visible exit, with concrete walls pierced with thick portholes, through which a dull bluish light was filtering.

Soon, the Chevrolet was completely free of the enclosing matrix. Akamatsu lowered his window and sniffed the air. He was holding his Beretta with a flexible wrist and the barrel of the automatic was in continuous motion.

As his hand took hold of the door-handle, Beffort whispered: "Don't get out, Yosho! This room must have the same function as a submarine's airlock. I'll wager that we'll have visitors momentarily."

The portholes suddenly turned red and began to flicker frenetically, while a bizarrely modulated signal sounded stridently, with the same rhythm as the flicker.

"I have the impression," said the Japanese man, "that we're being called to order. We have to do something—but what?"

Beffort turned a taut expression toward him. "We're in this trap voluntarily, and until now no one seems to have detected our presence. Stay calm. Someone will have to come and see what's happening here."

Akamatsu made no reply. He switched on engine and the headlights, and blasted the horn. Simultaneously, the portholes returned to blue and silence fell. The back wall of the room, which was illuminated by the headlights, pivoted slowly, unblocking the entrance to a narrow corridor. Portholes cast their pale light on its concrete walls, and the grilles of ventilation-shafts were distributed on the floor.

"Damn!" Beffort exclaimed. "You've activated the opening system."

Akamatsu smiled thinly. "That's a stroke of luck," he said. "Shall we make a move?"

Beffort got out and the Japanese man joined him after switching off the headlights and the engine. Together, the two men went into the corridor; they were in the middle of it when the concrete door closed behind them. They exchanged an anxious glance but remained silent. They were now in a place where everything was to be feared. There might be microphones hidden in the walls, and some of the portholes, duller than the others, looked like camera lenses.

Yosho Akamatsu was the first to arrive at a right-angled bend in the corridor. He examined the terrain prudently, after signaling to Beffort to remain hidden, then took a step back. "There's a staircase," he said. "We're probably on an intermediate floor of the building, for the staircase cuts across the corridor. What shall we do?"

"We'll go up." Beffort decided

"I agree," Akamatsu opined. "If our enemies have a sentry-post, it must be at ground level."

They went along the length of the corridor and began to climb the steps. The atmosphere grew sensibly heavier, and the two men began to sweat. After two floors, they emerged into a brightly-lit room and were transfixed by amazement.

Sam Forbes was standing in front of them, livid and stiff. His dilated eyes were devoid of expression, fixed on some distant point. His arms were extended beside his petrified body, as if he were standing to attention. It was a horrible sight.

"Sam!" said Beffort.

A porthole blinked. There was a crackle, and a feminine voice emerged from an invisible loudspeaker. "Your friend is dead, Mr. Beffort," it said, in an ironic tone. "He is presently under my control and will be set in motion when I direct the atom stream at him. He will take charge of killing you. I could easily do it myself, of course, but it seems much more piquant to have two FBI men murdered by one of their colleagues. When Forbes advances toward you, there will be no way to stop him, and your flight will not last very long. You will end up running into a wall, or going astray into a dead end. It will then be sufficient for Forbes to touch you for you to lose your life...."

The loudspeaker emitted a few crackles, and the vice resumed: "I shall follow your efforts on my television screen, gentlemen, but know that everything you can do will be in vain. The refuge in which you find yourselves has been empty for a couple of hours, and I am content to direct the operation from my personal shelter, some miles way. Tomorrow, the White House will be reduced to ashes, but tonight, my walking dead will spread terror throughout the United States, and nothing will be able to get in their way. Goodbye. Mr. Beffort. Goodbye, Mr. Akamatsu...."

Silence abruptly filled the room, and Forbes took his first step. Their throats tight, Beffort and Akamatsu watched him come slowly forward, with that terrible mechanical gait that nothing seemed able to stop, and the two men experienced a horrible feeling of emptiness and helplessness.

Akamatsu suddenly recovered his sense of reality. He gripped his companion's arm forcefully and dragged him toward the stairway. "We need to get away, Smith! If we let him get too close, we're finished!"

As white as a sheet, Beffort paused at the stairhead. "I can't believe it!" he murmured. Then he howled: "Sam! Wake up, old chap! Sam!"

Akamatsu slapped his face, and growled: "Don't be an idiot, Beffort! He's dead, as you know full well, and no prayer can bring him back to life!"

"I don't believe that!" cried Beffort. "Remember what Dr. Soblen said. He said that Maggie Fairbanks was acting in a hypnotic state, and Sam is surely...."

The Japanese policeman's Beretta spat fire, but Forbes did not even shudder under the impact of the bullets. A round hole appeared in the center of his forehead; others ripped through the fabric of his jacket at breast-height, but Forbes continued to advance, staring, rigid and frozen.

"Well?" Akamatsu demanded, sharply. "Are you convinced now?"

Beffort's lips began to tremble, and he recoiled toward the steps.

Forbes had crossed the room and they noticed that he was walking quite rapidly—and that the slightest error or the simplest obstacle might bring them within his reach.

"We have to get a head start," said Akamatsu, "and try to find an exit. Come on, Beffort!"

The federal agent finally emerged from his prostration and hurtled down the steps behind the Japanese man. They reached the landing from which the corridor they had already traversed departed, went down one further flight of stairs and stopped, cocking their ears.

Sam Forbes had to be in the middle of the first flight, for his footsteps were hardly audible. Akamatsu pointed at a corridor on to which several doors opened, and said: "That's exactly the kind of cul-de-sac we need to avoid. The solution of locking ourselves into one of these rooms would sign our death-warrant. Forbes is capable of waiting for us to come out again for weeks...."

"This way," said Beffort, rapidly. He had recovered his self-composure, and all of his habitual efficiency. Akamatsu followed him at a run, and they came into a long room cluttered with various materials. A corridor followed, at the end of which they found another room and larger dimensions.

Beffort stopped. "He'll get us for sure," he said, "If we can't find a means of stopping him. He's nothing in himself. He's being remotely controlled by the woman we heard. She's watching us through hidden television cameras, and that's where we have to strike."

Akamatsu nodded. "Agreed, but how? The cameras must be incorporated into the walls. To put them beyond use one after another would be a Herculean task!"

"We have to provoke a short circuit that will plunge the building into darkness!"

Akamatsu shook his head. "I thought of that," he said, "But it's no good. If Madame Atomos thinks that Forbes can't get to us, she'll kill us some other way!"

"Listen!" whispered Beffort, tautly. Forbes' footfalls were no audible in the corridor; although he was not yet visible, it could only be a matter of seconds.

Akamatsu suddenly went over to the wall and called to Beffort. "Look here!" he said, nervously. "Drums of gasoline."

The federal agent uncapped a drum, sniffed it and looked up again. "Do you think this might stop him?"

"We don't have any choice, do we?"

They emptied two drums in the corridor. The gas spread out over the concrete floor in waves, quickly forming an insurmountable pool.

Forbes appeared as Beffort was pouring out the contents of a third drum, and the federal agent leapt into the room.

"Get back!" Akamatsu ordered. He was holding a box of matches. He knelt down.

Forbes came into the danger zone without hesitation, his feet splashing in the liquid, which impregnated his shoes and the bottom of his trousers.

Akamatsu struck a match, and leapt to Beffort's side.

There was a dull explosion, and crackling flames rose up swiftly to attack Forbes, enveloping him in a red whirlwind. For an instant, the two men thought that even fire could not stop the dead man, but then the latter collapsed in a heap, without a shudder, like a steel girder crashing to the ground, while a frightful odor of charred flesh spread through the overheated air.

Akamatsu shook with silent laughter, and gripped Beffort's shoulder. "Do you know why we've succeeded, Smith?" And as the G-man interrogated him with his gaze, he explained: "Because Madame Atomos only has a limited number of cameras at her disposal! If she'd seen us preparing our life-saving operation, she would have stopped Forbes in time. It's probable that she doesn't know how her...robot came to grief, and that she has no eyes in this room. That gives us time, of which we must immediately take advantage, Come this way—we'll try to get back to the airlock...."

Chapter XII

The Boss had been calling Beffort continually for thirty minutes. Then, spitting out his cigar—reduced to a mere stub—he decided to execute the second part of his plan.

It required a further half-hour to get the heavy armaments ready to go to work, but when the artillery opened fire, the field, the Senator's house and the worker's hovel would be smashed by the shells. The watchers would see to it that Madame Atomos had no chance of getting out.

The bombardment lasted a quarter of an hour; then two hundred paratroopers were launched upon the terrain. They were armed with submachine-guns, grenades and flame-throwers and had received orders to give no quarter.

Akamatsu and Beffort were thrown to the ground by the force of the first explosions. At the same time, the lights went out, and a part of the subterranean shelter collapsed with the deafening sound of an avalanche.

A brief calm followed, then the pounding resumed, after which the rate of fire was controlled, at the rhythm of one shell per second.

The concrete crumbled in compact blocks around the two men, or disintegrated under the sustained fire, while shards as trenchant as razor blades stung the wall that had not yet given way, rebounding and whizzing away, whistling like a swarm of crazed wasps. Ten shells fell in the same place; like a nail driven into a plank, they hollowed out a giant funnel that divided Madame Atomos's lair into two shaking halves.

Stunned and covered in dust, Akamatsu and Beffort found themselves on the edge of a chaotic gulf, balanced on a narrow ledge, too astonished at being still alive to take an interest in the fall of the Chevrolet, which the explosion had hurled into the air.

Beffort perceived a glimmer light shining in front of him, and howled to draw Akamatsu's attention to the anomaly. The corridor opened in the flank of a crater. The ledge that the two men occupied led them to it, and as the bombardment was continuing, they urgently needed to find a shelter.

They ran into a tunnel under the hail of debris, getting into it just in time to escape a further collapse, and ran on while all hell was unleashed behind them. A shell struck the tunnel entrance, burying it under tons of earth; the ground shook and the light went out under the violence of the impact.

Guiding themselves along the wall, which was oozing moisture, the two men continued their blind course. Their lungs were on fire, and were obliged to pause when the ground began to slope steeply.

The explosions sounded very dull now, and when they ceased, the two men had the sensation of being buried alive.

"*Ikasa deska?*" said Akamatsu, reverting to his native language in the heat of the action. "How are you?"

"Not bad," Beffort growled, "but I'll be a lot better when I get out of this rat-hole. Strike a match, Akamatsu!"

The Japanese man took out his box, and a little dancing flame lit up the steeply-sloping corridor.

"In my opinion," said Beffort, "We've stumbled no one of Madame Atomos's evacuation tunnels. Without the bombardment, we'd never have found it. The Boss has done the trick!"

The match went out and Akamatsu slipped the box into his pocket. "We're not out of the woods yet," he said, gravely. "I'm wondering whether this corridor might take us straight to another lair."

Beffort started walking. "We can only go one way," he observed. "The tunnel's collapsed behind us, and I'm sure that the army occupying the field will fire on anything that moves. In truth, we're better off down here than up there."

They marched for some time in complete darkness, but when Beffort ran into an obstacle Akamatsu struck another match.

"A staircase!" he said. "We're getting there!"

They went up the steep steps, pushed a trapdoor, and emerged into the dining-room of an abandoned house. Looking outside, they ascertained that they were on the other side of the hill, at least two miles from the place they had just left.

The house was flanked by a large outhouse that had evidently been converted into a garage. Patches of fresh oil speckled the flattened ground, and there was a gas-can in one corner.

Beffort and Akamatsu went out on to the road, and started walking westwards, in the direction of Oakland.

At one o'clock in the morning, the Boss learned that Beffort and the Tokkoka agent had just reached Oakland. After a telephonic conversation with the G-man, he knew that Madame Atomos had escaped the bombardment and intended to launch a vast terrorist operation during the night.

The word *terror* took on its full meaning when it was employed to designate the diabolical Japanese woman's action, and the Boss did not take the warning lightly. The radio waves started humming incessantly over the entire territory, but preventative measures were concentrated on New York, Washington, Baltimore, Philadelphia and Boston.

At two o'clock, a conference in the Boss's office brought together those responsible for the security of the threatened regions, and Beffort and Akamatsu were invited to explain the situation.

Beffort spoke briefly, telling the story of how Sam Forbes had been transformed into an atomized robot, and had been neutralized by fire. Everyone present understood without further explanations that a means of destroying Madam Atomos's walking dead had finally been discovered. There was scarcely any objection to the agreement that flamethrowers were the best weapons of destruction, but it quickly became evident that there would not be enough of them to cover a tenth part of the cities that were under threat effectively.

General Dickson started talking about incendiary grenades and Molotov cocktails, but was dryly interrupted by the Boss. "We're not fighting the battle of Normandy, general," he murmured, "and it's not a matter of blowing up the Empire State Building."

Dickson raised a head like that of a plucked parrot. "You've already used artillery, bombers and parachutists!" he yelped.

"The target was a field," Beffort reminded him, softly.

Dickson looked daggers at him, but Beffort did not flinch. He had been a sergeant in the army, and was used to generals looking daggers at him.

"If the nation is calling on the army," Dickson roared, "it's because all the usual means have been shown to be ineffective! In consequence, it seems clear that it's the army that should have the honor of taking national defense in hand!"

The Boss groaned with clenched teeth, slumped in his armchair. What he had feared was happening: the army and the civil service were coming into grotesque conflict over a question of prestige and influence, and they were going to talk for hours, uselessly, perhaps requiring the arbitration of Congress, or even the President.

At the same moment, an old woman was walking silently along a dark street in Brooklyn. Her gait was mechanical, her head was held up straight in spite of the cold, and her rigid arms were flat against her sides. She passed under a street-light, turned ninety degrees by pivoting on her heels, crossed the road without pausing or looking to see whether any cars were coming, and then resumed her progress imperturbably, amid the gusts of wind.

A man encountered her a little further on, took three more steps after having passed her, and collapsed on the sidewalk. He remained motionless for thirty seconds, as stiff and cold as a cadaver, then got up and started following the old woman, who had continued on her way.

Twenty yards apart, the woman and the man walked alongside the dark walls, then cut across another street. They had reached the middle of an intersection when a stray dog approached. The animal raised its leg against a fire-hydrant, then went up to the old woman, wagging its tail—and fell on its side. It got up again as the man drew level with it, and followed him with the strange gait of a mechanical dog.

Further on, the old woman stopped in front of a door from which a pale light filtered. The man and the dog joined her and stopped beside her. Then the woman pushed the door and went into the vestibule of a night-club, followed by the man and the dog, who were hot on her heels.

The young woman half-asleep in the cloakroom woke up and her mouth rounded in surprise. She was apparently in good health, but fell softly on to the carpet as the little group passed in front of her.

Inside the club, a hundred people were trying to forget their cares by dancing and drinking to excess. They were very fashionable people, who put on airs, and there was nothing to be seen but low-cut dresses and well-tailored suits.

On a little stage, Niles Dunkett's orchestra was playing in a subdued manner, in order not to drown out the slightly raucous voice of Suzy Trenton, who was caressing her microphone. Multicolored streamers striped the smoky space, and the laughter of enervated women punctuated the dulcet melody that Suzy was intoning as she sucked her mike.

Earlier, the ambience had been explosive, but this was what they called the soft time, although it was only a state provoked by fatigue, drunkenness and the onset of boredom. To shake up this crowd, it would have required an attraction genuinely out of the ordinary, and when the old woman, followed by the man, the dog and the cloakroom attendant appeared on the threshold, an enormous gale of laughter ran through the assembly.

Suzy's laughter vibrated in the microphone, and the orchestra stopped playing. Men threw streamers at the old woman, but she continued to advance without showing any emotion, and the laughter abruptly ceased....

The old woman, the man, the dog and the hat-check girl were stiff-limbed and had staring faces....

The group went passed the first tables, and fifty revelers collapsed on the spot, under the terrified eyes of those who were still too far away to be atomized—and then got up, advancing in their turn toward the stage....

Five minutes later, a police car patrolling the quarter braked sharply as it reached an intersection. Kearney, the driver, jogged his partner with his elbow and pointed to a strange procession that was coming in their direction.

"Take a look at that, Bill!"

The man extended his neck, whistled, and rubbed his eyes.

At two thirty in the morning, in freezing cold, a hundred people in evening dress were silently following an old woman, a dog, a man dressed in workman' clothes and a pretty blonde girl molded into a black dress."

"They must be drunk!"

"For sure," Kearney agreed. "We'll have to have a few words with them...."

The two cops got out of the car and planted themselves in the middle of the intersection, twirling their nightsticks. A taxi appeared and braked. The driver leaned out of the window, and looked at the strange procession advancing along the narrow street. His takings were down, because he had hardly picked up a fare all night. He called his company on the radio, asking them to send a few extra cabs to the location.

"Well?" shouted Kearney. "What's this circus all about?"

The old woman arrived in the middle of the intersection. The two cops and the taxi-driver were subjected to an abrupt atomization.

Augmented by the three new recruits, the macabre procession headed toward Plum Island and the Naval Air Base at Floyd Bennett Field.

Three blocks behind, a car driven by a woman in a skunk-fur wrap followed slowly. In the passenger seat was a man armed with what looked like a fiberglass fishing rod, and on the back seat a square metallic device was humming softly.

Madame Atomos's Operation Destruction was under way.

Incredulously, Lieutenant Cook watched the enormous procession that was advancing toward the entrance to the base. He saw the sentries collapse, and realized that something abnormal was happening when the latter got up again and took their places in the disparate ranks that were invading the outer courtyard of the base.

Cook sounded the alarm, leapt to the telephone, howled a brief message, and raced outside, unknowingly running to sudden death, and the most atrocious afterlife that humankind had ever known….

Naval Air Base at Floyd Bennett Field attacked by enormous silent crowd. Sentries, troops and officers have joined procession. Request orders urgently. Signed: Officer of….

Admiral Kenilworth looked as if he had been struck by a violent electrical discharge. He read the message aloud and the Boss leapt to the telephone.

At the same time, General Dickson understood that this was not a time for sterile discussions, and gave orders over another radio link for a company armed with flame-throwers to be sent to the naval air base.

Beffort and Akamatsu left the office without waiting for orders and went down to the next floor. Davis was there, deciphering messages, accompanied by about fifteen G-men. Beffort and Akamatsu learned that a thousand people had been atomized, and that the number was growing by the minute, but that the tightly-packed procession was still confined to the southern part of Brooklyn.

They feared a disintegration that would render any intervention impossible. If the atomized dispersed through the city, a fantastic catastrophe might ensue. They knew that each dead person was contagious, and that animals were not spared. Soon, rats, dogs, cats and birds would spread throughout the region, carriers of death.

Beffort and Akamatsu hurtled downstairs, climbed into a service car and headed straight for the base.

Chapter XIII

At three o'clock in the morning, the glacial temperature climbed by five degrees and the snow made its appearance. At first there were no more than a few light flakes, spiraling gracefully in the harsh glare of the street-lights, and then a terrible blizzard descended on the city.

The military convoy transporting the flamethrowers ran into difficulties in the vicinity of Newark. The snow was accumulating on the windscreens, and the wipers were impotent to clear it away. Men were positioned to either side of each vehicle to carry out that work, but the speed of the convoy was considerably reduced.

In New York, particularly in Brooklyn, panic suddenly gripped the population. Alerted by the howling of sirens, the radio and television spat out a continual stream of special bulletins, which added to the panic, and the inhabitants leapt into the cars. Within ten minutes, monstrous traffic jams had been produced at all the important intersections, preventing the police services from descending on Plum Island.

The snowstorm reduced visibility to zero, and spectacular pile-ups began to occur all over the city. Many people abandoned their cars where they were, and set off on foot through the snow, beginning an incredible game of hide-and-seek. Groups formed in order to be certain of being among living beings, but retreated automatically as they met one another, fearful that they might be dealing with Madame Atomos's atomized people.

An infernal carousel started in Brooklyn, and the night was populated by furtive silhouettes, strangely similar by reason of the snow that blanketed them.

By three twenty-five half the population was circulating through the cluttered streets, while the other half had locked the doors of their buildings in order not to be submerged. Because of that, those who wanted to return to their homes found it impossible to do so, and were condemned to wander through the tempest, fleeing from one another.

It was a demented cavalcade, and Beffort was overwhelmed. The service vehicle, blocked in the vicinity of Prospect Park, was no further use, and the messages that the radio was putting out indicated that the situation was getting much worse.

The atomized were now so numerous that the FBI switchboard spoke of a veritable human tide. The procession emerged on to Homecrest, touched Flatlands and brushed Paerdegat Basin. The air base at Floyd Bennett Field had not responded for some time, and the military convoy carrying the flame-throwers had only reached Jersey City.

The Air Force was called in. Cargo planes stuffed with GIs and flame-throwers landed at Idlewild and were immediately directed to Paerdegat Basin.

A hundred flame-throwers went into action when the procession emerged on to Canarsie, roasting the first ranks of the atomized on the spot, but quickly had to give ground.

The soldiers aimed their flame-throwers at anyone who was not wearing a uniform; a group of the living became targets and were burned to a crisp. In the whirlwinds of snow the troop became disorientated, retreating before the innumerable dead who appeared to be rising out of the ground, and whose advance was unstoppable.

At three forty the flame-throwers ran out of fuel and the soldiers opened fire with submachine-guns, rifles and pistols. It was a puerile and utterly futile reflex. The dead continued their progress, sealing the two hundred soldiers in the jaws of a mortal vice and submerging them.

Beffort and Akamatsu knew all this by courtesy of the radio, and realized that, without a miracle, Brooklyn—and then Long Island and New York—would be solely populated by the marching dead.

Around them, there was a stampede. Deprived of information, the members of the crowd were rushing in all directions, bumping into one another, knocking one another down, lashing out indiscriminately. The weak were rolling in the mud and being trampled. The wounded and the dead strewed the swarming streets, and at the windows of houses and other buildings those whom prudence had kept indoors watched the apocalyptic spectacle in terror.

Beffort and his companion got out of the car and were borne away in spite of themselves by a howling group. They struggled in concert to get free, and eventually found themselves, breathless and bruised, in the relative calm of Churchill Avenue. The roadway as cluttered with abandoned vehicles, their doors wide open, and broken suitcases were spilling heaps of clothes and various other objects in the snow.

Ten-dollar bills were swirling around a lamp-post, and a woman with a bloody nose was trying to catch them, laughing all the while. A baby started to cry in one of the cars, and Beffort took a step in that direction, but Akamatsu held him back firmly.

"This isn't the time," he said, in a calm voice. "The child might as well be there as elsewhere."

They plastered themselves against a wall to let a frenzied group of people pass by, then started running in their turn. They were no longer thinking about anything but saving their own skins—and, if possible, getting back to FBI headquarters. There was nothing else they could do.

They reached the intersection of Churchill Avenue and Coney Island, and perceived a formidable human mass heading in their direction. The crowd was advancing slowly, silently and mechanically, taking up the whole of the avenue. An old woman was marching at the head of the procession, with a workman, a dog and a young woman immediately behind her. Further away came the group in evening dress, two uniformed policemen, and then a compact mass, so tightly grouped that they seemed welded together.

Beffort and Akamatsu retraced their steps, drawing away toward MacDonald Avenue.

Suddenly, Beffort spotted the Cadillac. He threw himself on the Japanese agent and pushed him behind a small truck. "Look, Yosho!" he whispered. "In that cream Cadillac, which looks as if it's been abandoned."

The Tokkoka man leaned out. At first he thought the car was empty, but then saw the fugitive red glow of a cigarette. He looked harder, saw that a man and a woman were sitting in the front seats, and pivoted uncomprehendingly. "So what?" he said. "What about them?"

Beffort's fingers dug into his arm. "That woman," he said, "is Lydia Watanabe—the woman who was in the Buick with Hisato Keichu, and who hired the houses on which the concrete towers were built!"

Akamatsu started. "If you're not mistaken," he said, "I…."

"Remember the Boss's description!" Beffort interjected, ferociously. "A young brunette woman, pretty, thirty years old at most, Asiatic! I've only seen her once, Yosho, but I'm absolutely certain that it's her!"

Akamatsu leaned out again, and then straightened up. "The girl is probably Eurasian," he said, in a flat voice, "And I've just seen a dark object on the rear seat."

Beffort took out his thirty-eight and cocked it. "Kill the guy!" he spat. "I'll take care of the girl—we need her alive. We'll attack from behind, you to the right, me to the left. Watch out for the rear-view mirror! Ready!"

Akamatsu was already clutching his Beretta. "Whenever you like, Smith."

They ran along the sidewalk, separated, ducked down and crossed the road, keeping to the shadows. In fifteen seconds they were behind the Cadillac, and came to a halt.

Beffort raised his arm, then lowered it, and the two men rushed the doors. Akamatsu fired through the glass, killing his man with a bullet to the head. Beffort broke the other window with a mighty blow of his gun-butt and smashed it into Lydia's chin. She crumpled in a heap.

"Look!" howled Akamatsu.

He pointed with his arm at the mass of the atomized, who were emerging into Churchill Avenue, still led by the old woman.

Beffort opened the rear door, heard the hum of the apparatus placed on the rear seat and searched feverishly for a means of switching it off. In the darkness, his hands wandered over the smooth surface, finally encountering a switch.

The humming suddenly stopped, with an imperceptible hiss, and a little indicator light went out.

At the same instant, on Churchill Avenue, in Brooklyn, Plum Island, Canarsie and everywhere else they were to be found, the atomized collapsed, and the streets were covered in corpses.

Later, nine thousand of them were to be counted, but for the moment no one realized the amplitude of the disaster. A great calm descended upon the city: a profound prostration that was to last for hours, in the course of which everyone tried to recuperate. No one knew how the drama had been brought to an end, and Beffort and the Japanese agent were too busy to think of explaining it.

With the aid of their neckties, they tied up the unconscious young woman securely, and Akamatsu set about bringing her round.

Lydia Watanabe opened her eyes after the fourth slap, and looked around in profound surprise.

"Can you hear me?" Akamatsu asked, softly.

The woman looked at him and nodded her head.

"I'm an agent of the Tokkoka," the Japanese man went on, and this man belongs to the FBI. What you need to understand is that your goose is well and truly cooked, and that you needn't expect the slightest mercy from us."

The Eurasian woman spat in his face, and Akamatsu slapped her with the back of his hand, without holding back. "Where is Madame Atomos?" he demanded, in his soft voice.

"I don't know who you're talking about."

"*Ah...so deska?*" He seized Lydia's arm, took hold of the index-finger of her hand, and twisted it slowly.

The young woman howled and struggled, but the finger broke cleanly and silently, like a wisp of straw.

"Now?"

Lydia bit her lips, but did not say a word.

"Your cigarette, Smith?"

Beffort obliged, and Yosho applied the incandescent end to the Eurasian woman's cheek. The hiss was confused with her howl of agony, and Lydia started weeping—but she did not open her mouth.

"Where is Madame Atomos?" Akamatsu repeated.

The Eurasian woman shut her eyes. "I don't know," she hissed. "No one knows where she's hiding."

Beffort glanced at the bodies of the atomized strewing the avenue, and turned to the young woman ferociously. "If you don't talk," he said, "you won't get out of that car alive! I don't normally hold with torture, but your crimes authorize me to cut you to ribbons with a clear conscience. For the last time, where's Madame Atomos?"

Lydia Watanabe stiffened, and her jaws contracted. The G-man's tone left no doubt as to his intentions, and Lydia had never been on the other side of the barricade. The power of Madame Atomos had always seemed so formidable to her that even at that moment, she could not believe that the American could succeed in making her talk. Before she succumbed to torture, Madame Atomos would intervene. That was obligatory, inevitable.

Akamatsu's voice brought her back to the present moment. "Let me do it, Smith. It's not a matter of killing her but of making her talk. Unfortunately, I'm well used to this kind of operation. No human being can resist certain agonies. The nerve-centers are extremely sensitive, particularly in this region."

His hands gripped the young woman's hips, and she howled like an animal. Akamatsu persisted, and Smith Beffort had to exert all his strength to keep the Eurasian woman in her seat.

Finally, Lydia stopped howling, and collapsed limply in the G-man's arms.

"She's fainted," observed Akamatsu, calmly, "but that's nothing. Would you place her arms behind the seat, if you please."

When Beffort obliged, the Japanese man methodically tore off Lydia's clothes, only leaving her the skunk-fur wrap, her stockings and shoes.

"Morally," he explained, "She'll be profoundly shocked. A nude woman can't hold out for long if the…interrogation is well-crafted." He glanced sideways at Beffort and added: "I'd prefer it if you left us alone, Smith."

Without replying, Beffort got out of the car. He dragged the body of the Eurasian woman's companion on to the sidewalk, lit a cigarette and tried not to hear the cries that emerged from the Cadillac, or to see Akamatsu leaning over the nacreous body of the girl.

Lydia Watanabe lay panting in a corner of the back seat, moaning dully and continuously, but Beffort had been able to observe that she was not marked by any wound.

The car was travelling in a westward direction. Akamatsu was at the wheel, sometimes pausing to wipe away the sweat that was still running down his forehead. A rictus of disgust was still on his lips, and it was in a colorless voice that he asked Beffort to light him a cigarette.

"It's a pity that we can't alert the Boss," Beffort said, regretfully. "We'll have to be content with reinforcements from the local police."

Akamatsu grunted. "She gave in very quickly. I'm wondering whether we're really going to find Madame Atomos's lair in that place."

Beffort frowned. "Tarrytown," he said. "Tarrytown…that's odd. That name seems familiar, but I can't remember when I've heard it before."

"It's on the bank of the Hudson," Akamatsu specified.

"I know, I know…."

"The town isn't far from New York, so it's entirely natural that you've heard of it."

"There's something else," said Beffort. "Something important connected with that name. Something unusual happened in Tarrytown recently…."

Akamatsu grimaced. "Since the beginning of this affair a whole host of unusual things have happened, Smith! You'd need a memory like an elephant to conserve them all…."

The Cadillac left the New York City limits and continued along the Hudson. There was no traffic, and the snow, which was no longer falling, formed a slippery muddy carpet on the roadway, which prevented them from exceeding a modest speed.

It was while they were going through Yonkers that the G-man suddenly remembered. "Tarrytown!" he exclaimed. "That's where Maggie Fairbanks and her parents lived!"

Akamatsu flicked his cigarette-butt out into the snow. "The abandoned Fairbanks house! A dream hideout for Madame Atomos."

Lydia Watanabe groaned more loudly to hide the click of the switch that she had just depressed. With the noise of the engine, the hum of the apparatus was inaudible, and she had placed her bare leg over the green indicator light."

Chapter XIV

The atomized of New York were unaffected by the radiation of the remote control apparatus, because it was now too far away from the city, but in Tarrytown, a hobo whose seemed to be asleep under a pier east of the Hudson woke up. He abandoned his haversack, went along the quay with his mechanical gait, climbed the steps and emerged on to the docks. The man was covered in snow; his clothes were disgusting, slimed with damp, and his feet dragged along the ground.

He had not been dead long and Madame Atomos had not anticipated that the radiation would put him in motion.

The hobo walked as far as Route 19, arriving at the exact moment when the Cadillac was going past. Drawn along by the remote control apparatus, the man turned around and departed in his jerky fashion toward the town, and the Fairbanks house.

The car arrived by means of its own momentum in the narrow lane, and stopped between two trees on the snow-covered pavement. Akamatsu let the engine tick over in order to maintain the distribution of warm air, for the cold was intense, but he switched off the headlights.

It was nearly five o'clock in the morning. The night was still dark and nothing was moving in the shuttered cottages. Brief gusts of wind brought down little clumps of snow that had accumulated on the bare branches, shook television aerials and whistled past the raised windows, helping the engine to cover up the muffled hum of the remote control, apparatus.

Huddled in the corner of the back seat, Lydia was now trying to slip out of her bonds.

Beffort jabbed a thumb in the direction of the Fairbanks house, which was hidden from their gaze by a thick hedge.

"In theory," he said, "the place should have been sealed after the death of its inhabitants, and if Madame Atomos is in the house she must have taken enormous precautions not to be noticed by the neighbors. One open shutter or puff of smoke emerging from the chimney, or any noise whatsoever, and the police would have been alerted." He studied the street, where a few cars were parked, and continued in a low voice: "Even an unfamiliar vehicle would attract attention. Can you believe, Yosho, that a woman like Madame Atomos would willingly blockade herself in that house, without a possible escape route?"

Akamatsu cast a suspicious glance at the Eurasian woman and, half-turning in his seat, said: "Madame Atomos must have been surprised by your organization's riposte, Smith. The woman is guided by hatred, a passionate desire for vengeance that has survived for years. It's possible that she launched her offensive without having made sure in advanced that her rear was quite secure. Her scientific temperament has given way to an exacerbated fanaticism that has carried her off in its irresistible whirlwind. However, to answer your question, I believe, in spite of what I've just said, that Madame Atomos has anticipated every possibility."

"Okay," muttered Beffort. "That's what I think." He took his thirty-eight from its holster, opened his door, and said: "Are we going?"

Akamatsu nodded, and got out in his turn. The two men glided like shadows along the hedge, without seeing that a slender barrel in the form of a fiberglass fishing rod was pointing in their direction from the first floor of the house.

The hobo was spotted by a police car at the corner of Benedict Avenue and Route 9, and the two patrolmen stopped the vehicle.

"Hey! You there! Come here a minute!"

The man continued on his way without even turning round and crossed the avenue dragging his feet.

"What the…!" swore one of the cops.

His colleague shrugged his shoulders, rapidly turned the car around, and quickly drew level with the hobo.

"Hey, granddad, are you deaf?"

The man continued on his way. He paid no heed to the police car rolling along beside him. His stiff stance and his livid, frozen face ended up intriguing the two cops.

"He's drugged, is all!"

"He's taking the Mickey!" said the more peevish of the two. "Hey! Stop, granddad, and show us some ID!"

"You'd better catch hold of him. This guy's looking to spend the winter in chokey. The angrier you get, the more awkward he'll get!"

Furious, the driver pulled on the handbrake and got out of the car with his colleague. The two men descended upon the delinquent. When they got to within a yard of him they were atomized, and fell down in the snow. They stayed there for thirty seconds, then got up and followed the man, adopting his jerky walk.

Further on, a milkman who was beginning his round was collected by the little group; then it was the turn of two sailors on shore leave, four housewives, a postman, and a pregnant woman and her husband who were getting ready to leave for the clinic in anticipation of the imminent birth.

The thirteen atomized individuals arrived thus in the neighborhood where the Fairbanks house stood, and went into the silent lane.

Lydia Watanabe waited for the two men to draw away, and then redoubled her efforts to free herself. She knew that Madame Atomos was on her guard. It had always been strictly forbidden to switch on the remote control apparatus in the vicinity of the refuges that the terrible woman had occupied, and that transgression of the regulations could only signify an urgent warning.

In that, the Eurasian woman was not mistaken.

In the Fairbanks house, three men and two women were putting the final touches to the apparatus designed to blow up the engines of destruction, as Madame Atomos had ordered. It was impossible to take the equipment away, but it was necessary at all costs to prevent the FBI agents from taking possession of it.

At the window, the sentry had seen the Cadillac arrive; since it was behind the hedge, however, he could only see its roof. The emergence of Beffort and Akamatsu had completely escaped him, and he shuddered when a silent group approached the car.

Lydia had just freed her hands. She opened the door, and abruptly found herself face to face with thirteen atomized individuals—who, deprived of directives, were automatically tracking the apparatus that had animated them. Lydia understood in a flash that she was doomed, uttered a frightful scream, and collapsed, thunderstruck.

At the same moment, the watcher pressed the trigger of his weapon. A lightning-flash lit up the night; the hedge, the car and the atomized people were instantaneously engulfed in flames.

Beffort and Akamatsu shot the sentry, leapt over the hedge and were rushing toward the house when it exploded. The two men threw themselves to the ground, and were showered with debris. When they were able to move again, the house was blazing like a torch.

In spite of the crackling of the flames, they distinctly heard the roar of an engine, understood that Madame Atomos was fleeing, and—in spite of the heat of the conflagration—ran into the garden extended behind the house.

Beyond the garden there was a dirt track, but the car had disappeared. Nothing remained on the damp earth but the double tire-track of the vehicle that had carried the terrible Japanese woman away.

The alarm was raised fifteen minutes later, and road-blocks set up throughout the region. By six o'clock in the morning more than thirteen hundred vehicles had been stopped and searched.

Six Asiatic women who were travelling by car on Route 9 were taken to the central police station in Tarrytown, and FBI headquarters was notified of these arrests.

Beffort and Akamatsu left for New York in order to save time. It was a matter of fetching the photograph and fingerprints of Kanoto Yoshimuta, alias Madame Atomos, which the Boss had retained, in order to compare them with those of the arrested women. This decision had been taken by reason of the dispersal of police and FBI personnel, who were occupied—along with other public services—in gathering up the corpses cluttering up the streets of Brooklyn.

The Boss seemed worn out, crushed by an intolerable burden, but his face cleared when Beffort and Akamatsu came into his office. "Glad you see you've come back alive," he said, bleakly. His features were transformed again, "It's a disaster," he said, passing his hand over the back of his painful neck. The count isn't finished, but the latest news was that there were more than ten thousand dead." He lowered his eyes, moved a pencil and added, in a hollow tone of which he would never again be free: "My wife is among the victims...." He raised his head again, and said: "We've lost six men too—old hands; guys who've been working with me since the beginning: Davis, Funk, Mitchell, Martin, Bernon and Twining."

"My God!" whispered Beffort, who was hard hit. After the death of Sam Forbes, it was the worst news he had heard in years. In the course of the night he had seen hundreds of corpses, but they had always been anonymous, representing nothing more than a heap of lifeless flesh. The names the Boss had just listed had imperishable memories attached to them, and the faces of the dead men were dancing before his eyes.

Akamatsu quietly intervened. "Six women are waiting in Tarrytown. We might, perhaps, find the person responsible for this tragedy among them."

Five minutes later, Beffort and Akamatsu were on their way back to Tarrytown.

Chapter XV

Chief Inspector Rooney was waiting for the two agents on the threshold of the central police station. He welcomed them as soon as they got out of the car and immediately made them party to his anxieties.

"Something strange has happened," he said. "The six women we've detained are all Japanese. They're all fifty years old and were either born in Nagasaki or lived there before coming to the United States."

Beffort and Akamatsu remained poised on the bottom step, mute with amazement.

Rooney scratched his nose and added: "Furthermore, all these females have been victims of accidents that have necessitated operations in cosmetic surgery, and they're all missing one of the fingers on their right hands."

Akamatsu started. "The index finger?" he roared.

"The index finger," Rooney confirmed. "That's the missing one."

Beffort took the photograph of Kanoto Yoshimuta, alias Madame Atomos, out of his pocket, and waved it under Rooney's nose. "Do any of them resemble this photograph?" he demanded.

The inspector studied the print carefully, and finally pursed his lips in perplexity. "There's a similarity," he said. "I think it would be better if you took a look for yourself."

Beffort and Akamatsu started to climb the steps, but Rooney stopped them. "There's something else," he said, wearily. "Obviously, we took their names. They're all called…" He stumbled over the name, took a piece of paper from his pocket, and read: "Kanoto Yoshimuta." As his two interlocutors stood there with their mouths agape, he added, as if by way of excuse: "It seems that in Japan, it's a name as common as John Smith is here...."

They were not identical, but they all bore a family resemblance to the photograph of Madame Atomos. They lived in New York, had been in the United States for six months, but had neither relatives nor friends there. They were unemployed, were only passing through, were due to return to Japan soon, and had not met one another before being arrested by the police. Now, they were chattering away between themselves in Japanese, seemingly absolutely delighted with this unexpected little party....

Akamatsu howled an order in Japanese, and the six women fell silent, looking at him reproachfully.

"Separate them," the Tokkoka man demanded of Chief Rooney, "and make sure that they don't communicate with one another."

He pointed his finger at one of the women. "You, Madame Kanoto Yoshimuta, remain here."

The other women clucked in annoyance, and allowed themselves to be led away to other rooms.

"What were you doing on Route 9?" Akamatsu demanded.

The woman was not aggressive, but it was evident that her desire to cooperate was nevertheless very limited. She was of medium height—like the other five women—and would doubtless have passed unnoticed in a crowd. She had a black simulated leather bag in her lap, and Akamatsu observed that only the final phalanx was missing from her right index finger.

"I learned from my radio," she finally replied, "that Madame Atomos had just attacked New York. The announcer said that there were already many people dead, and that an immense procession of the atomized was threatening to overwhelm the city. I was afraid, and my one thought was to get away."

"Where were you going?"

"Anywhere."

"You don't have any baggage, do you?"

The woman smiled, with considerable irony. "If you had been in my shoes, you wouldn't have thought of anything but saving your life. It really was an every-man-for-himself situation!"

"What are your means of support, Madame Yoshimuta?"

The woman looked at her hands. "My husband had a big life insurance policy. When he was killed...."

"How was he killed?"

"He and my children were killed by the atomic bomb in 1945."

Beffort and the Tokkoka man exchanged knowing glances. This woman's past life coincided strangely with that of Madame Atomos.

"What is the reason for your presence in the United States?"

The Japanese woman hesitated; then, still looking at her hands, she said, slowly: "I was curious to see the Americans at close range. It seemed to me that the people who had destroyed Hiroshima and Nagasaki could not be like everyone else. I've realized, of course, that I was mistaken."

"Do you detest Americans, Madame Yoshimuta?"

In her native tongue, the woman replied: "You're the same race as me, sir. You know as well as I do that the Japanese detest Americans."

Akamatsu translated for Beffort's benefit, and said: "Do you approve of the actions of Madame Atomos?"

"I can't deny it. I merely regret having been arrested before my task was complete."

Exclamations burst forth, and Akamatsu had to raise his voice. "So you admit to being Madame Atomos?"

"I admit it."

A great confusion burst out in the police station. The woman was handcuffed, journalists and photographers were admitted into the room, and in less than five minutes, the population of the USA learned that Madame Atomos was in the hands of the police.

Shortly afterwards, the *coup de théâtre* became manifest. All six women claimed to bed Madame Atomos, and each of the six swore that the others were lying, proudly claiming responsibility for the crimes that had been committed.

When a confrontation was attempted, they swore at one another, and if they had not been held back, they would probably have fought savagely. Then they were locked in separate cells and attempts were made to find a solution to the inextricable confusion.

It was the Boss who ordered, by telephone, that they be subjected to the judgment of truth serum.

This is an extract from the record made of the interrogation to which the six women were subjected, having been injected with truth serum, which was published on Thursday February twenty-eighth in the New York Herald and read aloud by Sydney Barrow of the ABC television network.

(1)   What is your name?

Responses: None of the women named herself Yoshimuta; they were in reality Mrs. Kawaguchi, Tanawa, Myamoto, Ilyinskaia, Kuanru and Sudinyo.

(2) *Where were you born?*

Responses: Nagano, Himeji, Kushiro, Gifu, Chiba, Yawata.

(3) *Who asked you to pretend to be Madame Atomos?*

Responses: Lydia Watanabe.

(4) *Why did you agree?*

Responses: Miss Watanabe offered me ten thousand dollars.

(5) *How and why did you come to the United States?*

Responses: A year ago, Miss Watanabe paid me to remain at her disposal. She was the one who brought me to the United States and proved me with a residence in New York and a car.

(6) *How did you meet Lydia Watanabe?*

Responses: She contacted me in the town where I lived and told me that she was interested in my situation. I was without resources. Miss Watanabe seemed very interested in my facial surgery and the mutilation of my index finger, and my age also seemed satisfactory to her.

(7) *Who ordered you to travel on Route 9 this morning?*

Responses: I received a telephone call asking me to go to Tarrytown immediately. I was to drive around the town for an hour and then return to New York. If I was arrested by the police, I was to claim that I was Madame Atomos.

(8) *Do you know Madame Atomos?*

Responses: No.

(9) *Do you know what has become of her?*

Responses:

Mrs. Kawaguchi: She doesn't exist.

Mrs. Tanawa: She is Miss Watanabe.

Mrs. Myamoto: She's dead.

Mrs. Ilyinskaia: She's a man.

Mrs. Kuanru: She has escaped.

Mrs. Sudinyo: She's one of us.

(10) *Do you admit to having worked for Madame Atomos?*

Responses: No. I worked for Miss Watanabe.

(11) *You did, however, agree to pretend to be her?*

Responses: I thought it was a big joke and was certain that the police would never take me seriously.

(12) *Do you approve of the actions of Madame Atomos?*

Responses: Not at all! She's a criminal and merits an exemplary punishment.

(13) *Did you know that Lydia Watanabe was working for Madame Atomos?*

Responses: No. There was never any mention of Madame Atomos in the various conversations I had with Miss Watanabe.

(14) *What tasks had you previously carried out for Lydia Watanabe?*

Responses: None. She did not ask me to do anything except to remain at her disposal by my telephone, day and night.

(15) *Did you know that other women were in the same situation, and did you know who they were?*

Responses: I was completely unaware of their existence

An investigation conducted in parallel by the Tok-koka and the FBI revealed that the six women had told the truth, and after the hearing that took place six months later they were simply released. Nevertheless, they were deported to their own country, and the Tokkoka kept them under covert surveillance.

In the United States, the search for Madame Atomos continued, and the security forces remained in a state of alert for six months. As no further incident occurred during that period, it was eventually concluded that Madame Atoms had died in the fire at the Fairbanks house, and the affair was gradually forgotten.

Smith Beffort accompanied Yosho Akamatsu to La Guardia airport to see him off.

"Forget all this," the Japanese man advised him. "It's obvious that Madame Atomos is dead."

Beffort remained serious. "I don't believe so, Yosho. "That woman has slipped through our fingers, and when we've forgotten her, she'll be back!"

Akamatsu's laughter was forced. "Don't be so pessimistic, Smith...."

The flight was called, and the two men parted.

Beffort remained standing there for some time after the aircraft had vanished in the sky, thinking about Sam Forbes, his dead colleagues and the thousands of victims of the Brooklyn tragedy. Finally, he drew away with his head bowed, and lit a cigarette.

Perhaps it was only his nerves, but he was convinced that Madame Atomos, concealed in the crowd, was watching him....

ANDRÉ CAROFF

MADAME ATOMOS SÈME la TERREUR

ANGOISSE

Éditions
"FLEUVE NOIR"

MADAME ATOMOS SOWS TERROR

Chapter I

In his New York office, Smith Beffort was sweating lightly. The sun was ablaze over the city and not a single breath of air was filtering through the wide-open window. It was ten o'clock in the morning, and when Beffort tore off the top page of his calendar he observed—without annoyance but with no particular joy—that it was Wednesday February twelfth, which was a sort of anniversary.

Exactly a year earlier, he had first laid eyes on the file of Kanoto Yoshimuta, *alias* Madame Atomos, had met his colleague Sam Forbes, and had set off on the trail of Hisato Keichu, the obedient accomplice of the terrible Japanese woman.

Since then, Hisato had died, Sam Forbes had died, and thousands of innocent people had succumbed to the terrible blows struck by the sinister Madame Atomos—but she herself had disappeared, without paying for her crimes.

Beffort had not succeeded in forgetting, and he did not believe that Madame Atomos was dead. He knew that the day would come when she would manifest herself again, and was ever ready to oppose her projects.

Madame Atomos had sworn to subject the United States to blood and fire. She blamed the Americans for having murdered her family by dropping the atomic bomb on Nagasaki, and lived for the hope of achieving her vengeance: a terrible vengeance gat was to be exacted on a national scale, including all the citizens of the USA, regardless of age or sex.

Smith Beffort started sweating a little more copiously. Yes, if that diabolical woman were to reappear, the squabble really would be a fight to the death....

That same day, at the same hour, old Cal Pooley abruptly perceived that he no longer had a single reel of string.

Cal was sixty-five years old. He had been a storekeeper since the day he was born—in a manner of speaking, since his parents had certainly been engaged in that occupation before him—and sold anything that he could sell, provided that it was no bigger than a lawn-mower.

Cal's general store was on Route 175 between Sagoville and Dallas, Texas. It was a big wooden building with two gas pumps out front, a counter inside, and a store-room in back whose only door opened into a narrow yard. At the back of that yard, in another wooden shed, Pooley kept his reserve stock. That was not a whim on his part but a clause in his fire insurance contract.

So, that morning, Cal Pooley picked up a wheelbarrow, opened the door of his back room and headed for his reserve stock. The yard was exactly a hundred yards long by fifty broad. It was covered by short grass and bordered by trees. A path had formed spontaneously by reason of the comings-and-goings between the back room and the shed, and whenever it rained it became a veritable mud-bath.

Obviously, Cal could have had that pathway tarred, cemented or paved, but God knows where he would have found the money for that! If he had not done it, it was not out of stinginess. He had always known the path to be like that, and whenever he looked at it, he saw his entire childhood. He had taken his first steps there. He had cut his chin there when he fell over. To the left, the dinner table had been set up in fine weather, and a canvas awning had been set up between the corners of the back room and the main building to protect it from the sun.

In brief, Cal liked his wooden buildings, his dusty steps and his ragged yard.

Pushing the wheelbarrow in front of him, he reached the middle of the yard, and saw that the mushroom was still there.

It was an odd mushroom. Cal had never seen one like it, but he was convinced that it was not edible. He could certainly have torn it up and thrown it on the dung-heap, for it seemed to warrant no better, but he was surprised and slightly flattered that something had finally consented to grow in his yard.

His parents had once tried to grow vegetables there; the disastrous result had soon discouraged them. It seemed that the ground was incapable of nourishing anything but the meager grass—but now, all of a sudden, the mushroom had appeared without warning!

Cal abandoned his wheelbarrow, put his glasses on and leaned over. He was instantly astonished. The mushroom now had several stalks, and measured at least a foot across. It also seemed flatter, and its yellow color was turning very gradually to pink.

"Wow!" Cal murmured. "Yesterday morning it was no bigger than a cigar-stub."

He knelt down, and observed that the five new stalks were firmly anchored to the ground by a multitude of little roots, but that they were not driven into it. He

147

lay down on his belly and saw that the grass underneath the mushroom had completely disappeared, and that the soil was granular, as dry as tinder.

It was odd, but Cal Pooley did not attribute any great importance to it. He was a tradesman, not a farmer...

That same February twelfth, a young fellow built like a battleship had bought a pair of boots from Cal Pooley's store. The man in question was named Eliot Sughrue, and Cal suspected him of having a crush on his shop assistant, Susan Bigelow.

Eliot was size 45; there was one pair of boots in the store that fitted him, but Eliot didn't like their style. He wanted Mexican boots with gilt embroidery. Cal knew that if he had had them to hand, Eliot would have asked for something else in order to be alone with Susan. Purely for the sake of malice, he sent Susan to the shed instead of going himself, and laughed behind his hand when he saw Eliot's face grow longer.

"How's Pop Sughrue?" Cal asked, as he piled up sacks of rice.

"Okay," Eliot replied, peevishly. He turned round repeatedly, darting occasional glances into the back room.

"Don't get impatient, fella," said Cal. "Susan'll be back in five minutes."

At that moment, Susan appeared in the doorway. Her mouth was wide open. Cal looked at her round eyes and empty hands, and said: "Tssh! I bet you couldn't find them?"

"It ain't that, Mister Pooley—I can't get by"

"You can't get by?"

He was already rummaging around for the key of the shed when Susan said something surprising; "There's a contraption blocking the path. I could have gone around it, but I wanted to tell you first."

"A contraption? What contraption?"

The girl spread her arms wide. "A long, flat thing, all red. I don't know what it is."

Cal shrugged his shoulders, went through to the door of the back room, and saw that the mushroom had indeed acquired extraordinary dimensions.

"Will you look at that!" he said, in amazement.

"What is it?" asked Eliot Sughrue, who had followed him.

Cal turned round proudly. "A mushroom," he said, heartily. "In my yard, eh?"

Eliot, who had a good view, had the impression that the mushroom was spreading slowly toward the shed. He went across the open space, and Cal followed on his heels.

Seen from close range, the surface of the mushroom was flat, as smooth as a glass plate and blood red in color. Its perimeter was equipped with stalks whose roots were stuck to the ground.

"That's not normal," said Eliot. "You might think that that there plant was on the move…that it was crawling toward your shed, Mr. Pooley."

Cal burst out laughing. "You're mistaking the damn mushroom for a snake? Hee hee! You've had one too many, fella?"

Eliot paid no attention to him. He bent down, touched the mushroom, and got up again, grimacing. "I've never seen anything like it," he said. "You might think that it was made of rubber."

Old Cal stopped laughing, abruptly. He too had the impression the impression that the plant was moving. It was almost imperceptible, but Cal had been further away from the mushroom a little while before than he was now, and as he hadn't moved his feet an inch....

"There's something weird about this," he said, with much less assurance. He looked at Eliot, looked at his shed, frowned, and said: What are we going to do about your boots?"

"I've got plenty of time, Mr. Pooley. Don't you think you ought to get rid of the filthy thing?"

"Damn right—but how?"

"You've got an axe, haven't you?"

"Sure! I've got several."

A few minutes later, he attacked the mushroom with mighty blows of a woodcutter's axe—but the iron rebounded as if from a tire filled with air.

Then Eliot went in search of a crowbar, introduced it between the strange matter and the ground, and exercised a powerful pressure. It was as if he had tried to lift a railway locomotive.

"My opinion," growled Cal, "is that we'll have to set fire to it."

The two men went back into the shop and filled four gas cans. Three customers came back with them and helped them spread the gas over the mushroom. When that was done, Eliot struck a match. There was a brief explosion; the gas caught fire and burned for five minutes. Then the flames diminished and went out. They all observed that the mushroom was absolutely intact, not even blackened.

At that moment, they heard a crack coming from the shed, and saw that a plank situated at ground level had just broken under the pressure exerted by the mushroom.

Old Cal howled in anger, climbed on to the thing that neither axe-blows nor fire had dented, and started running. Eliot and the three customers followed him to the shed, whose foundations were creaking.

Further away, a tree cracked.

Astounded, the four men watched old Cal defend his storage shed with axe-blows, but it was obvious that his efforts would be futile. After a few moments of sterile conflict, Cal threw away the implement. He was sweating, staring with dilated eyes at the edge of the extraordinary creeping plant that was attacking his cabin. When he turned round, he saw that the trunks of the tress surrounding his yard had already disappeared and that no grass was visible anywhere.

"You'd think," said one of the customers, "that someone was pulling an immense blanket over the ground. We'd better notify the authorities immediately!"

Eliot came back an hour later in a police car. He had had unexpected difficulty in persuading the cops to get off their behinds; they thought it was a hoax.

In the meantime, the landscape had changed, and the two policemen were stupefied. The Pooley Mushroom—as they had jokingly named it—had grown considerably. Now it covered the trees, the shed and Cal's store and was spreading into the rod. A group of people standing on the roadway was retreating as the Pooley advanced. Three cars had stopped on the far side of the uncrossable zone.

Old Cal was in despair. "There's nothing left of my house!" he croaked, "And it hasn't finished. Look at it expanding, the filthy thing!" He turned to the police car and said: "Well? Arrest that thing!"

Without a word, the driver turned the car around and launched it in the direction of Dallas. At the first glance, he had realized that the matter was much more serious than it had appeared....

At four o'clock the Pooley—by that time no one was calling it anything else—measured three-quarters of a mile in diameter. Cal's land was the center of the vast moving disk, which was flexible but as hard as steel. Discernible beneath its red surface were the forms of trees, houses, fences, embankments and six cars that had already been submerged.

On Route 175, which had been cut in two, powerful explosive charges were laid, which the Pooley was allowed to cover. At four twenty a mighty detonation rang out, and debris was flung six hundred feet into the air, while a thick cloud of dust eddied in the sunlight. When the dust had settled it was observed that the Pooley had been shredded over a considerable extent, but that the road had been literally volatilized by the explosion.

The remedy seemed worse than the disease—all the more so when, thirty minutes later, the Pooley had entirely reformed and had resumed its invasive progress. An enormous crowd gathered at the location. Radio, television and photographs, as well as journalists, had whipped up excitement.

Almost no one noticed the departure of Eliot Sughrue for hospital in Dallas. The young man's right hand was curiously swollen, very red and completely insensitive, and the inexplicable paralysis was spreading along his arm. No one, least of all him, thought of making a connection between that brutal infection and the Pooley—but Eric had been the first person to touch the terrifying substance on old Cal's land. Since then, many others had done so....

Eliot Sughrue died at seven p.m. of a general paralysis, and three hundred people presented themselves at various clinics and hospitals in Dallas. They all had swollen hands, red and insensitive. By midnight, the death toll had reached four hundred, and two hundred sick people were receiving treatment that was utterly ineffective.

Throughout the country, people were kept up to date with the ravages caused by the Pooley. It now measured seven miles across, and was threatening Dallas and Sagoville; it had engulfed dozens of dwellings and vehicles, but had been inexplicably interrupted by the Trinity and East Fork rivers.

At half past midnight, Smith Beffort was watching television. The presenter, Doug Willington, suddenly appeared and said in a cracked vice: "I've just received some horrible news...." He lowered his eyes, unfolded a sheet of typescript, and continued: "This is a copy of a message received by President Lyndon B. Johnson, and this is its text: *After a year's absence, I have reminded you of my existence by sending you the Pooley. I am certain that I shall attain my goal this time. Hiroshima. Nagasaki. Compliments of Madame Atomos....*"

For a second, Smith Beffort remained as fixed in place as Doug Willington, but he was out of his apartment before the presenter had resumed speaking.

Chapter II

Madame Atomos had not counted on the fantastic capacity for labor that Texans have. Perhaps she had not anticipated that her indestructible mushroom would recoil from water. Either way, once people were certain that the Pooley could not set down its roots on inundated land, thirty bull-dozers designed for laying pipelines were sent to Dallas. The enormous machines went into operation at three a.m. By seven o'clock, as the sun was rising, a narrow artificial river stopped the northward progress of the Pooley, and the city of Dallas breathed easy.

The danger remained for Sagoville, however, which was situated south-west of Dallas between the Trinity and East Fork rivers. As the Pooley was approaching the town, and it would have taken too much time to relocate the bulldozers, three thousand volunteers accompanied by troops and the crews of twelve fire stations were deployed between Sagoville and the two rivers.

At eight a.m. thousands of flamethrowers, water-hoses, pails, watering-cans and various containers poured tons of water on the foremost roots of the redoubtable plant. In the meantime, the bulldozers were brought into position, divided into two groups, and began the excavation of a second artificial river.

The Pooley, slowed down by the water-soaked ground, was unable to advance at more than six feet an hour. Its roots groped the soil like a blind man's fingers, retracting in response to the effects of the damp and setting forth again in search of dry ground, in a vile swarm.

By ten o'clock the second trench was hollowed out and abruptly flooded with water from the Trinity and East Fork rivers. A helicopter belonging to a TV network flew over the immense rectangle, and the viewers saw a bumpy desert region with no trace of life.

The Pooley had been stopped, put out of action. Although the water prevented it from advancing further, it was unable to force its retreat. Dynamite tore it apart temporarily, blasting enormous holes in its blood red flesh, but it reformed within a few minutes, as if nothing had happened.

The Pooley was no longer advancing, but it was holding its ground, and no one knew how to destroy it.

The Boss, an immediate colleague of J. Edgar Hoover, the FBI's overlord, strode back and forth in his office like a tiger in its cage—a tiger chewing a cigar, suffering from rheumatism and wearing a black armband on the left sleeve of his coat.

A year earlier, when Madame Atomos had attacked New York, the Boss had lost his wife. She had been caught by the rigid herd of the atomized, had been killed and had risen to her feet to follow the formidable procession of the walking dead. Later, after Smith Beffort had switched off the remote control apparatus, the Boss had found his wife on the sidewalk in Churchill Avenue. He was not ready to forget that atrocious spectacle, any more than he would forget the great and likeable Sam Forbes, killed, along with his fiancée Maggie Fairbanks, by Madame Atomos. There were also Davis, Funk, Mitchell, Bernon, Martin and Twining....

The Boss shook himself, took the cigar out of his mouth, at down in front of Smith Beffort and Dr. Alan Soblen, and said: "The message to Lyndon Johnson was sent from the central office in Dallas. The President received it at fifteen minutes past midnight. Five minutes later, I was alerted, and by twenty-five past midnight all communications coming out of Dallas were filtered. At present, sixty-five Asiatic women have been questioned, but identity checks haven't revealed anything. There's no need to tell you that Madame Atomos's picture is on every wall. Beffort, you'll leave immediately for Dallas—accompanied, of course, by Dr. Soblen. I don't think Madame Atomos will stay there. The Pooley is blocked, but we must expect to see other Pooleys developing virtually anywhere in the territory.

The Boss went to suit at his desk, and pressed one of the buttons on his intercom. "Has the man from Dallas arrived?"

"Yes, sir," replied a precise voice. "He's been waiting for three minutes."

"Send him up." He got up again, picked up a telegram, and said: "By the way, the Tokkoka tells me that Yosho Akamatsu will be here at eleven o'clock—which is to say, in a few minutes' time."

Beffort clicked his fingers. "Good," he said, with satisfaction. "Yosho hasn't lost any time. I suppose he'll be coming with us?"

"Obviously. If he could strangle Mother Atomos, he wouldn't leave the task to anyone else...."

At that moment the door opened and Cal Pooley appeared on the threshold. The agent accompanying him steered him gently into the office and closed the door behind him.

"Come in, Mr. Pooley," said the Boss, "and take a seat."

Old Cal grimaced. "Don't call me Pooley," he said, dejectedly. "My name disgusts me since it's been given

156

to that damn filthy mushroom. I'll sit down, but call me Cal...."

The Boss pulled out a chair for him and offered him a cigar, which Beffort lit. Old Cal relaxed slightly. He had taken a nap on the special plane, but his taut stomach had refused to accept any nourishment. Moreover, his head was buzzing, full of new and bewildering images. There had been too many novelties in quick succession for a man who had never left his home town before.

"Well, Cal," the Boss began, "tell us a little about how all this began."

Old Cal shrugged his shoulders. "It was yesterday morning," he said. "No, the day before yesterday...damn! What day is it? I've lost track, with all this going on...."

"Today's the fourteenth," Smith Beffort told him.

Cal nodded. "Right—then it was the morning of the twelfth when I saw the mushroom for the first time. It was no bigger than a cigar-stub."

"What kind of store do you have?" Beffort asked.

"I sell anything. My stock has all sorts...."

"Have you a loyal clientele? I man, are your customers regulars, almost friends, whom you recognize with no possibility of error?"

Old Cal raised his eyebrows. "For sure I know them. I'm not senile. I talk to my customers whenever they come in—the ones who buy gas, for instance."

Beffort lit a cigarette. "How far from the road was the mushroom, Cal?"

"I don't know exactly. Maybe fifty or sixty yards— yes, I'd say sixty. When is all this going to end? I've already told the story a hundred times to a whole heap of guys. You're the only one don't know it! I can't say what I don't know!"

Smith Beffort smiled at him. "Cal, we think that this mushroom didn't get on to your land by itself. Someone came into your home to plant it on a spot chosen in advance...."

"No way!" Cal said, indignantly. "No one's been on my land, especially not this damned Mother Atomos!"

The Boss coughed. "Cal," he said, "We're pretty sure that Madame Atomos didn't do it in person. She doubtless has a company of fanatical followers, as she did twelve months ago. They're probably Japanese, who lost their families in 1945 at Hiroshima or Nagasaki, and dream of nothing but getting revenge on our country. The question, therefore, is this: on the day of the eleventh, or the morning of the twelfth, did you serve a customer, male or female, of an Asiatic type?"

As old Cal remained mute, his forehead furrowed by a violent effort of concentration, the Boss added: "There's no need to tell you how precious such information would be to us. To put our hands on an accomplice of Madame Atomos would be to draw a bead on that terrible woman."

Old Cal pursed his lips. "I didn't see one," he said. "No, I didn't see one. You'll have to ask Susan."

"Who's Susan?"

"She works for me. She's in the shop more often than I am. She's a nice-looking girl and a lot of guys take a fancy to her. Poor Eliot Sughrue...."

"Susan what?" Beffort interjected. "Where does she live?"

"Susan Bigelow. She lives in Dallas in...."

"Just a second, Cal...."

Smith Beffort took his notebook from his pocket and wrote down Susan's name and address. Then he put it away again and said: "How long has the young woman been working for you?"

Cal passed a hand over the bulging veins in is tanned face and said, after thinking about it: "It must be two months now. Yes, poor Mildred died in November...."

"I find it surprising that Susan Bigelow, who lives in Dallas, where there's no lack of opportunities, decided to travel all that distance, morning and evening, to work at your place...."

"Tssh!" interjected old Cal. "If you suspect her, you're badly mistaken, my lad! Susan's a good kid, and when she saw the mushroom in my yard, her eyes were as round as pies!"

The intercom buzzed, and the Boss went around his desk to press a button.

"Mr. Akamatsu is here," articulated the secretary's precise voice.

"Send him up," said the Boss.

"Right away, sir."

Smith Beffort judged that there would not be time to resume Cal's interrogation before Yosho's arrival, and went to open the door. There was a rapid footfall in the corridor, and the Tokkoka man appeared on the threshold. Yosho was five nine and a hundred and a hundred and sixty pounds, with square shoulders and slim hips. Dark haired, with a long face and prominent cheekbones, he possessed an incontestable virile charm.

"*Hai!*" said Beffort. "*Isaka deska*, Yosho?"

"Very well," said the Japanese man, with a thin smile. "I needn't ask you how things are going here, need I?"

The special agent of the Tokkoka spoke the language of Uncle Sam with almost no accent, and his rapid speech never stumbled over any current expression. His voice was like a running stream, with brief changes of intonation, and he had a freedom of gesture surprising in a man of his race. Beffort know him to be tightly wound, straight as an arrow in his morality, overflowing with enthusiasm and unfailing in his courage.

Come in," said the Boss, holding out his hand. You're just in time to leave with Beffort and Soblen.

Akamatsu shook hands all round, put his black leather briefcase and his small suitcase down in a corner and said: "I presume that we're leaving for Dallas?"

"You're well-informed," said Beffort, approvingly. "How much do you know about the affair."

"Almost everything. We received hourly updates on the situation on the plane. I know that there are numerous fatalities already and that the Pooley...by the way, where does that strange name come from?"

Beffort turned to Old Cal. "This is Mr. Cal Pooley," he said. "It was in his yard that the mushroom was found, and where it grew...."

"And which it ended up covering!" Old Cal finished. Then, pointing at the Japanese man, he said: "I know you!"

"That surprises me," Yosho replied, politely, "but it's not impossible...."

"Mr. Akamatsu belongs to the Japanese police," Beffort put in. "He was occupied with Madame Atomos last February and his photograph appeared in all the daily newspapers."

Cal shook his head stubbornly. "It wasn't in a rag that I saw him," he said. "I think you came in to buy something from my store."

Yosho smiled. "I've come directly from Tokyo, and…."

"Hold on!" the Boss interjected. "Cal, are you sure that you've seen our friend in your store?"

"Sure would be putting it a bit strong. At any rate, if it wasn't him, it was someone who looked very like him."

The Boss understood that the special agent's arrival had stirred up the old man's memory—an entirely accidental release produced by the vague resemblance that all Asiatic faces seem to have in the eyes of white people. "Let's suppose," he said, "that it was him. When did you see him?"

"Oh, not long ago. He'd broken his fan-belt and I had to go out to me shed…hold on! That's what you were asking me just now. It's come back to me all of a sudden! It was Thursday morning, and I'd just opened up. Yes, I know that because Susan hadn't yet arrived, because she'd had car trouble…."

"What time was it?"

"No later than seven a.m."

Were you in the shed for a long time, Cal?"

"Quite a time, yes, because the fan-belts were right at the back….."

The Boss winked. "In sum," he said, "while you were searching for the fan-belt, the Japanese man was alone in the shop?"

"Yes, sure…."

"Do you think you would have seen him if he'd come out to plant the mushroom in the middle of your yard?"

Cal's features froze. "Damn it! No, I sure wouldn't have seen him…."

Yosho picked up his briefcase, opened it hastily and took out a thick envelope. Without a word, he took four photographs from the envelope and showed them to Cal Pooley. "Is that him?" he asked.

Cal only hesitated for a second. "That's him!" he exclaimed.

Akamatsu gathered up the photographs, put them back and said: "Mikonosuke Watanabe, aged thirty-eight, born in Nagasaki, brother of Lydia Watanabe, killed outside the Fairbanks house by the atomized of Tarrytown."

Smith Beffort started. "Son of a bitch! How come you have a photograph of the guy?"

Yosho smiled. "On returning to Japan after the disappearance of Madame Atomos, I gave orders to for the photographs to be sent of all suspect persons who had left Japan for the USA. I have a very interesting little collection of photos here. Like you, Smith, I never believed that Madame Atomos was dead...."

Chapter III

A few miles from Dallas, the Pooley was no longer on the move; its roots remained absolutely still. The sunlight was reflecting from its mirror-smooth surface, but everyone had the feeling that the Pooley was merely dead matter that would slowly decay. They waited for the first manifestations of the decomposition that was bound to occur, but Saturday went by without the immense fungus changing its appearance.

On the other side of the Trinity and East Fork rivers, and the two artificial rivers, an enormous crowd had gathered. Mobile tradesmen were selling ice-creams and hot dogs, and the ground was littered with greasy pieces of paper. It was a gigantic fairground, where nothing was audible but laughter and the discordant braying of hundreds of transistor radios. The Pooley was no longer exciting anything more than curiosity, and was even disappointing newcomers.

What! It was that inert plant that caused all last night's death. Come on, tell that to kids, but not to us! The whole thing's probably some fantastic publicity stunt!

The previous year's drama had already been forgotten: the thousands of corpses lying in the streets of New York, the burning of the large department store in Brooklyn, the deaths in Chinook, the robbery of the Dubinsky jewelry store....

Simpletons threw stones at the Pooley, and cameras filmed the impressive red expanse, but the general opinion was inclined toward an inexplicable, but natural phenomenon....

At six p.m. the whisper went round that Madame Atomos was well and truly dead, and that a practical joker had sent a hoax message to President Johnson. A television cameraman sent images of the crowd to the studio, made a rapid tour of the horizon while the commentator provided a voice-over, and ended up with a spectacular zoom. He focused on old Cal's store as the sun set, although the Pooley-covered building was no more than a slight bump.

Suddenly, something in the distance moved.

The movement was perceptible because everything else was still, but no one could make out exactly what it was. The camera however, remained fixed on the suspect point, and all the small screens in the United States displayed the image. The weather was very clear, and from New York to San Francisco people saw some sort of smoke or mist floating at ground level.

If the phenomenon had been produced over the entire extent of the Pooley the cameraman would doubtless not have persisted. A light mist often spread over the region in May—but this one was limited to old Cal's property.

A television helicopter took off from Dallas airport and rapidly reached the suspect place. The machine was equipped with a camera, and as well as the operator it carried the journalist Dick Slatt, who was renowned for his cool head.

The helicopter hovered, and descended toward the ground; the images seized by its camera were immediately transmitted, as an impressive tracking shot. People saw a grey extent, and divined a row of trees covered by the Pooley.

Dick Slatt's clear voice rang out: "We're flying over the exact spot where the Pooley manifested itself for the first time. Like me, you can make out the silhouette of Old Cal's place...." Dick Slatt interrupted himself abruptly, then howled: "I've just seen a fantastic creature! A gigantic spider! And there's another...and a third...."

On the screens, people found themselves looking at a monstrous spider, and the wide shot caused a terrible emotion. The Pooley had opened up, and a fourth monster was hauling itself up through the rip on to the vegetal surface. There was no point of comparison by which to estimate the size of the spiders, but some people were convinced that they were as big as elephants. That impression was confirmed when the first spider passed over Old Cal's house. The enormous black mass swayed in a horrible manner on its eight think hairy legs, seemingly moving rapidly north-westwards.

The helicopter gained height. Dick Slatt repeated that it was unimaginable, and that he could not believe his eyes, for the most part leaving the images to speak for themselves. Indeed, the spectacle did not require any commentary.

A line of six spiders was heading for Dallas, while other monsters surged forth from the rip in the Pooley, taking the same direction in an orderly manner.

The helicopter circled above this nightmare vision for twenty minutes; then, as darkness fell and everything vanished into the gloom, the machine head back to Love Field, Dallas's municipal airport.

The city was silent. Americans everywhere were sitting in front of their television sets, waiting. The evening meal was forgotten; the cinemas and theaters did not open their doors, and automobiles remained stationary. The United States was partially paralyzed—and that was Madame Atomos's first victory. No one had succeeded in such a *tour de force* before.

Beffort, Soblen and Akamatsu were watching the astounding procession in the FBI offices in Dallas. It was an otherworldly vision, and each of them had to make an effort to admit that it was happening not far from the city, and that it was not the climactic sequence of some futuristic film.

Dr. Soblen recovered the power of speech before his companions and said: "Those spiders are obviously remote-controlled! Madame Atomos has succeeded in creating biologically monstrous creatures, but has evidently not been able to develop their intelligence to the point of making them act as an organized company!"

Smith Beffort looked at the scientist. "One question bothers me, Doctor. Why did Madame Atomos choose Old Cal's property?"

Akamatsu put his hand on his friend's shoulder. Like me, you've noticed that the Pooley opened up spontaneously. That opening is situated in the center of Cal's yard, exactly where the mushroom emerged from the ground on Wednesday February twelfth…Smith, I don't suppose you've been idle with regard to Madame Atomos this last year?"

"Of course not! The investigation has never ceased. Every American citizen has participated in the hunt, without knowing it. Everyone is now familiar with Madame Atomos's face, symbolized by an atomic mushroom-cloud!"

"In that case," said the Japanese special agent, "how do you imagine that she has escaped your search?"

"If I know her, she's been locked away for a long time. What are you driving at, Yosho?"

Akamatsu lit a cigarette, and offered his pack around. "I believe," he said, firmly, "that Madame Atomos has been living underground. I think that, after having slipped through our hands, the diabolical woman took refuge in a haven prepared for that eventuality. A subterranean shelter, situated far from the location of her exploits.

"Beffort let out a whistle, and said: "Under Cal Pooley's yard, for example?"

"Yes. Cal hasn't cultivated his land and no livestock has grazed it. Cal never ventures beyond the path linking his store to his shed. Restocking the shed is done via the dirt road bordering the land. This, the delivery vehicles never go into the yard. Besides, old Cal has no children...."

"No children capable of discovering and interfering with the machinery supplying the shelter with fresh air. I'm beginning to believe that you've hit the bull's-eye, Yosho!"

Dr. Soblen immediately agreed. "It's the only way to explain the appearance of these giant spiders," he said. "They're coming directly from Madame Atomos's subterranean laboratory, having been subjected to a fabulous transformation. We still have to figure out what objective Madame Atomos is pursuing by releasing the spiders on to the surface of the Pooley."

There was a pause, and Maxwell, the chief of the Dallas office, took advantage of it to say: "If there really is a laboratory hidden there, why not bombard it?"

Smith Beffort turned slowly toward him. "I thought of that, Maxwell," he said. "Last year, artillery destroyed the Oakland refuge, but that wasn't protected by the carapace of a Pooley and Madame Atomos had abandoned it a short while before. If we were to launch a single shell today, I'll wager that it would explode before touching the ground."

Dr. Soblen wiped his spectacles. "It is, indeed," he said, "necessary not to forget that Madame Atomos has an uncommon arsenal at her disposal. It includes the thermal weapon and the paralyzing ray, not to mention the electromagnetic ray, the freezing fog and—most of all—the domestication of atoms. If that woman wanted to destroy all life on the Earth's surface at a stroke, I'm convinced that she could do it—except that, where the United States is concerned, Madame Atomos is, so to speak, tempered by her hatred. Before killing the Americans, she wants to starve them, subdue them and render them mad with fear. That. My friends, is why we're still alive."

Maxwell considered Alan Soblen with rounded eyes. "You're forgetting," he spat, "that we represent the most formidable atomic power on the planet! Why not reduce Madame Atomos's lair to ashes?"

Smith Beffort laughed. "And that's the explanation for our enemy's implantation in this region," he said, bleakly. "Drop an atom bomb on that terrain, Maxwell, and you'd also blow up Dallas and its environs."

Maxwell clenched his fists. "Surely there's something we can do!" he roared. "It seems to me that you're giving up very easily!"

Cut to the quick, Smith Beffort retorted, severely: "You were there when Kennedy was assassinated in your own city, Maxwell! Once the bullet had left the barrel of the killer's weapon, only two interventions were possible: to stop it or to get the President out of the way immediately. In the present case, we can't get the United States out of the way, so it's absolutely necessary to stop the bullet. Now, that bullet is represented by Madame Atomos; it is her, and her alone, that it's necessary to neutralize—and without any delay, before the Pooley covers the territory completely.

"It's incapable of crossing the rivers!"

"Unless a bridge is constructed for it! Tell me, Maxwell—what's the principal objective of a spider?"

"To spin its web, of course."

"Say no more! An army of spiders can weave webs over rivers!"

No one had thought it necessary to keep watch on the Pooley by night, and an hour was lost in bringing searchlight batteries from Dallas.

Old Cal's property had indubitably become the vital center of the USA. It was like a heart that might stop beating at any moment, or a large explosive charge that, in blowing up, might annihilate the vital forces of an entire country.

No one knew where the giant spiders were, but heavy machine-guns were disposed around the entire perimeter of the Pooley. Almost at the same time, the searchlights traced white furrows through the dark night, searching the shadows for any sign of the monsters created by the demonic Japanese woman.

The crowd had retreated. The incredulous individuals of the afternoon who had joked while sucking ice-creams were now stationary on the hoods of their cars. They army had taken up position, and the soldiers had their fingers on their triggers.

Police cars were driving back the recalcitrant, forcing them to respect a wide no-man's-land around the now-strategic zone.

At eight p.m. the searchlight batteries in the north-west corner fixed their beams on three gigantic spiders advancing toward the East Fork River. The surprise was total, because the monsters had been expected on the northern artificial river protecting Dallas.

There was a moment of frightful panic; then an order was barked and a machine-gun began to stammer. Tracer bullets were seen to strike the leading spider and ricochet off what seemed to be a thick carapace, to vanish into the night.

Other automatic weapons were brought into play, but the enormous creatures continued their progress without seemed to be inconvenienced by the infernal fire that fell around them. They quickly reached the East Fork, set foot on the other bank, and came to a halt. Their massive bodies swayed lightly above the river at a height of about three stories, and their eight legs were as thick as tree-trunks.

Suddenly, an extraordinarily shrill sound drowned out the crackle of the machine-guns, without anyone being able to discover its source, and the three Dante-esque creatures crashed down into the river.

There was a pause whose dramatic intensity was prodigious, and the army risked an advance into no-man's-land. It was thought that the spiders had succumbed to the gunfire, but doubt overtook the soldiers when they were better able to make out the carapaces that protected them. In the white glare of the searchlights, they resembled plates of articulated steel, and although no bolts or any other systems of attachment were visible, many had the feeling that they were confronted by armored robots that nothing could destroy.

The first Jeep had arrived in proximity with the river when the Pooley, slowly but inexorably, resumed its progress over the bridge formed by the incredible spiders of Madame Atomos. At the same moment, other monsters surged out of the darkness, and a sergeant counted a dozen of them advancing at the speed of a galloping horse.

Horrified, the troops moved back while the 12.7 machine-guns fired over the soldiers' heads, with no more success than before. Then the Pooley flowed on to the other bank like a tongue of lava, immediately spreading out like a pool of oil, covering the ditches, the road and the trees.

Machine-guns mounted on trucks continued firing in a kind of desperate frenzy on the spiders, which were now crossing the East Fork in their turn. A searchlight battery and the truck carrying it, which happened to be in the path of one of the monsters, was overturned by a powerful foot, and trampled by others. The men fled in terror, abandoning their weapons. In the blink of an eye, the little convoy was pulverized. The searchlights and headlights went out, thus plunging the area into darkness, and nothing could any longer be heard but the screams of the wounded and the shrill sound of a jammed horn....

Chapter IV

Dr. Alan Soblen was not what is normally thought of as a man of action. He was small, puny, grey-haired, and wore steel-rimmed spectacles. He had volunteered to work for the FBI, initially with Sam Forbes and then with Smith Beffort, following a personal request from J. Edgar Hoover. Alan Soblen was purely a scientist. Although he was not unfeeling, neither was he liable to be distracted by his feelings—to the extent that it was often said of him that he was no more than an electronic machine.

In fact, he was like one of those generals who consider the result of an attack without worrying overmuch about the losses sustained.

While Maxwell, Smith Beffort and Akamatsu tried to find out whether the convoy had sustained fatal casualties, he covered a page in his notebook with barely legible writing.

"What are you doing, Doctor?" asked Beffort, with a hint of annoyance.

Soblen's keen eyes gleamed behind his lenses, and he said: "Madame Atomos's spiders come from Guyana. They belong to the genus *Theraphosa*, native to South America, which includes the largest known species of spider...."

Interested, Beffort sat down beside Soblen. "What's their maximum size?"

"A hand's breadth, feet included. The thickness of their bodies can reach two inches. They're usually black in color. They're quite rare, and not much is known about their way of life."

Beffort lit a cigarette. "Glad to know it," he said, "but how does this information get us any further forward?"

Soblen smiled indulgently. "At least we know that the monsters aren't robots. Madame Atomos can't create life, in spite of all her scientific knowledge. The spiders have been subjected to a remarkable transformation, which renders them extremely resistant, but they remain mortal nevertheless. Given their size, it's obvious that machine-guns are no more use against them than pea-shooters are against you."

"All right," said Beffort. "So what? We already know all that, Doctor...."

Soblen interlaced his fingers and jabbed his chin at the map representing the zone covered by the Pooley. "Firstly," he said, "let's call this spider by its name. It's a *Theraphosa blondi*, as named by Pierre Latreille. I repeat that its size rarely exceeds that of a human hand. Whatever the dimensions of Madame Atomos's base might be, it certainly can't contain a herd of monsters as gigantic as these!"

"Probably not," Beffort agreed. "So what?"

It follows logically that each *Theraphosa* is subjected to transformation on the threshold of the subterranean hideaway. To put it another way, Madame Atomos presently possesses a stock of spiders that could easily be crushed underfoot!"

Beffort laughed. "Provided," he said, "that we could get into the base!"

"What a troop couldn't envisage," the scientist replied, very seriously, "a lone man might perhaps contrive. Give me a few sticks of dynamite and I'll take it upon myself to destroy that devil woman's installation."

Akamatsu, who had been listening silently, intervened with his habitual authority. "You're dreaming, Doctor. If Madame Atomos wanted to, she could wipe us out with a blast of radiation!"

"Exactly," said Soblen. "She doesn't want to. She knows that she's infinitely superior and has her entire lifetime before her. We must take advantage of that state of affairs. At present, Madame Atomos has only played two cards: the Pooley and the spiders. She's obviously waiting for the results before taking radically destructive measures. If we let her act, events will overtake us. I suggest that we intervene very rapidly, before the situation becomes desperate."

Maxwell started. "I'm on your side, Doctor! If you wish, I'll go with you. We can move freely over the Pooley, provided that we don't touch it."

"It's madness!" cried Smith Beffort. "What will you do if a *Theraphosa* attacks you?"

Soblen looked at him coldly. "A year ago, Smith, you and Akamatsu didn't hesitate for a second before introducing yourselves into the secret refuge in Oakland, although you knew that your lives were at risk. Today, then, let us attempt in our turn to do what you succeeded in doing so well...."

Smith Beffort cut through the air with a violent hand gesture. "The situation isn't the same, Doctor! Now we know how Madame Atomos builds her shelters. We're sure that two or three subterranean tunnels will lead away from the refuge and open several miles away. We only need to discover the entrance to one of these tunnels to...."

"Perfect!" Soblen interjected. "Look for a tunnel! In the meantime, Maxwell and I will go directly to the source!"

Smith Beffort looked at Akamatsu, Maxwell and Soblen; then, to the great surprise of the Japanese agent, he capitulated immediately. "All right," he said. "Since you're determined, I'll give you a free hand...."

While the four men were establishing their plan of attack inside their headquarters, terror took brutal hold of south-eastern Dallas. The Pooley advanced toward Forney, submerging solid bodies and going round liquid ones, breaking fragile branches, grass-stalks, and telegraphic and telephonic wires beneath its weight. A high-tension cable suddenly gave way, and the entire area was instantly plunged into obscurity. In the pitch dark, however, Madame Atomos's remote-controlled spiders, were not progressing blindly. They came up the East Fork, grouped together at Mesquite, and spun a large web over the river.

The observers, having noticed that the Pooley was following the route traced by the spiders, sent tanks mounted with flame-throwers to the critical point. Three months earlier, the army had stopped the people atomized by the sinister Japanese woman in that manner, and it was hoped that fire might put an end to these monsters too.

The *Theraphosae* were advancing rapidly, but not rapidly enough to escape the vehicles, and an interception was anticipated within minutes. However, when the Pooley arrived once more on the west bank, the spiders melted into the darkness. The expected encounter did not, therefore, take place, and it was understood that the *Theraphosae*'s only role was to intervene when the Pooley was interrupted by a watercourse.

At eleven p.m., the Pooley—whose speed was increasing steadily—cut between Forney and Mesquite, submerged Sunnyvale and Route 80, and threatened Route 67 and the little township of Rose Hill. Hundreds of houses were swallowed up by the terrible red substance, and thousands of homeless individuals fled toward Dallas, which had been mysteriously spared.

The United States and the entire world were following the progress of the terrible scourge in anguish, and Dick Slatt declared in front of the television cameras that the situation was going to become absolutely critical. The victims could no longer be counted, but everyone was retreating before the Pooley. Factories, railways, roads, dwellings, hundreds of head of livestock and cultivated fields were going to be absorbed by the Pooley. Already, the disaster victims could not be accommodated; already, food supplies were running low. What would happen if not way of checking this unforeseeable invasion was discovered? Soon, the Pooley would pass over watercourses, using bridges. Would it be necessary to blow up the bridges? There was no longer any question now of digging ditches and flooding them to create artificial rivers. The Pooley could go anywhere, surging through the streets of Dallas, obliging more than a million people to retreat.

It was insane and incredible, but real!

At eleven thirty the high command decided to take the offensive, in spite of the efforts of Smith Beffort, who advocated an immediate and systematic search for tunnel entrances. Akamatsu intervened, reminding them of the catastrophe at Oakland, but for once the army and police were united. It had all happened too quickly, and the final authority of the FBI in this kind of matter was not universally accepted. Then again, having recognized his weakness, a man had to fight....

Twenty armored vehicles thus climbed on to the Pooley, using the last stub of 175 as an approach-route. The vehicles made headway amid a thunderous roar, and when their caterpillar-treads bit into the edge of the Pooley many people had the impression that the strange matter was bound to burst asunder.

The vehicles had left their tracks on tarmac, on concrete, and on metallic plates, but they did not dig into the Pooley.

On the far side of the artificial river, people remained in radio contact with the tanks, and at Love Field Airport in Dallas a squadron of bombers laden with napalm bombs was readied for take-off.

The armored vehicles headed straight for old Cal's land without encountering any opposition. The *Theraphosae* had disappeared, doubtless dreading the mortal jets of the flame-throwers, and the leading tank was no more than two miles from its objective when Madame Atomos counter-attacked.

First of all, the Pooley swelled up like an overcooked pancake—but each of its blisters was ten feet high and far more resistant than steel. In front of them, the vehicles discovered an insurmountable barrier, tried to move backwards in order to go around the obstacle, and perceived that they were literally surrounded by a tall grille with innumerable bars—and it seemed that each bar was continuing to press forward.

Three tanks raced to the attack. They were capable of knocking down walls six feet thick as they moved, making anti-tank barriers made out of railway sleepers fold up like wisps of straw and crushing everything that happened to bed in their way with their formidable weight. In consequence, they went at top speed, hurtling into the bizarre obstacle as one, and the noise generated by the collision was audible for miles around.

The Pooley's stalks did not even shiver under the shock, but each tank seemed to have fallen from a height of ten stories. A dull explosion resounded. One tank meekly caught fire, was surrounded by black smoke, and blew up with unexpected violence, with a deafening racket. Its gas-tanks were on fire and its ammunition exploded in a chain reaction. Reddish sparks striped the night, whistling and humming like dozens of spinning tops.

Amid the smoke and the noise, the other tanks attacked the thick forest that surrounded them with cannon-fire and flame-throwers. For ten minutes, there was a fiery inferno; then the order to cease fire was given, in order to assess the results.

When the thick cloud of smoke had dissipated, the soldiers observed in amazement that they were enclosed within a vast bell, and that the shells had crashed down on the Pooley without provoking the slightest breach.

The smoke accumulated beneath the upper wall of the bell, but did not appear to have any orifice through which to escape. Captain Stockman had the engines stopped and sent a radio message to the high command, but could not obtain any reply. They tried several times before admitting that radio waves could not penetrate the Pooley.

Three tanks had been destroyed, eighteen soldiers killed, and a hundred men trapped beneath an impenetrable bell were going to die of asphyxia if they were not rescued....

At the headquarters of the general staff the advance of the armored column had been followed through binoculars, until the moment when the alteration in the terrain had hidden them from the observers' eyes. That had been anticipated. The configuration of the ground was known, and the route mapped out with common accord by Major-General Stuart and Captain Stockman cut straight through a wide basin.

The observers waited without impatience, therefore, for the column to reappear at the crest of the far slope—but the minutes went by, and not a single tank appeared. When the first explosion rang out and a red glow lit up the sky, they thought that the tanks were taking on the spiders. The cannon-fire reinforced this hypothesis. Then the detonations became less violent, and were muffled, as if the battle had become more distant, and finally died away altogether.

For a long interval, the most complete silence reigned over the advance lines. In order not to attract Madame Atomos's attention, it had been agreed not to use the radio except in case of emergency, and that ominous silence was inevitably prolonged before General Stuart gave the order to contact the column. When no response was received, a reconnaissance plane took off from Dallas and flew over the exact position where the armored vehicles should have been.

By radio, the pilot let it be known that the surface of the Pooley was as bare as the back of his hand, and that he could see no evidence of fire, nor of any vehicle, stationary or moving.

The aircraft flew close to the surface, but its searchlight illuminated nothing but the red substance for miles on end. That bloody uniformity prevented the pilot from observing with precision, and from noticing that a depression in the terrain had been mysteriously filled in. He saw nothing of that phenomenon, any more than he perceived the two minuscule silhouettes that attempted to avoid the vast luminous roundel of his searchlight.

When the plane had disappeared and the darkness was restored, Soblen and Maxwell raised their heads again. "I'm beginning to believe," Maxwell said, "that we made a mistake in leaving without telling anyone."

The little doctor shrugged his shoulders. "It would have dragged things out. Besides, I think all that noise must be monopolizing Madame Atomos's attention. Do you still have your gloves, Maxwell?"

"Yes, and the dynamite. Shall we go on?"

"No. I have an idea that that imbecile General Stuart will send in the bombers. It's best if we wait a little while. By the way, do you know what became of the tanks?"

Maxwell sat down, still holding the bag containing the dynamite. "I don't know any more than you," he whispered. "They must be awaiting orders before going back—but I wonder what they were firing at?"

Soblen did not reply. He installed himself comfortably against what had once been an embankment, making sure that no part of his face came into contact with the Pooley, pulled his trousers up and looked up at the sky.

Coming from the direction of Dallas, an enormous hum filled the night. Major-General Stuart had sent his airplanes to attack Madame Atomos's lair!

Soblen closed his eyes and stiffened his body, clenching his jaws. He knew exactly what was about to happen....

Chapter V

And it happened in exactly that fashion. As at Oakland, the bombers described a circular arc, coming closer to the ground, and three blazing rockets soared into the air over old Cal's property. Then the bombers, which had just finished their half-turn, abruptly dived.

Explosions rent the air, and Major-General Stuart, along with all his aides, saw to their horror that the aircraft were exploding, one after another.

It was as if the bombers had disintegrated, but—by contrast with what had happened at Oakland—no debris reached the ground. The napalm, pulverized in mid-air, lit up the terrain with a flamboyant glare; then a deathly silence was established and darkness fell again.

Dr. Alan Soblen tapped Maxwell on the shoulder and stood up. "Now," he said, "we'll have a moment's calm. If you need to speak to me keep your voice low, and don't make any sound as you walk. Madame Atomos possesses ultra-sensitive microphones, radar and an entire advanced detection-system. In truth, Maxwell, we only have one chance in a hundred of reaching our goal. If Madame Atomos spots us, she'll send a *Theraphosa* or disintegrate us with a ray-gun. Are you still determined?"

Maxwell grimaced. "Stop babbling, Doc," he said, amicably. "You seem like an intelligent chap. If you're here, it's because you think you have a chance—so let's go see what's happening over there."

Soblen made sure that the sticks of dynamite were secure in the straps of his satchel, but spoke again before moving off. "You're married with two children, aren't you?"

"Don't keep on, Doctor. I've got very good life insurance."

Soblen smiled. "Okay, we're going; from now on, not a word unless absolutely necessary…oh! Just one more thing, Maxwell."

"What?"

"If one of us falls into the hands of Madame Atomos, he must pretend to have come alone—understood?"

Maxwell shrugged his broad shoulders "You're not very optimistic, and I don't know what you're waiting for, but if the Jap broad catches me, you can count on me. I'll tell her that I came to pick mushrooms."

Soblen nodded and set forth. He was certain that his companion did not really believe that he was risking his skin in the adventure. Maxwell was a positive thinker. He had a thirty-eight under his arm and a satchel full of explosives on his back, and nothing would stop him except a bullet between the eyes. He was not exactly a hero, but simply lacked imagination. Some people anticipate events, seeing death beforehand and ending up being totally paralyzed by panic. Maxwell did not think like that; he lived in the present moment, sensing his muscles rippling under his skin, and was convinced that he represented a force that was difficult to neutralize.

In a sense, Alan Soblen envied Maxwell. The doctor knew that he had a chance, but only one. It resided entirely in the mad temerity of the enterprise. Tanks, bombers, artillery and weapons of every sort had been utilized without result. How could Madame Atomos imagine that two men would dare to attack her formidable refuge?

Then again, the Japanese woman must be interested in the progress of the Pooley. Soblen assumed that the invading substance must also be remote-controlled. Madame Atomos was probably monitoring it in her laboratory. Her slanted eyes would certainly be following the Pooley through the medium of judiciously-placed cameras—unless the cameras were being operated by accomplices....

Maxell suddenly grabbed Soblen's arm, silently pointing at a dark mass outlined before them. The shadow was enormous, more imposing than any of the buildings covered by the Pooley. In addition, it seemed that the motionless mass was hovering in mid-air, and something indefinable indicated to the two men that they were looking at a living being.

The thing moved one of its feet, raised itself up silently, then settled back into its initial position.

Soblen and Maxwell went on side by side, trying to hold their breath. The spider was standing guard, and it was necessary to conclude that the other *Theraphosae* were watching over Madame Atomos's lair.

Maxwell, whose eyesight was better than the doctor's, detected another motionless mass further away to the right, and explained by means of signs that the distance separating the two monstrous creatures permitted an infiltration.

Soblen put his mouth to his companion's ear. "We can get by," he whispered, "but watch out. I'm sure that all these spiders are linked together by a network of sticky threads. In this darkness, how can we remain safe?"

In his turn, Maxwell spoke into the doctor's ear: "I know this area well, Doctor. Since the Pooley is perfectly fitted to the form of the terrain, we'll find a sunken road a little further on, which will inevitably pass underneath the spider's web."

"What if the threads also follow the lie of the land?"

"Hmm…do you think these monsters can possibly spin a web with meshes so fine that we can't step over them?"

"We'll have to see, Maxwell. At any rate, remember that if we brush a single thread, our goose is cooked."

Maxwell nodded his head, and Soblen saw in the semi-darkness that his face was terribly taut. The man was visibly aware that the slightest error might be fatal. Paradoxically, that reassured Soblen, who had, until then, feared an excess of temerity. The fact that Maxwell was permeable to fear, as he was, reinforced their chances of staying alive.

"I understand, Doc," whispered Maxwell. "Follow me."

Bending low, they covered the distance separating them from the sunken road silently, and slid into it. At that moment, the clouds parted. A white round moon appeared, seemingly as cold as a lemon sorbet in its cone. A yellowish light illuminated the ground, and the two men were rooted to the spot.

In a uniformly blood red lunar landscape, the threads of an enormous web sparkled. Soblen had never seen anything like it. Every thread was as thick as a cable and must be virtually unbreakable. According to all evidence, the barrier was designed for tanks and airplanes. A hedge-hopping fighter intent on strafing Madame Atomos's lair would be bound to run into the gigantic snare.

A deadly ray disintegrated bombers flying at high altitude. A web stopped fighters, tanks and vehicles of any other sort. The Pooley—although Soblen did not know it—could also swallow up a column moving over its surface. Who could tell what the sinister Japanese woman had set out for humans?

While Soblen and Maxwell were getting ready to cross Madame Atomos's first barrier, the Pooley was ineluctably pursuing its destructive task. Although people could escape it without difficulty, there was no question of "saving the furniture". The Pooley continually changed direction, and Dallas, which had been thought to be out of danger, was now under threat.

Refugees were invading the streets of the city, blocking the traffic and creating a confusion that did nothing to calm minds. The army attempted to evacuate the new arrivals to Denton, Grand Prairie and Fort Worth, but ran into a general lack of cooperation. No one believed that the Pooley had covered the fields and houses permanently. Everyone hoped that the army, the FBI, the police or the scientists would find a way of stopping and destroying the unknown substance.

In truth, only the scientists could find a solution, and a team directed by Professor Nelson Manning was examining a fragment of the Pooley. The fragment came from the first intervention carried out by means of explosives, while the Pooley was slowly nibbling away at Route 175.

Nelson Manning was one of Alan Soblen's best friends, and he had asked after his colleague several times, but in vain. In seething Dallas it seemed impossible to think of meeting up with the little doctor, but Manning was tenacious. He was convinced that Soblen could lend him valuable assistance. If they could discover what the Pooley was made of, it would then be easy to manufacture a product capable of destroying it. Manning was a great chemist, but was not unaware that Soblen was an order of magnitude better.

At one o'clock in the morning, Manning learned that his colleague was on a top secret mission. He could not obtain any precise information from the sub-director of the FBI, no matter how hard he tried, demanded to speak to Maxwell, and was told that he too was on a mission.

Confronted with this conspiracy of silence, Maxwell lost his temper. He left his laboratory and went, with enormous difficulty, to FBI headquarters. Smith Beffort agreed to see him.

The atmosphere was dismal. Major-General Stuart was slumped in an armchair, and seemed to have aged terribly. The disappearance of his armored vehicles and the loss of his bombers represented, in his eyes, an irremediable defeat. The soldier was disarmed, the man embittered—and very conscious of the error he had made in not following Beffort's advice.

As for the latter, who remained cool and methodical, his eyes never left the map on which the Pooley's advance was being tracked. Like Akamatsu, he had an ironclad faith in the famous tunnel exits, and expected information on that subject at any moment.

Nelson Manning planted himself between Beffort and the map. "Can you listen to me for a moment?" he said, in a tremulous voice.

Beffort lifted an appeasing hand. "Don't get excited," he said. "Everyone's teeth are set on edge, and that isn't helping at all. Who are you and what do you want?"

"Nelson Manning, chief of the Dallas laboratory...."

"Good," interjected the G-man. "Can you do anything to stop the Pooley?"

Manning calmed himself, as he understood that his interlocutor thought that the Pooley came before everything else. "I'm in the process of analyzing a fragment of the substance," he said. "I think I'm alone in possessing a sample of the Pooley. I know that Dr. Alan Soblen is in Dallas. It's necessary that he come to my laboratory immediately."

Beffort looked at the professor wearily. He had been on his feet for twenty-four hours, had eaten nothing but sandwiches, and felt that he could not keep going much longer without a little sleep.

"Why do you need Soblen so much?"

"Because he's the top man in his field. Because it's necessary to ascertain the chemical composition of the Pooley as quickly as possible, in order to destroy it. Without Dr. Soblen, it'll be days before we each our goal. With him, we might reach a solution in a matter of hours. I hope that I'm making myself clear?"

Beffort and Akamatsu were dumbfounded. Nelson Manning took their silence the wrong way, and exploded. "I'm sick of this so-called top secret mission!" he spat. "Find me Alan Soblen immediately and bring him to my laboratory! If you refuse, the lives of millions of Americans will weigh heavily upon your conscience—if you escape with your own lives, of course!"

Manning crossed the room nervously, and went out, slamming the door.

Major-General Stuart stood up. He knew approximately where to find Soblen and Maxwell, and suddenly thought that his role might not be finished. "Presently," he said, pointing to Madame Atomos's refuge on the map, "They must be approaching this point. I propose that a helicopter be sent immediately to pick them up."

Beffort turned on his heel. "All right," he said. "I'll go with you. Yosho, you stay in communication with the search-teams. If anything new comes up, let me know by radio." He put on his hat, picked up his coat and followed General Stuart, who was already running downstairs.

The street was black with people. Women holding babies were sitting on the sidewalks; lost children were wandering through the indifferent crowd; police cars and Red Cross vehicles were distributing food and hot coffee; and the confusion of a disturbed ant-hill reigned over everything. Stuart and Beffort realized that it would be impossible to travel by car. They set out on foot along Hines Boulevard, and reached the airport in reasonably quick time.

Stuart introduced himself, and commandeered an aircraft.

Ten minutes after Nelson Manning's warning, the helicopter took off.

Chapter VI

At the very moment when Stuart and Smith Beffort took off, Dr. Soblen and Maxwell were slipping under the web extended across their path.

Thanks to the providential moonlight, the two men were able to distinguish the lower threads of the web quite clearly. It hung down perceptible into the sunken road, but the few feet that separated it from the roadway was largely sufficient.

Maxwell was the first to stand up, and shrug his shoulder to adjust the satchel, which had a tendency to slip. He waited until his companion had joined him.

They were now no more than a mile from old Cal's house, and the road they were following climbed slowly to terminate at a curtain of trees framing a farm. All of that was, of course, covered by the Pooley. The trees had the form of immense candles and the dwellings resembled squat cubes.

In spite of his perfect familiarity with the area, Maxwell had the feeling that he was in an unknown and virgin territory. In that he was correct, for no one before him had ventured so far into the condemned zone.

Soblen caught up with Maxwell and leaned close to his ear. "It's one thirty," he whispered. "If we hope to obtain any result we must be in place before three a.m."

"What do you mean, Doctor?"

"We've taken longer than I expected. I'm afraid that the High Command might get impatient. For the moment, the spiders are fixed in position; Madame Atomos has transformed them into pylons and their role consists of maintaining that vast web. If artillery or armored vehicles intervene, though, what will happen?"

Maxwell shook his head.

"We've done the hardest part, Doctor. From now on, we'll have trees, bushes and houses, behind which we can take cover. If you want my opinion, I think that Madame Atomos can stop any attack whatsoever without utilizing the *Theraphosae*." He looked in the direction of Dallas and added: "As for the artillery, if it opens fire, I'll wager that not a single shell will get past the limits of the web. You saw what happened to the bombers a little while ago."

Soblen reflected momentarily, and fixed his dilated eyes on Maxwell. "Do you know that we're in the middle of an electromagnetic field, and that without the *Theraphosae* we'd already be dead?"

Maxwell's face was a picture. "How do you know that?" he asked, still in a low voice.

"To tell the truth, I'm not certain that it's an electromagnetic ray," Soblen admitted, "but whatever it might be called, it's evident that it passes over the spiders. Thus, it follows that there is a neutral zone in which we're moving. I imagine that the ray is emitted from a point situated on the ground, and that it rises up to a point B set at an altitude of about thirty yards."

"An inverted funnel with no outlet?"

"That's right, Maxwell! And it's exactly because it emerges at ground level that we'll never be able to approach Madame Atomos's lair."

"My God!" groaned the Dallas FBI chief. "*Now* you think of that!"

"Shh! No point getting carried away, Maxwell. We have a problem; let's find a solution."

Maxwell grimaced. "Listen to me, Doctor: while we're talking, the Pooley is advancing and Mother Atomos must be cackling like an old witch. I don't know whether or not my house is under that red substance, and I have absolutely no idea what's become of my wife and kids. I've got this far and, ray or no ray, I'm going to throw my sticks of dynamite into the lair of that accursed Jap broad!"

"It's suicide. Stay here with me. In the present conditions, we have no chance."

"It doesn't matter, Doctor. I'm going on."

Soblen held on to the G-man's sleeve firmly. "Don't be an imbecile!" he begged. "It would be a futile sacrifice."

Maxwell understood that he could not tear himself out of the little doctor's convulsive grip. He raised a soothing hand and said: "Okay, okay…you're right. Let me go now."

Soblen obeyed, was instantly knocked out, and fell into Maxwell's arms. The latter laid him down, making sure that he was not in contact with the Pooley, and—for the sake of extra safety—took off his overcoat and slid it under his victim's head. That way, Soblen was in no danger of making contact with the paralyzing substance.

Maxwell took possession of the doctor's satchel, placed it on his back and moved away rapidly along the sunken road. He had fought in the war in the Pacific and had battled against the Japanese in jungles. He knew the traps, the feints and treacheries of guerilla warfare. He had a thirty-eight and five ammunition-clips, dynamite and courage. He was sure that he would get out in one piece.

Maxwell's house was equidistant from Dallas and Balch Springs, between 175 and 80, at the exact spot where the Pooley suddenly veered westwards.

May Maxwell had turned thirty at the beginning of the month. She was the kind of woman of mediocre height who seems fragile at first glance but who proves extremely resistant and stubborn when confronted with a difficult ordeal. May's physique was rather banal; in a mundane gathering she passed unperceived until you had spoken to her directly; afterwards, you realized that she reasoned swiftly and coolly, that her conversation was pleasant, and that she was a remarkably well-balanced person.

May drew on that serene calm in her home. She loved her house, its furniture, its plants and its garden. She adored her husband and her two sons. Besides which, May liked other people, as a general rule. Life had never treated her badly, and no one had ever done her any harm. May was neither suspicious nor bitter. She trusted people, at first, ready to ignore them if her judgment subsequently proved false.

Thus, until this moment, May had not really believed in the existence of Madame Atomos. It seemed implausible to her that a woman could hate an entire nation for so long and with such intensity. In addition, there were certain things that the young woman could not admit—death, for example. To be sure, she was not unaware that hundreds of people died every day in Balch Springs, Dallas and elsewhere, but they were events that unfolded outside of her own life and did not concern her directly. May still had her parents, her grandparents and numerous male and female cousins; thus far, none of the people she loved had died.

That does not seem particularly significant. People who find themselves in the same situation as May Maxwell shrug their shoulders and say: so what? But, especially when one is in May's situation, one forgets that human beings are destined to die as soon as they emerges from their mother's womb. One forgets that the grave is where everyone inevitably ends up, come what may, and one behaves as if death were something that only happens to other people.

May was no exception to the rule.

The Pooley was advancing toward her house. The neighbors were fleeing, for the "red tide" was close at hand. Its velocity had increased noticeably. No one knew what the cause of that acceleration was, but it was now about ten miles an hour. Obviously, it was not yet a lightning invasion; by sprinting, anyone could easily escape it, and May's sons were exceptionally quick on their feet.

Jack and Greg Jr.—who was named after his father, Gregory—were eight and ten respectively. They had red-blond hair, like their father, with freckles on their noses, and played football for the school team. Like their father, they were not afraid of anything much. When they got cold feet, they remembered that Papa Maxwell was the chief of the FBI and that they were morally obliged to put on a brave face, and by dint of doing so, they had become genuinely brave—to a point that was often not far short of recklessness.

Thus, while Maxwell Senior was knocking out little Dr. Soblen, the Poole was gaining ground and had almost reached the garden of the Maxwell house. May was already in the Tangleys' car with her two sons by her sides. Mr. Tangley was ready to drive off when May uttered a cry. Mrs. Tangley turned round and said: "What's the matter?"

It was a trivial thing, but if the stout woman had not asked, Mr. Tangley would have put the car in gear and nothing would have happened.

"I've forgotten my suitcase!" May lamented.

Mr. Tangley hesitated, then turned to face the young woman. "Is it important?" he asked.

"All my cash and jewels!"

Jack and Greg Jr. pricked up their ears. They knew that the money was not very important, but that the jewels had great sentimental value in their mother's estimation. They looked at one another, and got out of the car simultaneously.

"We'll go, Momma!" Greg shouted.

Mr. and Mrs. Tangley had no children. They also lived a little apart from their neighbors, and literally choked at the sight of children of that age acting on their own initiative in such circumstances. As for May, well used to the decisiveness of her sons and seeing the always get themselves out of the worst scrapes, she hesitated markedly before shouting: "No! It's not important! Come back!"

Jack and Greg Jr. did not hear her. They were already in the living room, searching it with the aid of an electric torch. It is necessary to remember that the electricity had been cut off by the breakage of a high-tension cable, and that at the moment when the Maxwell boys were unconsciously risking their lives, it was about two o'clock in the morning.

Outside, Mr. Tangley uttered a scream on perceiving the Pooley, which flowed on to the street, climbed over the little enclosing wall and suddenly fell from the roof of the Maxwell house like a curtain descending on a stage. That meant that the entire rear of the house was covered by the terrible substance, and that Jack and Greg Jr. only had a few seconds to escape the horrible trap.

May understood brutally, and tried to get out of the car, but the stout Mrs. Tangley took hold of her solidly. While May struggled vainly, Mr. Tangley sounded his horn to summon the children. Having done that, he watched the Pooley, which flowed rapidly along the roadway, ran down the façade of the house from top to bottom, and reached the ground floor windows.

"My children! My children!" howled May, in a demented voice. "Let me go, Mrs. Tangley. Let me go, I beg you!"

Mr. Tangley saw that the "red tide" had just swallowed up the Maxwell house, and that it was almost touching his rear wheels. He threw the car into gear and moved off savagely.

May Maxwell had just lost her two sons, and Madame Atomos had just made an implacable enemy, perhaps more ferocious than herself....

The helicopter was flying at low altitude, following an imaginary line. That line represented the route that Dr. Soblen and the G-man Gregory Maxwell ought to have followed.

General Stuart had been informed of the precise point at which the two men had crossed no-man's-land, and from that, it was easy to reconstruct the most direct itinerary for the use of two pedestrians.

The apparatus was flying with no lights, almost skimming the Pooley, which was bathed in sinister moonlight. The pilot was not confident, and did not try to pretend otherwise. "Do you intend to go far like this?" he asked.

"As far as possible," Smith Beffort replied, "but keeping risks to a minimum. Our objective is to pick up two men, not to get down ourselves."

General Stuart allowed Beffort to direct the operation. He contented himself with scrutinizing the ground attentively, and it was he who first noticed the strange glimmer given off by the spider-web. The *Theraphosae* themselves were confused with the accidents of the terrain, and the three men genuinely believed that Madame Atomos had suspended an interception network between prefabricated mounds.

"Why the net?" asked the astonished Stuart. "An aircraft can easily get over it."

"You don't know the Japanese woman," Beffort groaned. "I'll bet that if we try to pass over, our machine will fall prey to some ray or other."

The pilot reduced speed and got even closer to the ground. He had seen how the bombers had been disintegrated, and conserved a memory of it that gave him goose pimples. Two hundred yards from the net he swerved, and began to move along its edge, keeping his distance.

Suddenly, Smith Beffort made out a minuscule flame straight head of him, and thought he saw a gesticulating silhouette profiled against the faint gleam. He notified the pilot of his discovery, who immediately set a course for the little flame.

Three minutes later, the machine set down ten paces from Dr. Soblen. Beffort leapt down on to the Pooley in order to help his friend climb into the cabin, but Soblen beckoned him over. "Come and see this, Beffort. It's rather surprising!"

Smith ran as far as a heap of ashes, and Soblen said, excitedly: "Look! I set fire to my notebook in order to attract your attention, and that brief flame has caused the Pooley to melt!"

Beffort struck a match and leaned over. "Better than that," he said. "One would think that the Pooley had retracted in order to escape the heat! My God! Your notebook was just paper, though, Doctor?"

"Of course. Surprising, isn't it?"

Beffort straightened up and looked round. "Surprising," he conceded. "Where's Maxwell?"

Soblen pointed to his chin, where a bruise was blackening. "He hit me hard enough to knock out an ox and headed for the refuge, taking my dynamite. By now, he's a long way beyond the net; in my opinion, he's got one chance in a thousand of getting out again…."

"We can't get to him, or wait for him to come back?"

Soblen gestured toward the web. "I hear you, Smith, and I deplore Maxell's recklessness as much as you do, but to stay here would be suicide. These big dark masses you can see between each section of the net are *Theraphosae* and the net is a gigantic spider-web! In all sincerity, I confess that I don't understand how you were able to reach me without Madame Atomos….."

The pilot shouted a summons, and the two men turned round. They saw that the Pooley had become agitated around the helicopter. A stem formed, and then another, and another….

In a flash, Smith Beffort understood that Madame Atomos was launching the bloody matter in an assault on the machine. He shoved Soblen ahead of him, hoisted him into the cabin and leapt up in his turn.

The pilot took off immediately, gained height amid the desperate whistling of the blades, cleaving the air, and, as the engine executed a rapid glissade, was out of range in two seconds.

Transfixed, the passengers watched the stalks of the Pooley form a cage, which folded over the place where the helicopter had been moments earlier.

While May Maxwell was witnessing the horrible disappearance of her two sons, her husband was stealthily approaching Madame Atomos's lair, Soblen was being collected by the helicopter and the Pooley was making inroads in Dallas, Yosho Akamatsu received one of the agents sent in search of tunnel entrances.

The man was exhausted. He had been obliged to go around the vast area covered by the Pooley, struggle against a counter-current to clear a path through the surging flood of refugees heading west, and he was too weary at first to pronounce a single word.

Akamatsu let him recuperate, while blackening the eastern district of Dallas on his map, the Pooley having invaded it. Having done that, he went back to the man and offered him a cigarette. "Well?" he said, simply.

The agent used his sleeve to wipe away the sweat that was running into his eyes and licked his lips. "I think," he said, "that we've discovered the entrance to one of the tunnels."

Akamatsu grabbed hold of the man, pulled him across the room and set him before the map.

"Show me the location," he ordered, in a voice that contrasted with his previous agitation.

The agent set his finger on a point representing the center of a triangle formed by Sagoville, Crandall and Forney. "It's here," he said. "The farm was rented by a Jap, but no one lives there. We discovered the entrance to the tunnel in the barn. It's hidden by planks covered

198

with freshly-spread straw. It was the last detail that attracted our attention—it looked bizarre on a seemingly-abandoned farm. As you ordered, we put everything back in place. Two of my colleagues are watching the barn. They're waiting for you.

Akamatsu abandoned the tiller to the deputy director and left the office like a tornado. He headed straight for the airport.

Chapter VII

Gregory Maxwell had not made much headway when the helicopter came to pick up Soblen. The G-man was certainly not very far from Madame Atomos's lair, but he was progressing so prudently that he was virtually crawling.

From the crest of a rise Maxwell saw the minuscule fire lit by the little doctor, then heard the regular throb of the helicopter just as it came into his field of vision. For a moment, he dreaded that it might attempt to reach him, but the machine took off shortly thereafter and vanished into the gloom.

The G-man breathed out. He suspected vaguely that Madame Atomos might have a great deal of difficulty realizing his presence. It seemed reasonable to think that the Japanese woman would find it impossible to detect a lone man, because her radar apparatus would only react to the sound of motors and the movements of massive objects.

Maxwell crept along the side of a workshop and emerged on the edge of a large open space that must have been a crop-field. He went around the field, moved like a shadow between two rows of small trees, and suddenly froze. The silence was so dense that it was becoming oppressive. Maxwell had never known anything like it. Even in the densest jungles there was always the chatter of a monkey, the cry of a bird. Here, there was nothing.

This patch of land drowned by the Pooley prefigured the future of the United States, if no one intervened.

Maxwell moved forward again, went through a small wood and emerged a hundred yards from Cal Pooley's store. The telegraph poles set alongside 175 no longer carried their wires, but still indicated the exact position of the road. Maxwell adopted it as a point of reference, quit the edge of the wood and sprinted as far as 175. There he stopped again, knelt down and got his breath back.

He thought that if Soblen had got it right, the electromagnetic ray must be passing a few feet over his head. From this moment on, therefore, he had to go on his hands and knees as far as old Cal's store, and then crawl as far as possible.

As far as possible would put him within range of Madame Atomos's lair. For Maxwell, that range was limited by the strength necessary for a twenty-yard throw. To be sure, he was capable of throwing an object further than that, but the sticks of dynamite had short fuses. He had, in consequence, to get as close as that maximum.

Maxwell checked his satchels, emerged from his hiding-place, and crossed the road on all fours. Still in that position, he went as far as the gas pumps, and moved on to old Cal's property.

Then he lay down on his belly and started crawling slowly. At the far end of the yard he could make out the dark mass of the shed, the surrounding fence and then, to the right and the left, the trees bordering the property.

Abruptly, a metal tube emerged from the Pooley a few inches from his face. Maxwell froze, holding his breath. His heart was beating furiously.

The tube looked like a tobacco-pipe, and the black hole of its bowl was angled toward the G-man. Maxwell lowered his head instinctively, then started when a derisive laugh split the darkness.

"Mr. Gregory Maxwell!" said a feminine voice, in an ironic tone. "The chief of the Dallas office of the FBI in person! I didn't think I'd capture such a big prize!"

The laughter rang out again, and Maxwell, seized by an abrupt fit of rage, tried to get up. He tensed his muscles, but experienced the sensation of being caught in a matrix of steel. His chin settled into his two hands, and remained stuck there in spite of all his efforts.

"Futile, Mr. Maxwell," said the vice. "You are the target of my paralyzing ray, and no force in the world could extract you from that unfortunate situation. Dr. Soblen proved to be more intelligent than you. I don't know what aberration led you to believe that you could get to me without my being aware of it, but you must recognize that you've signed your own death-warrant. Last year, the G-man Sam Forbes made the same mistake. You know what happened to him, don't you?"

Maxwell tried to speak, but was incapable of separating his jaws. He understood then that he was entirely at the mercy of Madame Atomos, and was submerged by a vague despair. How, indeed, had he been able to believe that he could out an end to this diabolical woman?

"You are going to ask yourself many questions, Mr. Maxwell," the voice went on. "Certainly as many as the atomized people of Hiroshima and Nagasaki whom your bombs didn't murder on the spot! Do you know that Japanese people are still dying in consequence of their burns? Do you know that the children of those injured people do not know whether they will die prematurely?"

Maxwell heard heavy breathing, then Madame Atomos, having calmed down, continued: "You are a murderer, Mr. Maxwell! The United States is inhabited by a population of murderers! Your country is a realm of corruption, gangsterism, vice, racism and crime! Your women do the housework for you and get drunk in bars! You kill men like Lincoln and Kennedy, when no foreigner would have touched a hair on their heads! Mr. Maxwell, you will die slowly, and you will be able to watch yourself die! Your muscles are already dead. Soon, your nerves will be; then your blood will coagulate in your veins. Your heart will cease to beat, but for a few seconds, your brain will continue to function. Those few seconds will be horrible, Mr. Maxwell—horrible! And I hope you enjoy them!"

The demented laughter tormented the G-man's eardrums as well, and the hate-filled voice of the sinister Japanese woman threw at him, by way of farewell: "Compliments of Madame Atomos, Mr. Maxwell!"

Then there was silence—an interminable and profound silence, which was to become, for the man nailed to the ground, an eternal silence.

Already, the G-man sensed that his extremities were losing sensation. He felt as if his chin was resting on a block of ice, and no longer felt the weight of the satchels on his back or the contact of the butt of the thirty-eight under his arm.

His death-throes were exactly as Madame Atomos had described. The man suffered horribly, and his body was cold by the time his soul departed. Providence, however, had shown him the mercy of leaving him ignorant until the end of the death of his sons, and Gregory Maxell's final thought was for them and May.

As for May, the tranquil little housewife of Balch Springs had lost all her reasons for living in less than an hour.

Yosho Akamatsu ran toward the helicopter as it landed and rapidly brought Beffort up to date with the discovery of the tunnel. In spite of his fatigue, the federal agent decided that it was worth immediate verification. He asked General Stuart to accompany Dr. Soblen to the laboratory, and climbed back into the apparatus with the Tokkoka man.

Seen from the sky, Dallas resembled a city gone mad. A dense crowd was flowing through the streets, fleeing the Pooley—which had, however, clearly slowed down. In fact, hundreds of flamethrowers were spitting water at the accursed plant, and veritable streams were preventing the roots from getting a grip on the ground. The city was being defended foot by foot, but in spite of its inhibition, the "red tide" was nevertheless continuing to advance. Then again, if its development had been halted in Dallas, it was continuing freely in a northward direction. Rose Hill and Rowlett were submerged and Garland under threat. Inhabitants were fleeing everywhere. The roads were disappearing beneath a flood of vehicles, and monstrous gridlocks were blocking the traffic in places.

The water-supplies were diminishing at a prodigious speed, and it was obvious that the city could not be defended indefinitely.

He helicopter flew over the whole covered extent, left Forney—which the Pooley had brushed but not engulfed—to its left and landed next to the indicated farm. Smith Beffort instructed the pilot not to get out of his machine, and drew away with Akamatsu.

The two federal agents came to meet them; they declared that one had gone into or come out of the barn, and that no vehicle had approached the farm.

"Have you been here long?" asked Beffort.

"Since two o'clock, or thereabouts. The most difficult part was to get a message to you. Do you intend to go into the tunnel?"

"Naturally."

The man turned his head toward the barn. "In that case," he said, "and if it won't inconvenience you, I'd like to go with you. My parents were atomized last year in New York…."

Sam turned him around again. "What's your name?"

The man forced a smile. "Eddie Witter," he said. "My father was a motor-cycle cop. He's the one who was disintegrated on Route 22—remember?"

Beffort remembered. He had only just escaped the deadly ray of the thermal weapon wielded by Lydia Watanabe himself.

"As for my mother," Witter went on, "she was in the street when Madame Atomos's walking dead headed for Plum Island. Needless to say, if I could corner that damnable Jap..."

He did not finish his sentence, but his large hands mimed strangulation. It was sufficiently explicit.

"Okay," said Beffort. "You can come with us." He turned to the second agent. "I suppose you must also want to take a trip in the tunnel, but you'll have to give up on that, old man. Someone has to warn the Boss if things turn sour."

"All right," said the man. "What are the orders?"

"First of all, prevent anyone from getting into the barn. Then, wait for us to come back. If none of us gets back here in two hours, climb into that helicopter and go back to Dallas airport. Then find a way to contact the Boss…."

"The telephone lines are down," the man objected.

Beffort gestured impatiently. "Listen," he said. "Get this straight: if we disappear, you become the most important person in the territory. If we're kayoed, Madame Atomos, knowing that she's in danger, will be in a tearing hurry to take flight. Thus, you have to move very quickly. Use a radio, requisition a jet-fighter, but the Boss has to know what the situation is within an hour. Got it?"

"Got it."

Beffort made sure that Witter had an electric torch, and headed for the entrance to the tunnel.

While Smith Beffort, Witter and Akamatsu set off into the bowels of the earth, May Maxwell arrived at FBI headquarters in Dallas.

The Tangleys, trapped in their car, had not been able to escape the current dragging them westwards, and May had been obliged to cross the city, sometimes struggling furiously. The young woman was virtually stupefied. She could not get rid of the vision of her sons going into the house, and of the Pooley settling conclusively over the windows and the front door.

May tried to focus her thoughts on her husband. She knew that she would go mad if she continued thinking that Jack and Greg Jr. were not yet dead. It was necessary to consider them as such. They would asphyxiate slowly, with frightful suffering. How long would it take for the oxygen contained in a two-story house to be completely polluted? May had no idea.

In a film, she had once seen a submarine resting on a bed of sand at the bottom of the ocean. Little by little, its oxygen supply had been exhausted, and the men had died choking. Their mouths had been wide open. Sweat had inundated their bodies, and their hands had clutched their throats. It had been atrocious. Then, still in the same sequence, a diver had gone down to the submarine and rapped on the hull. The survivors had recovered hope and....

May uttered a scream, and stood still, leaning against the wall.

The telephone!

The electricity was no longer working, but that did not mean that it was the same for the telephone.

May ran up the stairs, forgot to knock and came into the office like a whirlwind. The room was full of smoke. Men were going in and out continually. Others were shading a map of the region and sending radio messages, and deputy director George Cooper was on the telephone.

As no one paid any attention to her, May crossed the room and planted herself in front of Cooper. The man raised his eyes, smiled wearily and removed his cigar from his mouth. "Good evening, Mrs. Maxwell," he said, hoarsely. "You've been forced out too?"

May leaned toward him. "Mr. Cooper," she said, "I need to phone my home."

Cooper raised his eyebrows. "Hold on," he said. "If your house is under the Pooley...."

"My sons are in the house," May said, in a voice that seemed to come from a long way away. Tears ran down her taut face. She made no move to wipe them away, and Cooper was quite certain that she was unaware that she was weeping.

He got up, offered her his chair and pointed to the telephone. "Go on," he said. "Some lines are working, others aren't. We don't know why. You might have a chance, but it would surprise me...."

"Where's my husband, Mr. Cooper?"

"On a mission," he deputy director replied. "He's with a man named Soblen. I don't think he'll be long...." He drew away in the direction of the rest room. May picked up the phone and dialed her own number. She waited for some time, her heart hammering, and during that terrible moment her gaze remained fixed on a photograph pinned to the notice-board. It was a portrait of a Japanese man. The caption said that his name was Mikonosuke Watanabe, that he was thirty-eight years old and that he was one of Madame Atomos's collaborators.

The silence on the line was complete, and May hung up without ceasing to study the Japanese man's face. She thought that the windows of the house had still been open, that the Pooley would certainly have penetrated into the upstairs rooms, and quickly invaded the entire dwelling. Jack and Greg Jr. must have been dead for some time, and it was better thus.

Yes, that was much better.

The telephone rang, and May picked it up mechanically, putting the receiver to her ear. She was still looking at the photograph of Mikonosuke Watanabe, unconsciously memorizing every aspect of his physiognomy.

"Hello?" said a harsh voice. "Is this the office of Deputy Director Cooper?"

"Yes," said May, indifferently.

"Then put him on! What are you waiting for?"

"He's gone out for a moment."

"In that case tell him that one of Mother Atomos's spiders has deposited Gregory Maxwell's corpse in no-man's-land. Hello? Hello? Did you get that?"

The telephone was dangling at the end of its wire, and May resembled a marble statue.

Chapter VIII

May was walking along Lancaster Avenue. She knew that she was in Fort Worth, but had forgotten how she had got there. All she could remember was that her sons and her husband were dead, and that Deputy Director Cooper had spoken softly to her while holding her by the shoulders. He had also given her money—a good deal of money—and then had returned to the telephone.

Now she was walking along Lancaster Avenue, in the midst of a silent crowd. She was a few miles for Dallas, but could not say how she had got there, or where she was going.

Besides, it was all the same to her.

An old woman grabbed her arm. The woman had white hair. She was alone, and seemed to be exhausted. "Excuse me," she whimpered, "but I can't go on…"

May did not reply. She put her arm under the woman's and supported her as best she could.

"Come on!" a man shouted. "Get moving, you two!"

They moved on with the crowd, which paused impatiently at an intersection for long minutes while another human herd passed by. May realized then that policemen were directing the traffic.

Some people were moving southwards. Others were heading westwards. When a policeman spread his arms, people stopped. When he opened the way, they set off again.

"Do you think we'll all be able to get into the buses?" the old woman asked.

"I don't know," said May.

The old woman noticed her indifference and looked at her, immediately thinking that she must be ill. She tried not to put so much weight on her arm. "Where are you going?" she asked.

May looked at her. "I've forgotten. I don't care. My children and Gregory are dead...." She smiled mechanically, and added: "Gregory was my husband. He was in the FBI. Madame Atomos killed him."

"Poor child," said the old woman. "Poor child...."

May felt a lump forming in her throat and drew apart from her companion slightly. If anyone tried to console her, she would certainly start weeping, and she did not want that. She tried to pull herself together, knowing that she was among distressed people who were accepting their fate without fighting it. The night was dark, but the young woman could make out men and women immobile on the sidewalks. They were watching people go by, but did not seem to have any desire to leave themselves.

Why go any further, then?

May let go of the old woman's arm. "I'm not going with you," she said.

"You're not taking the bus?"

"No. Excuse me. Goodbye...." She cut through the crowd, left the procession and stepped up on to the sidewalk. A policeman she had not noticed approached her. His helmet was titled back and his uniform as covered in a thick layer of dust.

"Where are you going?" he asked, without any great interest. "The buses are assembled in the center."

May turned to face him. "I'm not taking the bus," she said firmly.

The policeman pulled a face. "In that case," he said, as if he were reading from a set of regulations, "you have no business here. Go where you want, but don't get in the way of people who have…."

"Exactly!" cried a shrill voice. "We've got enough trouble already! Send the broad home!"

Other people began to shout, and May drew way rapidly, took the first turning and started running. She reached a little square, silent and deserted, and let herself fall on to a step. The stairs went up to a house with closed shutters, behind which a family was presumably asleep.

May set her handbag on her knees and turned up the collar of her coat. She was neither tired nor hungry. She felt empty and abandoned, having realized that people were not as good as she had imagined. Just now, the policeman had been hostile. Someone had called her a broad, and everyone had stated complaining. No one knew her, though. She had just lost her house, her husband, her children.….

At the end of her tether, she started weeping in the dark, and threw herself back against the wall when a car drew up, scraping the sidewalk. She felt ashamed of being there in the dark, mourning on her own, and did not want to be seen.

She raised her eyes, however, when the sound of the engine died away. The car had stopped ten feet from the steps. May saw the face, and clearly made out the gesture that the driver made to switch on the ceiling light. The interior of the car lit up, and May felt a violent shock.

The man who was leaning forward in order to get a close look at a map was Japanese. His name was Miko-nosuke Watanabe, and he was Madame Atomos's accomplice.

May knew that she was not mistaken. The face of that man was engraved in her mind in an indelible manner. She had been looking at his picture when an unknown man had told her about Gregory's death, and the face with the slanting eyes and prominent cheekbones was forever linked with that atrocious memory.

Looking at Watanabe, May abruptly discovered the hatred that was brooding within her: a terrifying hatred that replaced her blood, impregnated her brain and lacerated her heart. May was momentarily terrified, then understood that she would henceforth live solely for that new sentiment, whose existence and power she would never have suspected until now.

She drew back further into the shadows, let out the air that filled her lungs, and tried to discipline her thoughts, to envisage a plan of action. She was alone and without weapons, which automatically excluded violence.

Watanabe was dangerous. To confront him head on would be the equivalent of a bullet in the head. What, then, could she do?

A metallic click restored all the young woman's lucidity. She leaned forward, and saw that the Japanese man had got out of the car and gently closed the door again. He was acting with every precaution, evidently not wanting to attract any attention. He checked that the parking lights on his car were off, left the sidewalk and crossed the street. He was holding a rectangular box fitted with a strap, and kept his right hand in his overcoat pocket. May could see that he was not hesitant. He made an almost-complete circuit of the square, and suddenly disappeared, level with a building that was under construction.

May saw the discreet light of a torch going upstairs; then Watanabe appeared on the uppermost platform. Then the torch went out and the young woman could no longer see anything.

She stood up straight and went to the car. The rear door opened without difficulty. May got into the Mercury, closed the door quietly and lay down on the floor between the back seat and he backs of the front seats.

A few moments passed, then Watanabe got back into the car. Without turning round, he deposited a walkie-talkie on the rear seat, started the engine and swiftly drew away.

From the turn that the Mercury executed, May deduced that the Japanese man as heading due south.

They had gone down nearly thirty steps before the ground became horizontal again, and Witter's torch revealed a concrete-lined corridor. It was in perfect condition, was about ten feet wide, and followed a straight line in a westerly direction.

"If this tunnel really leads to Madame Atomos's hideout," Beffort murmured, "it must go under the East Fork River. I wonder how the she-devil was able to carry out such work without attracting attention.

Yosho Akamatsu laughed humorlessly. "Madame Atomos has undoubtedly been laboring for years on American soil. Everything we discover now is the fruit of slow and colossal labor. Last February, we were certain that our enemy had been conclusively vanquished. The Oakland refuge was destroyed, the concrete towers discovered. See, Smith, how wrong we were!"

Beffort shook his head. "The woman has tremendous means at her disposal," he murmured. "She has no lack of money or accomplices."

Witter fixed the beam of his torch on a curious and still-distant protuberance. Beffort saw it and hastily grabbed the G-man's arm. "Switch it off!" he said. "Now! That's an automatic camera."

Witter obeyed in a flash. "My God!" he said, in the darkness. "How did you know? It looked like a porthole."

"Keep your voice down!" hissed Akamatsu. "If there are cameras, there must also be microphones."

Witter fell silent. He had suddenly realized that the Japanese woman was an extremely redoubtable adversary, and that her madness was merely a form of genius—an evil genius, to be sure, but directed in a permanent manner. Madame Atomos wanted to raze the United States, and Witter, who had never previously been able to believe in such an eventuality, began to wonder. To be sure, America had no lack of scientists or money—but nothing had been put in place capable of combating the terrible Japanese woman effectively. Her threats, her crimes and her fantastic skill had been forgotten as soon as her disappearance had seemed certain.

"You can switch on now," Beffort whispered. "We must have passed the camera—but act prudently. A brief flicker first, to check…"

Witter sent forth a rapid beam, and switched off immediately.

"It's all right," said Akamatsu. "Nothing alarming."

Witter switched on the light, and the three men picked up their pace. At regular distances the round lifeless eye of a camera was directed across the path, and the G-man switched off spontaneously. After twenty paces, he switched the current on again, and the trio resumed the march.

After ten minutes, a slight dampness filtered through the walls, informing the men that they were passing under the East Fork River.

"Watch out!" Beffort warned. "We're approaching our goal. Silence, and no light!"

Witter switched off his torch again, but kept it in his hand. At the same time, he took out his automatic, and flicked off the safety-catch.

"Good God!" Beffort exclaimed, in low voice. "Put your gun away!"

"But...."

"Silence! If Madame Atomos decides to kill us, she will. Our only chance consists of passing unnoticed. Walk on tiptoe, young man, and try not to sneezes if you want to see daylight again. As for your popgun, leave it in its holster. For the moment, it's an obsolete weapon— an antique...." Beffort interrupted himself, listened momentarily, and drew closer to Witter to add: "Above all, don't lose your nerve if anything unexpected happens. Don't light your candle for any reason, and don't talk. Okay?"

"Okay."

Akamatsu felt his way along the wall, keeping his left hand on Beffort's shoulder; the latter, in his turn, maintained contact with Witter. Without letting go of one another, the three men traveled nearly half a mile in the most absolute darkness before hearing the faint hum of a motor.

Without a word, they went on, but their nervous tension increased markedly. Beneath his fingers, Beffort felt Witter's shoulder become wooden. The young G-man must have been as tense as a steel blade. The slightest incident might plunge him into a disastrous panic, and Beffort regretted having accepted him into the expedition.

Yosho Akamatsu came to an abrupt halt, stopping both of his companions at the same time. Beffort felt the Tokkoka man lean toward him, and heard his voice very close to his ear: "Careful, Smith—there's a bend in the corridor."

Beffort did not see any need to warn Witter, and urged Akamatsu to proceed with the pressure of his hand. The Japanese man understood the invitation, and resumed walking without hesitation.

As soon as they had passed the bend, the three men knew that the end of their difficult journey was imminent; a pale nimbus parsimoniously illuminated the extremity of the concrete corridor, along with a portion of a staircase that appeared to divide into two.

They moved forward cautiously, Smith Beffort taking the lead, and reached the end of the corridor. The light had no visible source, seeming to emerge from the granulous walls. Two camera lenses aimed their dead eyes toward the corridor, forbidding any ingress.

Beffort and Akamatsu exchanged a glance, and the Japanese agent took out his weapon. He fitted a silencer, took rapid aim and pressed the trigger. Two faint detonations rang out, instantly followed by a sound of shattering glass.

Witter watched his motionless and mute companions, and had difficulty swallowing his saliva. He was stuck to the wall, and felt that obscure and unimaginable forces were prowling around him. The sly and silent struggle made his skin prickle. He had prepared himself for a forced entry into the Japanese woman's refuge, and felt disarmed and particularly vulnerable—far from the tranquil certainty that Beffort and Akamatsu possessed.

The spy-lenses had been destroyed, but the silence was just as profound, and even though there was no indication of it, the imprecise threat seemed to be drawing nearer.

Abruptly, the light went out, and Witter jumped. Beffort's hand gripped his shoulder ferociously.

"Calm down, boy," whispered the G-man's voice. "The sudden breakdown of two cameras has made Madame Atomos anxious, but she doesn't know yet exactly what it signifies. Putting out the lights is a simple preparation for the check that will follow...."

The end of the sentence was punctuated by a formidable release of electricity. The room was striated by fiery blue streaks of lightning. It was a bombardment that no human being could have withstood. The air quivered under the power of the discharges, and when silence felt again the three men were dazed.

Then a whistling sound lacerated the excessive silence, and Madame Atomos's voice sprang forth from a loudspeaker. "Mr. Beffort? Mr. Akamatsu?"

There was a momentary pause. Beffort took hold of his two companions and dragged them back along the tunnel at top speed. "Let's get out of here!" he whispered.

He did not know what instinct he was obeying, but he divined that they had to get away as quickly as possible.

"Answer me, gentlemen!" Madame Atomos demanded. "I know you're there...."

"Faster!" ordered Smith Beffort.

The three men raced over the concrete floor, while behind them—already distant, but perfectly audible—the hoarse voice of Madame Atomos continued: "I'm a long way away from this shelter, Mr. Beffort, but it will nevertheless be my hand that provokes your death! You'll never get out of that tunnel. In a few minutes, there'll be an explosion, and the waters of the East Fork River will flood the tunnel. You'll be drowned, obviously, but the Pooley won't suffer any consequences…."

Beffort, Akamatsu and Witter were sweating.

"Faster!" the Japanese agent urged. "We must be under the river by now!"

In the distance, they could still hear the voice of Madame Atomos, but could no longer make out the meaning of her words. The fact that the sinister Japanese woman was continuing to talk to them clearly indicated that she thought that they were still in close proximity to the room. The three men redoubled their efforts. It had taken them a long time to make the outward journey by reason of the precautions they had been obliged to take, but the return was made at top speed. It was a desperate flight, a race against time, against death.

"You can switch on your torch," Beffort gasped.

Witter obeyed, and the luminous beam revealed the first steps of the staircase that led to the barn. They were no more than ten yards away when an explosion shook the ground. Immediately, a dull rumbling sound burst out in the tunnel, while the waters of the East Fork River flowed through the vast breach.

A tidal wave of unexpected violence sped along the tunnel, but Madame Atomos had spent too much time talking. Beffort, Akamatsu and Witter were out of range when the wave crashed into the steps. It was the Japanese woman's first mistake.

Chapter IX

In Dallas, and everywhere else that the Pooley was gaining ground, an enormous sigh of relief was released when the storm announced itself.

It was Monday February seventeenth, and the clocks marked five o'clock in the morning when the first raindrops hit the ground. For a moment, it was feared that it might not last; then, while the thunder rumbled, torrential rain poured down on that part of Texas.

Believers filled the churches in order to thank the Lord, and the rest tried to get their strength back in re-parative sleep. The reports coming from George Cooper's headquarters indicated that the Pooley had been literally stopped on all fronts.

In fact, such a deluge had not fallen on Dallas for years. All the rivers started to flow rapidly, and both the Trinity and the East Fork flooded in several places.

The observers keeping watch on Madame Atomos's lair noted that the *Theraphosae* were unusually agitated. The spiders remained in place, but the protective web had broken in several places. This unusual occurrence was debated, and flame-throwing canons were being made ready when one of the *Theraphosae* reared up on its legs and set off toward old Cal's property.

Soon, other spiders executed the same maneuver, but their movements no longer manifested the same syn-chronicity. The enormous creatures came together, abandoning their web, and ended up clustered around the orifice from which they had emerged. From a distance, their legs were seen agitating madly, and General Stuart realized that the marvelous apparatus remotely controlling the monsters had broken down.

Suddenly, thanks to the torrential rain, the situation took an unexpected turn. Nature had succeeded in doing what humans had not been able to achieve: stopping the Pooley and rendering freedom of movement to the *Theraphosae*.

Stuart felt that the time had come to attempt a lightning attack. He telephoned the airport and ordered that a bomber be dispatched immediately. The commander of the Air Force bristled once again. "No!" he said, categorically. "Use the artillery if you think that will have any effect on the Pooley, but none of my aircraft are taking off!"

Stuart tried to forget that he was the senior officer. "I understand your reluctance," he said, "but you evidently don't know that the rain has altered the balance of power. At present, the Pooley isn't gaining an inch, and the *Theraphosae* have gathered around Madame Atomos's refuge...."

"That won't stop the ray from working," the commander interjected. "The Air Force isn't scared of the Pooley and the spiders, but it's not the same where the ray's concerned. You're forgetting our recent losses, general!"

Stuart kept calm. "While the spiders are directly above the refuge," he said, "I'm convinced that Madame Atomos can't use any of her usual weapons! Besides if you were here, Commander, you'd be able to see as well as we can that something's gone awry in the Japanese woman's lair."

The commander remained silent momentarily, and finally confessed the real reason for his refusal. "General," he said, reticently, "My men are refusing to fly over the Pooley. They remember the disaster of the other night, and the one last February in Oakland. In all humanity, I can't send them to their deaths!" There was another pause; then the commanded added: "Nevertheless, given the exceptional circumstances, I'll pilot the plane myself. Napalm bombs?"

Stuart breathed again. "Yes," he said, "but act quickly!"

"It's ten past five and my plane's ready to go. You can expect my intervention in six or seven minutes."

The command hung up, and Stuart stood there, holding the receiver, stupidly. He hoped that he was not mistaken, and that the man to whom he had been speaking would not perish in the adventure.

Around him, Stuart sensed the utmost disapproval. He replaced the receiver in its cradle meekly, and just as meekly lit a cigar. In spite of his efforts his hands were trembling, and a drop of cold sweat ran down from his armpit, flowing interminably all the way to his hip.

Stuart shivered, left the office that served as his headquarters, and took refuge under a tarpaulin that the soldiers had extended between two trucks. Squalls of rain pattered on the bodywork and splashed on the ground, which was dissolving into sticky yellowish mud, darkening the nascent daylight.

For a few moments, the rain fell in sheets, reducing visibility to a few yards. Stuart grabbed his binoculars and aimed them toward the east. Now he could scarcely make out the enormous moving mass formed by the *Theraphosae*, and wondered whether the bombardier would be able to pick out his target.

Suddenly, the airplane flew overhead like a lightning-flash, its jets making an infernal racket, completed its curve, released its chaplet of bombs, and shot across the sky like a meteor.

The earth shook as the bombs exploded; then a fantastic glow lit up the gloom, while the napalm grilled the *Theraphosae* where they stood. Everyone saw their feet twisting in the furnace, and thought they could hear the sound of carapaces splitting. Then the mighty conflagration lost its intensity, and finally expired in a ridiculous heap of ash that the rain did not take long to clear away.

The bomber made a triumphant pass above Stuart's headquarters, and returned to its base. A formidable ovation saluted the exploit, and Stuart, his legs buckling, let himself collapse on a case of ammunition.

The Mercury had not been moving for very long when the storm burst. Mikonosuke Watanabe switched on his windscreen-wipers, and the rhythmic sound blended with the gentle purr of the engine. Soon, the two sounds were replaced by the hammering of the rain on the roof and hood, and May could not hear anything else.

She lay on her back, perfectly inert, sometimes perceiving trees through the window that was facing her—but those fugitive visions vanished when the rain increased in violence.

Watanabe uttered a groan and lightened his foot on the accelerator. The road disappeared under water and the windscreen-wipers were no longer adequate to their task. Between sweeps of the blade, the windscreen bristled with undulating wavelets that blurred visibility, making the landscape tremble.

The Japanese man slowed down further, and May had the feeling that the car was only advancing at walking pace. She was astonished by the quietness of the roads the Mercury took. Since she had left her home every inch of terrain had been occupied by the crowd, and she had imagined that the entire country must be consumed by the same agitation. Now, she realized that less than twenty miles from Dallas, in a densely populated area, the inhabitants were enjoying a lazy Sunday morning. Not far away, people were spilling on to the roads after losing everything they owned, and sometimes people dear to them, but those who had not been affected remained indifferent.

May experienced the sensation that combatants feel on returning from the front, which translates itself into a profound sense of injustice.

Jolts disturbed these reflections, and she saw trees again through the window. They were very close to the car, as if it had turned into a narrow pathway that was scarcely navigable. That impression was confirmed when the rear wheels started to skid.

The heavy vehicle slipped sideways; its rear end bumped into the embankment and it came to a halt. Watanabe swore, and restarted the engine, which had stalled. The wheels hissed in the mud. The Mercury vibrated, slid forward, and moved off slowly, while the engine roared. Finally, the tires gained purchase on more solid ground, and the vehicle leapt forward.

Surprised by the violence of the take-off, Watanabe maneuvered the steering-wheel feverishly. By mistake, he pressed the horn, and May heard it howl. Her nerves were jangling. She was not cut out for the adventure on which she had just embarked, and knew that she would weaken at the critical moment. She was already regretting her decision. Back in the little square she had not had time to reflect, but now she could see quite clearly that she should have taken possession of the vehicle in order to alert the police....

Watanabe started to sing in Japanese—and, bizarrely, that enabled May to calm down.

The Mercury continued through the heavy rain for some time without leaving the narrow road, and came gently to a halt beside a wall.

Watanabe left the engine running, grabbed the walkie-talkie with a swift movement and brought it back to the front seat. May saw the apparatus brush her knees, and for a brief but terrible instant the Japanese man's chin showed over the back of the seat. A few moments before, she had not been afraid, but her jaws were now clenched in panic.

Watanabe leaned out of the window, deployed the antenna of the little apparatus, and pronounced a few words in his native tongue. The response was immediate; Watanabe folded up the antenna again and resumed his position behind the steering wheel.

A few seconds went by, and May heard the grating of rusty hinges. Immediately, the Mercury moved off again, crossed the threshold of a metal gate, the bottle-green tint of which May glimpsed, rolled over gravel briefly—May recognized the noise because the driveway to her own garage was similarly garnished—and was abruptly engulfed by darkness.

Watanabe switched off the engine, got out, closed the door and disappeared.

May waited for her eyes to become accustomed to the gloom and sat up. She found that she was in a garage whose door was still open. Beyond the threshold the young woman could see a gravel path, an exceedingly green and well-kept lawn, and the base of the trunk of an enormous tree.

Facing the hood of the vehicle was a small window, a closed door and a table on which tools were scattered.

Underneath the table was a row of six gas cans, four spare wheels and two worn tires. May's gaze returned to the car's interior, and her heart leapt. The glove compartment was open, exposing the light brown butt of a Colt automatic.

May was nothing but a good homemaker, but her husband had been in the FBI and she knew a firearm when she saw one. She leaned forward, picked up the forty-five and pressed the button that freed the ammunition clip, which fell into her open hand. It contained seven bullets. She checked the breech and found, as she had expected, that there was an eighth bullet in the chamber. She replaced the ammunition-clip, put the weapon in her handbag and got out of the Mercury. She hesitated momentarily, then took the forty-five out of her bag again and kept it in her hand, having taken off the safety-catch. She had no plan of action, knowing only that if anyone surprised her, she would have to defend her life fiercely.

She walked on her crepe soles to the back door and slowly turned the handle. The batten pivoted silently, opening into a room with a cement floor. It contained a broken-down washing machine and a quadruple set of wires running along the wall half way up. A window, black with grease, opened in the wall to the left, and there was a door with flaking paint at the back of the room. Between the window and the door there was a tub filled with disgustingly murky water. It had obviously been a long time since anyone had done any laundry there; the dust covering the machine and the ground was clear evidence of its dereliction.

May closed the door behind her, went to the window and scraped a corner of the pane clean. She saw then that the garage and the laundry-room were separated from the main building by a lawn punctuated with trees. Through the trunks she made out a three-story building. All the shutters were closed and the house seemed abandoned.

May leaned forward. Her angle of vision changed, revealing four concrete buildings without doors or windows, whose flat roofs were bristling with antennae. The blockhouses were situated behind the house. There was an alleyway between them, and there was a man in the alleyway armed with a curious apparatus resembling a fiberglass fishing rod, who was pacing back and forth in the pouring rain. He was wearing a black raincoat with a hood and rubber boots, and when he turned round May saw that he was Japanese—or Asiatic, at least.

May remembered the disintegrator "rifle" mentioned by the newspapers during the previous year's affair, and understood immediately that the guard was equipped with that terrible weapon. By comparison, her Colt seemed a derisory plaything, and she shrank back into the shadows.

Chapter X

It was raining hard when Beffort, Akamatsu and Witter returned to the surface. They emerged from the barn and found the man on guard anxious as to their fate. He had seen a geyser rise up from the East Fork, and a bomber had released his munitions on Madame Atomos's lair almost simultaneously.

"Merciful heaven!" cried Beffort. "At least our intervention has done some good! It's now proven that the Japanese woman can't have eyes everywhere."

"What do you mean?" asked Witter.

It was Akamatsu who replied: "Madame Atoms said explicitly: *I'm a long way away from this shelter.* You remember that, don't you?"

"Yes," said Witter. I found that quite extraordinary! How can she survey the region, and direct the Pooley and the spiders, if she's not here?"

"It's not, strictly speaking, so very difficult," Akamatsu assured him. "The rockets we're sending to the moon are controlled remotely from Earth, and Madame Atomos is a good enough technician to direct from a distance the various items of apparatus that, in their turn, direct the Pooley, the *Theraphosae* and a whole set of paralyzing, disintegrating and electromagnetic rays. Our presence in the tunnel, however, claimed her total attention. We represented a danger that it was necessary to counter at any price, and she took charge of it personally. She hates us intensely, for Beffort and I were close to arresting her in Tarrytown…." He turned to the other G-man and asked: "Do you know whether the bombardment proved effective?"

"Through this tornado," the man replied, "I could only make out the glow of the fire—I don't know what was burning…."

Akamatsu turned up the collar of his coat, pulled down his hat and told Beffort what he intended to do. "I don't think there's anything more we can do but return to Dallas, Smith. This underground complex has been destroyed, but I don't think that will affect Madame Atomos unduly."

"Evidently not," Beffort growled. "The tunnel hasn't been used since the construction of the refuge. Madame Atomos reached old Cal's field by that means, where she installed her automatic laboratory, unknown to anyone. The spectacle was staged on the farm, in fact—that's where the excavation ends up. Concrete was manufactured there, workmen lived there, and there must have been an incessant traffic of trucks. The farm is isolated, of course, but how is it possible that none of the neighbors noticed anything? That amazes me."

Akamatsu looked at his watch and yawned. "Don't you think," he suggested, "that we need a little sleep?"

Beffort scowled. "You're right, Yosho. Let's go back to Dallas."

"What about us?" Witter asked.

"Climb into your car and then get some sleep yourselves. Rendezvous at ten o'clock in Cooper's office."

Witter made as if to turn away, hesitated, and said: "I'd rather stay with you, Mr. Beffort."

"All right," Smith said, gruffly. "You can keep us company—but drop the Mister. Go with your pal and get some sleep, and be at the rendezvous. If Madame Atomos isn't here, we have to find her—and believe me, my lads, that won't be a piece of cake! Go home, now!"

May Maxwell was the only one actively involved in the affair during the next two or three hours.

The rain was still falling as heavily, and everyone in Dallas was recuperating. The Pooley remained absolutely inert, the spiders had been burnt to a crisp and there was nothing to indicate that Madame Atomos was planning a new offensive. With the elements unleashed, it seemed that nothing could be attempted. The bad weather pinned people down, swelled the rivers, flooded the fields and rendered the roads dangerous, if not impassable.

More than one war had been stopped by nature, and this conflict was no exception. Everyone was waiting, except May Maxwell.

It is true that the young woman was in the heart of the enemy camp, that her presence had not been detected and that she knew that her actions might be decisive. The certainty of her importance had, however, almost paralyzed her. She tried to imagine what her husband would have done in her place, but only came up with answers that far surpassed her capabilities.

Gregory would probably have knocked out the guard, blown up the concrete buildings and destroyed the house—unless he would have escaped without attracting attention in order to summon reinforcements.

May passed her moist hand over her drawn face. She was tired, but understood that she could not abandon herself to sleep without risking the loss of her life. She was safe in the laundry-room, but for how long? It would be sufficient for someone to open the garage door, for any reason whatsoever, for all to be lost. In the final analysis, the little building was more trap than refuge.

On the other hand, by remaining passive, she was playing into Madame Atomos's hands.

May went back into the garage and took the keys to the Mercury, thus depriving her enemies of one means of escape. She darted a glance over the deserted grounds, and saw the high enclosing wall and the closed gate through the trees. She presumed that the gate must open automatically by means of a system situated in the main house.

She emerged from the garage, made sure that the guard could not see her, and ran across the lawn. She dived between two clumps of bushes, stopped and listened. Nothing was perceptible, but the patter of the rain had to be drowning out all other sounds.

The young woman opened her handbag, took out the money and identity papers it contained, dug a hole in the soft ground and buried it. She slipped the money and documents into her coat pocket, gripped the butt of the forty-five and, now freer in her movements, made a further run that took her under the veranda.

Indecisively, she plunged into the heart of another clump of bushes, and peered through the leaves at a thick wooden door situated at the top of a flight of steps. With that door, its smooth walls and its closed shutters, the house seemed impregnable. May knew, however that she had to get inside if she hoped to do anything effective.

A long moment went by without the young woman finding a solution, and then the door suddenly opened. Mikonosuke Watanabe came down the steps, turned the corner and disappeared.

May left her hiding-place and went up the steps, her heart beating rapidly. She breathed deeply, thought of her sons and Gregory, and then pushed the heavy batten. She went in and closed the door quietly. A long corridor extended in front of her, ending in a staircase. There were several doors to either side of the corridor. Two of them were wide open, and absolute silence reigned everywhere.

May told herself that Watanabe might return at any moment, and also saw that her clothes, drenched with rainwater, were leaving an evident trace on the parquet floor. She moved forward rapidly in the semi-darkness and went into the first room. In spite of the gloom, she made out a long table, shelves laden with books and a low divan placed in a corner. May was still hesitating when she heard the footsteps of the Japanese man on the steps.

She slid along the wall, crouched down behind the divan, which was not separated from the parquet by any gap, and held her breath.

The entrance door opened and closed again, but the Japanese man's footfalls hesitated and fell silent. May immediately assumed that he must have stopped in front of the pool she had imprudently allowed to form. Perhaps the prints of her shoes similarly marked her passage. If Watanabe had the slightest suspicion, she was done for.

She crawled on her knees as far as the corner of the divan, positioned herself more comfortably, and risked a peek. She was thus able to see the door of the room where she was hiding, a section of the corridor and a closed door. By reason of the closed shutters, the house was bathed with a diffuse light that blurred objects and formed disquieting banks of shadow everywhere.

May heard the rustle of clothing, and Watanabe resumed walking, passed through the young woman's field of vision, and drew away. He had not darted a glance into the room, and May realized that he had stopped in order to take off his raincoat and hang it up in a cloakroom that she had not noticed.

At that moment, she perceived that she had only experienced a moderate fear, that her forefinger was riveted to the trigger of the Colt, and that the slightest false move on the part of the Japanese man would have signed his death warrant.

She also realized that, until now, chance had smiled upon her. In fact, she had just succeeded in doing what all the federal agents in the land had been trying in vain to do for three months: discovered Madame Atomos's secret hideout. To be sure, she had not yet seen the terrible Japanese woman, but the concrete-clad buildings, the strange antennae bristling on their roofs led her to conclude that this was the place from which the waves departed that animated the various weapons spreading terror through Dallas and its surroundings—unless these installations were merely relay stations.

Suddenly, the chandelier lit up and light flooded the room. May thrust herself backwards. Two men armed with disintegrator rifles appeared in the doorway; May could see them in a mirror situated beside a telephone. The men were short and yellow-skinned, with slanting eyes and a suspicious gaze.

"Come out here!" ordered one of the Japanese men, with a frightful accent.

May realized that they did not know exactly where she was hiding—but it was obvious that the men could not fail to discover her. That would happen in the next few seconds. Then they would open fire and destroy the divan.

A fit of rage took hold of her. She let herself fall on to her side and pressed the trigger twice. Gregory had taught her to shoot, and both her bullets hit the target.

The little yellow men were thrown back by the impacts and folded up like accordions emptied of air. At the same time, the shots split the silence and echoed through the building, reverberating from wall to wall an in apocalyptic din. May leapt forward, grabbed the disintegrator rifles, shoved the corpses into the corridor, closed the door and drew the bolt.

Her momentum enabled her to run to the telephone, put one of the rifles down beside it—while she kept the other in her hand—and dial the number of the FBI office in Dallas with a feverish finger. It was the number on which she was accustomed to call her husband, and it was engraved in her memory. She did not know whether it would be possible to get through from this house, but she made the attempt for want of anything better.

The bell rang at the other end of the line—once, twice….

May bit her lips until they bled. She was trembling like a leaf, not knowing whether it as fear or excitement—but the rifle remained solidly wedged under her arm.

Blows made the door shake, and a shadow appeared against the oblique cracks in the shutters of the nearest window. May directed the barrel of the weapon at the window and pressed the button that she could feel beneath her finger.

There was a brief flash, and the window, the shutters and the man who was crouching there disappeared as if rubbed out with an eraser.

Stupefied, May almost failed to respond when the hoarse voice of George Cooper said; "FBI here. I'm listening."

May pulled herself together, swallowed her saliva and said, rapidly. "May Maxwell here. Listen hard, Mr. Cooper. I'm in Madame Atomos's house…."

"What!"

"Shut up and listen. Hurry up and trace this call, because I don't know where I am. I've just killed two men and…." She felt a sudden weakness and her throat seized up.

"My God!" howled Cooper. "Talk, Mrs. Maxwell!"

My opened her mouth—but at the same moment, the door split apart, showering splinters.

"Where are you, Mrs. Maxwell?" cried Cooper.

May pressed the button of the rifle. The door and the man wielding the axe were disintegrated. "I don't know…." she said.

There was a click, and May realized that someone had just cut the telephone line. She threw the apparatus away, seized the second rifle and retreated toward the window. Overlapping shouts rang out in the house. A woman was howling orders in Japanese, and there was a sound of running feet on the floor above.

May was certain that the woman could only be Madame Atomos. Her desire to run away vanished on the spot, and she ran toward the blackened door-frame, whose shreds were still clinging to the wall, by some miracle. Conscious of having a fantastic means of destruction in her hands, May raced like a shadow along the corridor, reached the foot of the staircase and climbed the steps rapidly.

She stopped on the first landing, her ears pricked, but it suddenly seemed that the building had been emptied of its occupants. Suddenly, there was a crackling sound behind her and the first flight of stairs collapsed, smoking. One of her enemies had evidently made use of the disintegrator ray too. May moved back, spotted a room, and took refuge therein. With a blast of the ray she made the window disappear, panes and shutters alike, and leaned out into empty space. She found herself facing the concrete buildings, from the first floor. Beneath the pouring rain, the grounds seemed deserted.

Behind her back, the walls were transformed into smoke, and another flight of stairs collapsed noisily. The young woman understood then that Watanabe, or Madame Atomos, was prepared to destroy the house in the hope that she would be killed by one of the discharges of the terrible weapons.

She crouched down as low as possible, let the rifles fall on to the grass, climbed out of the window and, after suspending herself by her fingers, let herself fall in her turn. She landed without injury, grabbed the rifles and ran to take cover beside one of the outbuildings.

At that moment, the roar of an engine burst forth. May started to move toward the garage, but the house exploded in a fantastic conflagration, and the debris that whistled through the air obliged her to throw herself back behind the thick wall.

Deafened by the violence of the explosion, May was incapable of moving. Incandescent splinters were crashing to the ground continually, and an immense glare sprang up from the fire-ravaged house.

Finally, the rain of debris ceased, and without waiting any longer, May raced over the lawn, making a large detour. It seemed to her that a century had gone by since her leap from the first floor, but it could not have been longer than a few seconds, for she perceived a cream-colored car speeding along the winding driveway.

May raised the barrel of her weapon and pressed the button—in vain. She realized that the fuel-supply was

235

empty. She raised the other weapon and aimed it at the car. A row of trees evaporated in smoke, but the vehicle continued its course.

Thanks to the gap thus contrived, the young woman saw that the gate was now wide open, and that the cream car was approaching it at top speed. May fired again, pulverizing another row of trees and grilling the grass for a hundred meters, but the gate remained intact.

May persisted, before realizing that the mortal jet did not carry that distance; by the time she understood that, her weapon was empty. Powerless, she watched the car go through the gate and disappear behind the enclosing wall, bearing between its flanks Mikonosuke Watanabe and Kanoto Yoshimuta, alias Madame Atomos.

Alone in front of the building, which was still ablaze, May felt empty. The murderess of her sons and Gregory had succeeded in fleeing without any opposition being raised to her project!

Suddenly, May remembered the Mercury and the bunch of keys that she had dropped into her pocket. She raced to the garage, climbed into the car, switched on the engine and backed out at a furious speed.

A minute later, the Mercury went through the gateway, turned right, and set off in pursuit of Madame Atomos.

Chapter XI

It took exactly fifteen minutes for Deputy Director George Cooper to locate the place from which May Maxwell had sent her SOS.

During that interval, his assistant went to find Beffort, Akamatsu, Witter and the latter's partner, Cadogan.

The telephone call had come from a property situated south of Fort Worth, in a relatively deserted area not far from Godley, which was named White Mountain.

By radio, Cooper alerted the police at Cleburne and Stephenville, who set up road-blocks on Routes 67 and 377 and sent a substantial company of men to White Mountain.

Simultaneously, a helicopter took off from Love Field Airport in Dallas. The three federal agents and Yosho Akamatsu were aboard.

Beffort could not believe the news. "It's unimaginable!" he repeated, "unimaginable! It's probably a hoax!"

Akamatsu knotted his necktie, which he had just recovered from the depths of his holster, and said: "Cooper knows Mrs. Maxwell well. He recognized her voice. Do you know, Smith, that the woman lost both her sons before learning unceremoniously of the death of her husband? Cooper's assistant told me how that happened in the FBI office."

Beffort scowled. "Exactly," he said. "That must have shaken her up. Perhaps she's gone completely mad. I wouldn't be surprised if she'd imagined this whole thing. You know the precautions with which Madame Atomos surrounds herself."

"Sometimes chance can accomplish miracles...."

"In this case, then," Beffort said, ironically, "chance has surpassed itself. To discover the refuge of Madame Atomos is a performance, but to succeed in getting into it and making use of her telephone smacks of magic."

It was still raining and the cloud layer was very low. The machine was flying at reduced altitude, struggling against a violent wind blowing at an oblique angle, and the pilot had to hold on tight to maintain his course.

Eddie Witter was the first to draw attention to the cloud of smoke climbing into the sky in a spiral.

"One would think," said Cadogan, "that the forest were on fire!"

The helicopter drew nearer and the fire became visible.

"It's White Mountain!" Beffort groaned. He glanced sideways at Akamatsu, and added: "I think you were right, Yosho. It's customary for Madame Atomos to burn any hideout that's no longer of any use to her!"

"Look!" cried Witter. "The cops are already here!"

The police had indeed just invested the grounds, and uniforms were swarming around the garage, the house and the concrete buildings.

The pilot descended further, made a pass and said, having examined the terrain: "We can land on that lawn, next to...."

Four brief but violent explosions cut his speech short, and the apparatus shuddered and slipped sideways, pitching in the turbulent air, finally stabilizing while a cloud of shards whistled through the air.

The four blockhouses bristling with antennae had literally blown apart, and a dozen shattered corpses were lying on the green lawn.

The garage and a few trees had been blown down, and a police car completely turned over. Men were running in all directions, and an ambulance was demanding passage with loud blasts of its siren. On the road, five fire-engines were arriving, preceding a group of vehicles loaded with policemen. All of them had already been on the way before the destruction of the blockhouses. They converged on the designated spot to collect the wounded and put out a further fire,

Perceiving several radio cars, Beffort told the pilot to open communication with the ground. This was rapidly done, and a dialogue began between the police and the helicopter.

"Do you need us?" Beffort asked.

"No. Apart from the dead we have only six men slightly wounded, who can wait."

"Any information regarding Madame Atomos?"

"We haven't found anyone here, but a message to all cars has just announced that a cream Chevrolet and a black Mercury are heading for Waco. They're traveling at top speed, and are presently on 144 between Walnut Springs and Meridian…."

The pilot veered around and immediately took the direction indicated.

"Do you think your colleagues can intercept them?" Beffort said into his mike.

"Not likely. The message is too recent and our forces are assembled here. On the other hand, Meridian's an important junction. There are five routes out of there. Have you a map of the region?" The pilot waved a packet of maps, holding one out to Beffort, who confirmed the fact to his interlocutor. "In that case, put our foot down and you've got a chance. We'll stay in contact with you, but if reception becomes poor, try to get hold of Waco HQ."

The helicopter flew over the Brazos River, leaving Lake Whitney to its left, and started following 174, which led straight to Meridian....

In the laboratory in Dallas, Nelson Manning and Alan Soblen were trying doggedly to isolate the chemical components of the Pooley.

They already knew that the strange substance was not vegetal, but had been manufactured, that it could not resist a fire produced by burning paper—but paper alone—and that water stopped its growth.

An hour earlier, a crew of civil volunteers had unloaded three tons of old newspapers next to the Pooley. The fire had not destroyed the substance, but had forced a retreat of fifty yards. Five houses, a road, fences and a car had been liberated. On examination, it was determined that the Pooley had not damaged anything—except that the grass had turned yellow.

May Maxwell had nearly crashed, so great was her haste to catch up with the cream-colored car; at enormous risk, she had kept it in view until it reached Route 144. Now the young woman was keeping her distance. It was necessary, above all, that she should not be spotted. She hoped that George Cooper had been able to trace her telephone call, and expected to see the cream car run into a road block shortly.

In the meantime, it was necessary for her to stay in touch, to forget her hatred, and to transform herself into a shadow. That was difficult in the bulky Mercury, but the weather made it easier.

One following the other, the two cars passed through Meridian and took 22. The cream Chevrolet maintained a hellish speed, and it required all May's skill as a driver to stay in its wake.

They went through Laguna Park like a whirlwind, with May almost two hundred yards behind. As they came out of the town, she put her foot down, went along the shore of Lake Whitney, and found out, on discovering a long straight road that was deserted, that she had lost the other vehicle. In mortal anguish, she made a rapid U-turn and went slowly back toward Laguna Park. That stretch of 22 was only a secondary road; it went through a wood, crossed the Brazos River and went along the lake-shore. Apparently, the Chevrolet could only have cut through the woods or plunged into the lake!

Discouraged, May stopped the Mercury on the roadside and switched off the engine. She was suddenly overwhelmed by fatigue, which drowned her will-power beneath a wave of bitterness that forced her to admit the futility of her efforts. She had disintegrated four men, but Madame Atomos had got away.

Madame Atomos always got away. She was an ungraspable creature, full of conning and intelligence, anticipating everything and disposing of vast means....

May plunged into that immense weariness without even being consciously aware of it. She had just reached the limit of her strength....

The helicopter flew over Meridian and described a large circle over the road-junction, but the two vehicles identified by Cleburne Central remained invisible. It as ten twenty and the weather was frightful, scarcely inviting to travelers. The roads were practically deserted;

even in Meridian there were few people about. People were prolonging their Sunday lie-in, and only a few of the faithful were hastening to church.

Beffort asked the pilot to make radio contact with Waco HQ, and when that was done he took possession of the mike.

"Beffort here," he said. "Can you hear me?"

"Three out of five," the HQ replied, "but we're up to date. Where are you?"

"Circling over Meridian. Haven't yet seen the suspect vehicles."

"They're sealed within the sector," HQ affirmed. "Since the message from Cleburne all the roads are closed off, but our road-blocks haven't given any indication. Patrols are heading along Routes 22, 6, 174 and 144. The country roads are being watched, as well as the secondaries. Got that?"

"All received. We're going on.

"Stay on the air. Over and out."

Beffort replaced the mike and the headset, and stretched his legs. "If Mrs. Maxwell's driving the Mercury," he said, "logically, she'll soon be able to give us news."

"Nothing is less certain," Akamatsu objected. "We don't know what happened at White Mountain, but Mrs. Maxwell is probably dead now. Cooper, who was talking to her, said that the communication was abruptly cut off. The Chevrolet and the Mercury probably belong to Madame Atomos, and are transporting her gang...."

"Unless," Beffort cut in, "the rattletraps have nothing to do with the affair. We don't know why the two vehicles were flagged. We'll look pretty stupid if it's a group of friends going fishing!"

The pilot had taken off the headset, and thrust it into Smith Beffort's hands. "It's Waco," he said, laconically.

The G-man put it on and grabbed the mike. "Beffort," he said. "I'm listening."

"Two motor-cycle policemen have spotted a Mercury stationary on 22, between Laguna Park and Whitney."

"Tell them not to approach it!" Beffort exclaimed.

"Already done," the man from HQ replied, dryly. "We'll leave it to you. Over and out."

Beffort shrugged his shoulders. It was the old rivalry between the police and the FBI flaring up again, but he didn't care. "Change course," he said to the pilot. "Head for Laguna Park."

The apparatus changed course and slowly lost altitude.

Beffort turned to his companions. "The car might be empty," he said, primarily for the benefit of Witter and Cadogan, "but we'll take the usual precautions. Madame Atomos's people have disintegrator rifles that can transform you into smoke with no trouble at all."

"I can see the Mercury!" the pilot exclaimed.

"Don't go any closer," Beffort instructed. "Can you put us down on the road, before that straight section?"

"Easily done," said the pilot. "If you're not particularly keen on the road, I can see a patch of land that's very suitable."

"Go on, then. The main thing is that your hull remains some distance from the car. In fact, take off as soon as you've dropped us. Stay in contact with Waco HQ, gain altitude and keep your eyes on us. If we're out of sight for more than five minutes, don't try to find us—we'll be reduced to smoke.

The pilot looked at Beffort with wide eyes, suddenly swallowed a wad of saliva, and asked: "What should I do in that case?"

"Inform Waco, George Cooper and Dr. Soblen. That's all. Now set down."

The helicopter went down and posed delicately on the muddy field. The four men leapt to the ground. The apparatus took off immediately, gained height and began circling.

Beffort led his little company to the turning, stopped before the straight stretch, pointed to the car a hundred yards away and said: "Let's not put all our eggs in one basket. I'll go alone to see what's simmering over there."

"No," said Akamatsu, softly but firmly, "You aren't going alone. I'm coming with you. We'll take one side of the road each, and Witter and Cadogan can cover us."

Beffort capitulated. Akamatsu was not under his orders, and had carte blanche from the Boss to act as he saw fit.

The two men drew away, their stomachs slightly knotted, quickly covered the intervening distance, and came up to either side of the Mercury, guns in hand. A single glance sufficed to tell them that there was no one in it.

Chapter XII

May recovered consciousness with a frightful slowness, somewhat after the fashion of the corpse of a drowning victim returning to the surface, and did not know at first whether she was still dreaming.

She remembered having fallen asleep in the Mercury, her retina retaining the image of a rainswept road, but now she saw before her a solid wall, with a strange bluish luminosity.

She was lying on a mat set directly on the ground, and was naked. Her nudity gave her a terrible shock. She stood up without difficulty and examined her prison.

The room was rectangular and had no windows. A steel door took up one entire side of the rectangle, and the ceiling was pierced by the opening of a ventilation shaft about three feet in diameter, fitted with a metallic grille.

May could not explain how she had arrived in this place, who had undressed her and why, but—without quite admitting it—she already suspected Madame Atomos of the outrage.

She made a tour of her cell and put her ear to the door. A faint hum was audible, but apart from that, the most profound silence reigned.

Vaguely scared, May looked round the room. Five paces by six, the ceiling was within reach of an extended hand; the temperature was somewhere between twenty-five and thirty degrees Centigrade.

Abruptly, the light went out and May was plunged into absolute darkness. The heat became more oppressive and the young woman drew nearer to the ventilation shaft, feeling the ceiling. Her fingers touched the metal. May knew that she was directly below the opening, but could no longer feel any draught. She waited for a while, began to sweat, had trouble breathing, and finally understood that the air supply had been cut.

"You are May Maxwell," said a woman's voice in the darkness, "and you have killed four of my men. You have as much courage as Sam Forbes had, and it's only fair that you be subjected to the same fate."

"Who are you?" May demanded.

"Madame Atomos, of course. That cannot surprise you, since you have been trying to catch up with me since dawn. Were you trying to do that because I killed your husband, Mrs. Maxwell?"

Sweat ran down May's body like water from shower. "You've also killed my children," she panted, in a weakening voice.

"You seem to be suffering," said Madame Atomos, ironically. "It is my intention to kill you, but your point of view interests me. Here is a little air, Mrs. Maxell."

The hum resumed, and a jet of fresh air fell upon the young woman's face. She breathed in deeply, thinking that the Japanese woman would supply her with air for as long as she found a way to cultivate her attention. But then what? That could not last forever.

"So," Madame Atomos went on, "I killed your children and your husband, and now you hate me. By virtue of that, you have some understanding of me. In 1945, at Nagasaki, you Americans also killed the members of my family."

"That was war!" May protested, furiously.

"That was your war," said the Japanese woman. "Now, this is mine. I am waging it alone, with the aid of a few desperate people who, like me, lost everything at

246

Hiroshima or Nagasaki. Our race has a profound scorn for death. Mrs. Maxwell, but cannot tolerate the coldly premeditated murder of thousands of individuals!"

Madame Atomos was still speaking, but the young woman was no longer listening. By contrast with what a man would have done, she had just exerted a horizontal pressure on the grille, and it had shifted slightly. It was like a sliding door, moving along its grooves. May could fit her arm into the gap she had created. She braced herself on the floor and pushed with all her strength. The grille retreated further, reaching the mid-point of the circumference outlined by the ventilation shaft.

May made a further effort, and the grille ceded again, creating a sufficient gap.

"If you were a man," said Madame Atomos, "I would already have killed you, Mrs. Maxwell. You remind me of what I was a few years ago...."

May took hold of the grille and hauled herself up painfully. She got her knees on to the metal edge, and her groping hand found a rounded iron rung.

"Hatred is an all-consuming sentiment that gives no respite to the person it afflicts...."

May put her foot on the rung, bent down and put the grille back in place. It ran quite easily now.

"But it is necessary to pursue one's vengeance to the end, no matter what...."

My held her breath, found another rung, and climbed up the narrow conduit. In the most complete darkness, she had no idea where she was going, but was certain that nothing could be worse than dying of asphyxia in a concrete cell.

She climbed up a dozen rungs and reached a turning. The conduit became horizontal, and the voice of Madame Atomos now only reached the young woman as a confused murmur. Her knees were bloody, as were her elbows, but the pain had no effect on her for the moment.

All of a sudden, the fresh air ceased flowing through the conduit, and May knew that Madame Atomos had grown weary of receiving no reply. She had the impression that she had been crawling for hours, and began to think that she would never reach the end of her ordeal. Furthermore, the oxygen was thinning out and May was beginning to pant again. The darkness was populated with colored lights, which danced before her eyes like myriads of luminous insects, and the young woman was convinced that it was all over when her hand bumped into a solid surface.

The conduit stopped there. She was a prisoner in a metal pipe and would asphyxiate slowly, as her two sons had been asphyxiated. With a supreme effort, she pushed the solid plate that she found in front of her. It emitted a slight click and pivoted creakily on a central axis.

May felt fresh air caress her face, saw a grey light a few meters away, and realized with boundless joy that it was daylight.

She made an attempt to squeeze past the shutter, became trapped momentarily between the axle and the wall of the conduit, and then succeeded in scraping past the obstacle. A last glimmer of lucidity made her put the shutter back in place, and she fainted, a few meters from liberty, but knowing that she was not longer at risk of asphyxia.

The police patrols had returned along Route 22 and a specialist had come to take fingerprints from the steering-wheel, gear-stick and door-handles of the Mercury. The telex had come into play between Waco and Dallas, and it had been confirmed that the prints were those of May Maxwell.

It was equally certain that the cream Chevrolet had not emerged from a narrow circle that had few inhabitants and offered no natural hiding-places.

"Unless she has a hideout under Lake Whitney," Smith Beffort growled, "Mother Atomos is bound to fall into our hands before the end of the day. All the houses in the vicinity are inhabited."

Akamatsu frowned. "Under the lake, you say?"

Beffort started. "I was joking, Yosho! You aren't keeping up...." The look that the Tokkoka man directed at him rendered him mute. After all, with Madame Atomos nothing was impossible! "What are you thinking?" he asked.

Akamatsu pointed at the Mercury. "Have you noticed, Smith, that the car isn't pointed in the right direction? Assuming, which is ninety per cent probable, that Mrs. Maxwell was driving, why would she make an abrupt U-turn while she was pursuing Madame Atomos's Chevrolet?"

Beffort bit his lip. "I wasn't paying attention," he admitted. "That is, indeed, odd...."

A detective approached the group. "Almost all the houses situated in the zone have been visited," he said. "None is empty, or occupied by Asiatics. We've also inspected the garages. We've found eight cream-colored Chevrolets, but none has left its garage for hours. With the rain and the mud, that's easy to verify...."

"In conclusion," said Akamatsu, "the suspect perimeter is now reduced to this road...."

"This section of road," the policeman rectified. "No more than the wood, a dozen villas and the strip of land separating the roadway from the lake. Before noon, it will all have passed through a sieve…."

"And the lake itself?" Akamatsu enquired, quite seriously.

Nonplussed, the detective scanned the liquid extent, and brought his astonished gaze back to the Japanese agent. "What do you mean? The lake's deserted. In this weather, the boats remain at their moorings. Even if Madame Atomos had crossed over with the aid of a motor-boat, she couldn't escape."

Akamatsu shook his head with gentle stubbornness. "That's not the question," he said. "Madame Atomos is capable of possessing a submerged refuge, or of having excavated a shelter underneath the lake. With her, nothing can be neglected. Will you give orders for Whitney to be sounded?"

The detective realized that he was not joking, said that he would make the necessary arrangements, and drew away.

Smith Beffort threw away his cigarette-end, and observed: "At least you follow through with your ideas, Yosho!" Then, addressing Witter and Cadogan, he added: "There's nothing left for us to do but to join the search, without breaking up our little group. Come on, lads…."

On Madame Atomos's orders, Mikonosuke Watanabe had cut the ventilation system supplying the cell in which May Maxwell was imprisoned. The American woman would die in about thirty minutes, and Mikonosuke knew that her death-throes would be particularly horrible. In the darkness, she would go mad before expiring. That was what Madame Atomos wanted. For her, death was not sufficient. It was indispensable that the subject should attain the limits of terror.

Mikonosuke had heard the story of the death-throes of the G-man Sam Forbes in a cell in the Oakland refuge. At that time, he had not yet joined Madame Atomos's crew; it was the death of his sister Lydia that had made up his mind. Mikonosuke had made the sacrifice of his life in advance. If the terrible Japanese woman demanded that he kill himself for the cause, he would do it without hesitation.

This May Maxwell could never suffer enough. Because of her, it had been necessary to abandon White Mountain, and now the final Texas hideaway was under threat. The construction was underground, but the house that stood over it might be invaded by police at any moment. Officially, the house was the property of a naturalized American couple, Polish in origin. For two years, Madame Atomos had held them at her mercy. The couple had an only daughter, whom Madame Atomos had kidnapped. It had been no more difficult than that.

Mikonosuke wore a little cruel smile. He consulted his watch and judged that the American woman would be no more than a corpse. He switched the light back on, switched on the ventilation system. left his sentry-post and headed for the second floor down.

At the end of a long corridor, he drew the bolts from a steel door, tugged at the heavy batten—and remained rooted to the spot.

The cell was empty!

Seized by vertigo, Mikonosuke was obliged to lean back against the wall. The mat was still there, but the American woman seemed to have evaporated.

The Japanese man went into the narrow room, examined the ventilation grille—which May had put back in place—and saw nothing abnormal. Besides, the air was coming through the conduit normally, and a human body would inevitably have obstructed it.

"Well, Watanabe?" the voice of Madame Atomos suddenly spat. "What's happening?"

Mikonosuke stretched his neck in the direction of the apparatus sealed into the concrete. "Mistress," he said, helplessly, "the prisoner has disappeared."

Silence fell, and then the calm voice of the Japanese woman said: "She can only have escaped through the grille. The cell has never been used and none of us has checked it out. Look more closely at the grille, Watanabe."

"Yes, Mistress."

Mikonosuke suspended himself from the metallic checkerboard, which did not yield by the slightest fraction of an inch. Then he shook it violently in every direction, and the grille suddenly slid sideways, unblocking the opening over three quarters of its circumference.

"The grille moves sideways!" Mikonosuke shouted.

"Close it again," Madame Atomos replied. "The ventilation shaft ends in a hollow tree on the edge of the bank, and the American must have got out some time ago."

There was a further pause, which Mikonosuke dared to break by proposing: "I could try to follow the conduit, Mistress?"

"No," said Madame Atomos, sharply. "It's too late. The police are surrounding us, and the vice is closing in on us. Blow up the ventilation shaft and make sure that the Lomakines don't make any mistake. Above all, don't show yourself, Watanabe. Where have you hidden the car?"

"In the underground garage…."

"Good," the Japanese woman interjected. "Use it to flee if the police discover the secret entrance in the Lomakine house. Don't worry about anything else. Rendezvous at point B in forty-eight hours. *Au revoir*, Watanabe."

"*Au revoir*, Mistress."

A click revealed that Madame Atomos had cut the connection. Mikonosuke left the room, and went back along the corridor to his sentry-post. On three screens he could see the Mercury stationary on Route 22, a group of armed policemen searching the little wood, and four men—one of whom was Japanese—advancing toward the Lomakine house.

Mikonosuke pressed a lever, and a muffled explosion told him that the ventilation shaft had now caved in. On the screens, he verified that the policemen had not reacted, and left the redoubt. He went up one floor, caused a fake bookshelf to pivot, and emerged into the Lomakines' drawing-room.

The two of them were waiting. The woman was nearing forty, and her face was racked by anguish.

"Pay attention!" said Watanabe, harshly. "The policemen are going to interrogate you. Act naturally. Don't forget that your daughter's life is hanging by a thread."

The woman nodded her head, but the man's face was set like marble. "We haven't had any news for a year," he said, in a glacial tone. "I'm sure that we'll never see her alive again. You're a killer, and you're not getting out of here!"

"Serge!" moaned the woman.

Watanabe made a gesture, but Lomakine pointed a little 6.35 at him. "If you move," he warned, "I'll kill you!"

Chapter XIII

While Lomakine was rebelling against one of Madame Atomos's representatives, the rain had stopped falling in Dallas ten minutes earlier. Although the saturated ground still conserved a certain dampness, it was not the same for tarmac or bitumen surfaces.

The Pooley agitated its roots, like some vile beast shaking its legs on awakening, and began a slow, groping creep on the surfaces that the wind had rapidly dried. The nightmare had resumed. As soon as he was notified of the fact, Deputy Director Cooper leapt to the telephone and dialed the number of the laboratory.

Dr. Soblen abandoned his test tubes, wiped the lenses of his spectacles, which had been mired by the sweat from his brow, and steered himself unsteadily toward the ringing booth. The little man had not slept since leaving New York, and was only standing up by virtue of an enormous effort of will.

"It's stopped raining, Doctor," said Cooper, feverishly, "and the Pooley's on the march again. Have you discovered a means of fighting it?"

"No, not yet...."

"I'll have to evacuate the city, then," Cooper said, sounding discouraged. "If the Pooley starts advancing as rapidly as last night, Dallas will be entirely covered by this evening...."

Alan Soblen let himself slump on to the stool. "Professor Manning and I are doing all that we can," he said, by way of excuse. "We bear a heavy responsibility, Mr. Cooper. You must count entirely on us...."

254

"Now," said the Deputy Director, "I can't count on you at all. Your laboratory will be underneath the Pooley in a few hours, and you'll have to abandon your research. Trains, trucks and airplanes are being loaded up all over the state, but by the time the paper they're carrying is delivered to us, the Pooley will have covered a vast expanse. All the paper supplies in the United States won't be sufficient then."

Soblen, who was falling asleep, made a violent effort to unstuck his eyelids. "After that storm," he said, "there's no lack of water. Shower the terrain. Slow the Pooley down as much as you can...."

Cooper roared in frustration. "That's not a solution!" he proclaimed. "You have to find something that will destroy it, Doctor!"

Soblen hung up without replying, went back to the laboratory and resumed work next to Nelson Manning. "What was that?" the latter asked, indifferently.

Soblen brought him up to date with the situation, and Manning shrugged his shoulders, "You told me that you'd stay here come what may," he murmured, keeping his eye glued to his microscope. No need to repeat that I won't abandon you, is there?"

Soblen shook a gaseous solution, added a pasty mixture, stirred it, and let a drop fall on to the fragment of the Pooley. Instantaneously, there was a crackle, and the surface of the strange material was visibly hollowed out.

"No progress," Soblen observed.

Manning examined the result of the experiment and said: "I'm not so sure. It seems to me that there's a definite amelioration."

"Was it caused by the nitric acid?"

"I think so."

Soblen muttered something between his teeth, added a measure of nitric acid, and carried out another trial....

Three miles away, a factory was standing by in a state of alert. It was linked to the laboratory by telephone and radio, and could start the manufacture of any product whatsoever in the blink of an eye. Indubitably, Soblen and Manning were the only ones who could stop the Pooley—except, of course, for Madame Atomos.

May Maxwell emerged from her brief fainting fit while Watanabe was discovering her escape. She remained still momentarily, wandering what she was doing in the narrow pipe, suddenly recovered her memory and was seized by a violent panic on hearing the ventilator fans operating again. That signified that her escape had been noticed, and that measures were about to be taken to recapture her.

She assumed a kneeling position, feeling very cold—which reminded her that she was as naked as a worm. She struggled against a desire for sleep that caused her to bow her head, and crawled painfully to the end of the conduit.

There was one last bend. May reached it, had the possibility of standing upright, and observed with astonishment that she was inside the trunk of a hollow tree. By hanging on to cracks, she hoisted herself up to the opening through which light was filtering, suddenly saw the whole extent of the lake, heard the patter of the rain and smelled the odor rising from the moist ground.

With a thrust of her hips, she installed herself on a ledge and leaned out. The tree was planted on the edge of the lake, on a hillock that was difficult to climb, and the young woman observed an isolated enclosure. It was made of metal pickets supporting wire netting. Evidently, the tree had been placed in the grounds of a private property.

At that precise second, a muffled explosion shook the ground. A cloud of dust invaded the hollow trunk. When it had dissipated, May saw that the opening of the ventilation shaft was filled with earth. She shivered at the thought that, a few minutes earlier, she would have been buried alive. A reflex of retrospective fear caused her to jump down on to the wet grass.

A nearby splashing sound made her turn around, and she saw with amazement that a periscope was cleaving through the water, heading for the middle of the lake. May realized with a heartfelt shock that it could only be one of Madame Atomos's inventions. The latter was fleeing yet again, and it seemed that nothing could stop her from getting away.

She remained rooted to the spot, and then began shouting in order to attract attention....

Mikonosuke Watanabe knew that Lomakine was not joking. The barrel of the 6.35 was aimed at his chest, and the man's forefinger was dangerously tight on the trigger. "If you play the imbecile," he said, slyly, "I'll probably be picked up by the police, but you can be sure that Madame Atomos will kill your daughter."

Serge Lomakine pointed to a chair. "Get away from that door," he said, "and sit down."

Watanabe obeyed, and Lomakine closed the fake bookcase without relaxing his vigilance. "Anna," he said to his wife, "the police are outside. Go fetch them."

The woman's eyes were moist with tears. "Serge! Think about Catherine!"

"Go!" growled the man, impatiently. "It's too late to go back now."

The woman understood that all discussion was futile. She left the drawing-room, opened the door at the front of the house, went through the garden and opened the gate.

On the road, Beffort, Akamatsu, Witter and Cadogan were approaching the house. Anna Lomakine materialized in front of them and raised her arms in the manner of a drowning man. Her mouth opened, but emotion prevented her from uttering the slightest sound.

"Something's going on!" said Beffort. Immediately, he started running, followed by his companions, and they quickly surrounded Mrs. Lomakine. Reflexively, Witter and Cadogan drew their weapons.

Anna Lomakine rolled her terrified eyes. She had been living in anguish for months, and suddenly had the sensation of having been suddenly transplanted back to Warsaw, to the ghetto of her youth, which the Nazi killers had crucified. "Go into the house!" she whispered. "My husband is with one of Madame Atomos's men!"

Akamatsu and Beffort rushed into the garden, ran into the house like a whirlwind and irrupted into the drawing-room just in time to see Watanabe collapse in his chair.

Serge Lomakine turned a distraught face toward them. "He's taken poison," he said. "I couldn't stop him."

At that moment, May Maxwell's cries burst forth.

Beffort looked at the 6.35 dangling from the end of Serge Lomakine's arm, and Watanabe's body, shaken by spasms of agony. "Who's that shouting?" he enquired, dryly.

"I don't know," the man replied. "It's coming from the grounds…my wife!"

"No," said Beffort. "It's not her. She's outside the front gate with two of our men. What was the Jap doing in your house?"

Lomakine collapsed into an armchair. "Madame Atomos's hideout is under the house," he said, bleakly.

Akamatsu started. "Where is she? Come on, answer me!"

"Staircases go down behind those fake book-shelves," Lomakine replied, "But we'd do better to get out of here immediately. Madame Atomos will blow everything up if she thinks she's in danger."

The door opened brutally, and Witter came in, carrying May Maxwell, wrapped in an overcoat. "It's Mrs. Maxwell," he said. "She's fainted, but she says that Madame Atomos has just escaped aboard a submarine. If I hadn't seen the periscope, I'd have thought that her mind was wandering!"

Cadigan came in, in his turn. He seemed distraught. "That's right!" he said. "A periscope was cutting through the water of the lake, heading north."

Smith Beffort roused himself from his confusion. "Evacuate the house," he said, "and take Mrs. Maxwell to the police cars. Come on, Yosho!"

They went out at a run, meeting Anna Lomakine, who was coming back like a sleepwalker, and started galloping toward the group of men whose were standing guard.

"Gather all your men!" Beffort shouted, as soon as he was within voice range, and have the lake surrounded!"

Chief Inspector Kellogg jumped. "Have Lake Whitney surrounded!" he protested. "You can't do that—it would take an army."

Beffort grabbed hold of him by the collar of his jacket. "Don't argue! Madame Atomos is in the lake right now. She's crossing it aboard a pocket-submarine, and if we let her do it, she'll slip through our fingers again!"

"A pocket-submarine!"

Beffort bared his teeth. "For now, Kellogg, it's necessary to believe in Father Christmas! Send a radio message to Waco demanding reinforcements. It's vital that the lake be surrounded within thirty minutes."

Kellogg saw that he was serious. He leapt to his car radio, sent his message, and repeated it at maximum volume, while a policeman recalled the searchers by shouting into his megaphone.

When the helicopter took off, Beffort and Akamatsu saw policemen already running along the shores of Whitney. "Stay at medium height," said Beffort to the pilot. "It's a matter of spotting a submarine and not losing sight of it again! It's steering northwards, and ought to be about a mile from shore."

The pilot did not ask any questions. He leveled out at a hundred and fifty feet and headed due north. The rain was no longer falling, but the lake was still dark, acting like a mirror reflecting clouds that were still charged with rain, and the helicopter itself, like a grotesque wingless bird.

The pilot pulled a face. "This won't be a piece of cake," he said, "And I'll soon be running short of fuel."

"We can fill up in Waco," Beffort replied, without ceasing to scrutinize the surface of the lake.

Abruptly, Akamatsu grabbed his sleeve. "*Ohe dai*," he said, excitedly—meaning "come here".

Beffort did not understand, but followed the moment and found his nose stuck to the port partition.

"Look," said the Japanese agent.

The G-man saw a thin wake, but the water as so dark that it was impossible to make out the form of the submersible. "It might be the fin of a fish," he said, unenthusiastically. Speaking to the pilot, he added: "Go further down and try to stay behind the wake. If Madame Atomos sees us through her periscope, she'll dive and change course...."

The apparatus came around. A large circle took it well behind the wake, on an axis heading due north, and it came back skimming the waves whipped up by the air displaced by its blades.

The pilot got steadily nearer, and the three men could clearly see the black tube surmounting a cylindrical shape traveling a few feet beneath the surface.

"It's really her!" Beffort exclaimed.

"Go back up," Akamatsu said, softly. "We can't do anything but follow that machine, Smith—we have to contact Waco."

The pilot had no need to be told twice. He called HQ, and passed the headset and mike to the G-man as soon as he had got through.

"Waco here," Beffort heard. "What's all this nonsense about a submarine?"

"It's not nonsense!" Beffort spat. "Have you sent the reinforcements?"

"Yes, but we don't have any torpedo-boats," said the HQ operator, sarcastically.

Beffort suffered an abrupt fit of wrath. "Listen, pal," he said, in the frigid tone that anger lent him, "We have the periscope of the submarine before our very eyes. Mother Atomos is in the process of setting sail, and I'm telling you that if the reinforcements haven't stitched up the lake before eleven thirty you'll be looking for a new job. How many guys have you sent?"

There was a strangled cough. After a pause, an authoritative voice vibrated in the earpieces. "This is General Ireland. Are you the one who's seen a submarine in Whitney?"

Beffort understood that nothing had been done. "General," he said, "I'm warning you that if two regiments aren't in place at the specified time, I'll have you court-martialed. I'm Smith Beffort, specially commissioned by J. Edgar Hoover to the Atomos affair, and as the temporary head of the FBI I have the right to requisition civilians, the police, the army, the navy and the air force!"

"But a submarine…!"

"Nothing less!" Beffort interjected, ferociously. "Get moving and send the two regiments I'm asking for immediately. Send artillery too, and alert the FBI office in New York. This is no hoax, Ireland—it's a matter of Madame Atomos!"

Chapter XIV

At eleven fifteen on that same Monday February seventeenth, a wind of panic swept through Dallas and its surrounding area. The Pooley was gaining ground everywhere, threatening Denton, Allen, Wylie, Royce City and Wills Point.

In Dallas itself, they were fighting at close quarters with flame-throwers, and tons of water were poured out in the streets—but that was a petty flood by comparison with the tempest of a few hours ago. The Pooley hesitated on the ground, but scaled the houses, coiffed buildings, extended over roofs and came down again along the facades like chocolate cream spreading over a rice-cake.

George Cooper had no need to order an evacuation. It was taking place automatically. Women, children and old men had left the city, and no one remained behind but the army, the police and a corps of civilian volunteers.

At eleven forty-five the Pooley formed a vast set of pincers biting into University Park and Highland Park to the north and bearing down on Fruitdale in the south.

A convoy of three hundred trucks moved into the city shortly thereafter. They were distributed along Harry Hines Boulevard and Zang Boulevard, and the tons of paper they were transporting were unloaded. Thus, Dallas was cut in two, and Love Field Airport sacrificed. An attempt was made to protect Arcadia Park, where Professor Manning's laboratory was located, and escape-routes heading west to Irving, Grand Prairie, Arlington and Fort Worth.

The paper was set alight, and a barrier of fire stopped the Pooley, even obliging it to retreat a few yards—but the witnesses knew perfectly well that it was only temporary.

"In less than thirty minutes," Cooper said, bitterly, "We'll have burned the lot."

"Other trucks are on the way," his assistant replied.

Cooper coughed in the smoke, and waved his arm broadly to indicate the horizon. "If the Pooley's blocked here," he said, "it's advancing everywhere else. I can tell you what will happen: we'll be encircled, without any way out, before mid-afternoon, and the trucks will no longer be able to reach us."

"Aircraft will still be able to parachute in combustible materials."

"And what then? One corner of Dallas won't be covered for a certain period of time, but will be abandoned as soon as the efforts of the scientists prove vain! Take me to the laboratory, Guderian—we're going to see what Manning and Soblen are cooking up!"

The G-man launched his car through the deserted streets and stopped outside the laboratory. Cooper leapt out. He found himself face to face with the two scientists, who were carrying a hermetically-sealed milk churn and a vaporizer pump.

"Where are you going?" Cooper asked.

"You've arrived at the right moment," Manning replied. "Do you know where we can find the....what's it called, Soblen?"

"The Pooley," said Soblen, without laughing.

Cooper jumped. "Do I know where you can find it!" he howled. "There's no one in the entire world who doesn't know!"

Manning and Soblen exchanged glances, and Manning said: "Then be kind enough to take us there, Mr. Cooper. We want to sprinkle a little of our product on it."

"You've found it!"

Soblen coughed. "We don't know yet. The fragment of the Pooley that we possessed suddenly went up in smoke, but we're not entirely sure which mixture obtained the result."

Cooley was dumbstruck.

"Don't worry," said Manning. "We've kept all the formulas, in spite of everything. Are you going to take us, or do we have to go on foot?"

Cooper opened the car doors, helped the two men to load the milk churn, took charge of the vaporizer, and the car set off again toward Zang Boulevard.

"What's making that smoke?" Manning asked.

"Fire, professor."

"Ha ha!" said Manning. "I suspected as much."

Soblen started laughing as well, and George Cooper had a sudden desire to hit them. He restrained himself, and added: "The fire that we lit to stop the Pooley in order that it wouldn't cover your lab. As we don't have your intelligence, you see, we use whatever comes to hand."

Soblen sniggered. "Paper, for example," he said. "But I was the one who first suggested it to you, wasn't I? Now, my dear Cooper, tell your man to put his foot down. My colleague and I are exhausted...."

Cooper realized that he had been unfair. After all, if the Pooley could be vanquished, it would be thanks to these two men. He and everyone else had done nothing but agitate vainly, spreading water and lighting fires like children playing Cowboys and Indians.

The driver slammed on the brakes and the car came to a halt behind the curtain of flames.

"Put that out for me!" said Nelson Manning, indignantly. "We'll choke in this smoke!"

Cooper gave orders for a passage to be opened and went back to his passengers, who were unloading their equipment. "Can I help you?" he asked.

"No," said Soblen, firmly. "Let us work in peace, please."

Cooper watched them work, seething. They opened the churn with infinite care, slowly tipped it over and transferred some of its contents to the vaporizer's reservoir. Then Manning sealed the churn again, while Soblen watched, and then pushed it gently up against the wheel of the car. Afterwards, he took a crumpled sheet of paper out of his shirt pocket, consulted it, and said: "Now that I think about it, I wonder if we really did keep all the formulas?"

Soblen took off his glasses, rubbed is eyes, put them on again and replied: "I think so. Are you going to carry this device?"

"That's what we agreed?"

"Put your mask on, then."

Manning rummaged in his pockets, opened his jacket, searched his waistcoat and trousers, and said: "I don't have it."

Cooper was scarlet with fury. "Listen," he barked. "Can this liquid destroy the Pooley or can't it?"

Manning and Pooley started laughing. "We don't know," Manning said. "We're here to try it out."

"Well get on with it!" Cooper howled.

"We will," said Manning, calmly, "but we need to find the mask."

Soblen took his handkerchief out of his pocket and found the mask rolled up inside it, retained by a knot. Manning puffed out his cheeks like an idiot.

Cooper finally realized that the two men were dead on their feet, drunk with fatigue. If he left them to it, they would doubtless vaporize their product in all directions and spoil their chance, if they had one. That observation suddenly calmed him down, and he changed tactics immediately. "Professor," he said, deferentially, "that reservoir looks very heavy to me."

"Don't worry, Cooper," said Manning, tottering. "I'm still capable of carrying it. I can carry it, can't I, Soblen?"

"Of course!" exclaimed the little doctor. "We've filled it. We've got it this far. Why wouldn't we be able to carry it?"

Manning had no succeeded in attaching the mask to his face correctly, and went to sit down on the footboard of the car. Soblen sat down on the churn, leaning back against the bodywork. Within two minutes, he was asleep. It was almost funny, but in the circumstances, things were in danger of becoming disastrous. Cooper signaled to Guderian. The later grabbed hold of Dr. Soblen, and deposited him gently on the back seat. Cooper picked up the mask that Manning had just dropped and adjusted it over his mouth and nose.

"Let them sleep," he said, for the benefit of the men who were approaching. "We'll wake them up if the product has any effect. Guderian, help me to fix his thing on my back."

The assistant lifted up the vaporizer. Cooper adjusted the straps, set his left hand on the lever controlling the pump, and took the nozzle in his other hand. He started walking, went through the passage that the volunteers had opened up in the barrier of fire, and approached the Pooley.

Everyone held their breath when he activated the pump. The liquid spread out in the air in a fine cloud, whose drops fell on to the Pooley.

For a second or two, nothing happened. Then, brutally, the bloody substance folded upon and retreated ten yards.

Cooper started again, further on, and the same phenomenon was repeated. Then he went back to the area that he had originally sprayed, and activated the pump again. This time, the Pooley disintegrated, fuming, and became nothing more than a formless paste, which a jet of water dissolved completely.

The men started howling with joy, and Cooper came back to the car. "Wake them up!" he shouted.

Soblen and Manning were roused unceremoniously from their sleep, set on their feet and shaken so ferociously that they opened terrified eyes.

"You've succeeded!" Cooper said, emphatically. "Now we need to send the formula to the factory."

Soblen pulled free vigorously. He seemed to have recovered all his lucidity. "Nelson!" he said to his colleague. "We need to go back to the lab. Cooper, get busy finding vaporizers like this one and prepare masks. Tell your men to use their handkerchiefs—they'll be perfectly adequate with the corners knotted. We also need reservoirs. The factory can put out five thousand liters of anti-Pooley an hour, and should reach twenty thousand after running in for a couple of hours...."

"We'll start right away," Cooper said.

"In that case, put a trustworthy man in charge of this churn. It contains twenty liters. If he can sprinkle it without wasting any of the product, we can work out from the surface area destroyed how much liquid we'll need."

Guderian put the straps over his shoulders, and attacked the Pooley while the car drew off.

Cooper left the two scientists at the laboratory after making sure that they had telephoned the formula to the chemical factory, and returned to the center of operations at top speed. A hundred vaporizers were already strewn on the ground. Stores stocking agricultural material were being cleared of such items, and men were patching on the nozzles of flame-throwers. Cooper had the cargoes of paper taken off the trucks and sent them to the factory in order to pick up supplies of anti-Pooley.

Having done that, he went to collect Manning and Soblen, and took them back to the place where Guderian had finished emptying his vaporizer. In fifteen minutes, a hundred square meters of Pooley had been reduced to harmless mud, which was being digested by the gurgling drains.

Chapter XV

At eleven thirty, as Smith Beffort had demanded, Lake Whitney was completely surrounded by armed men. There was a sentry posted every hundred paces. Batteries of rapid-fire artillery were distributed along the west bank, and four navy launches were plowing through the murky water.

The helicopter had been filled up in Waco, and was now criss-crossing the lake in all directions. Madame Atomos's submarine had not been seen again, but at the slightest sign of anything protruding from the water the alert was immediately sounded.

In the helicopter, Beffort and Akamatsu were becoming annoyed.

"In your opinion," Beffort asked the Tokkoka man, "How long can a submarine of that size remain underwater?"

The Japanese agent shrugged his shoulders. "I don't know," he said, "but it seems to me that it would be in danger after an hour or two."

He pilot turned round once again over the north shore, and said: "At any rate, the submarine will have to surface eventually. Time is against Madame Atomos." He pointed to the soldiers, the artillery, the trucks and the launches, and continued: "How do you expect her to deal with all of that!"

Beffort and Akamatsu exchanged glances. They both knew the diabolical cleverness of Madame Atomos, and would not swear to anything until the redoubtable woman was in front of them, dead or alive.

And even then…!

"No one has seen her face," Beffort murmured. "Those who have got close to her are dead, and we only have an old identity photograph. Mrs. Maxell was in the same house, and heard her voice, but is incapable of saying what she looks like...."

Yosho lowered his eyelids. "It doesn't matter," he said. "Madame Atomos is in the submersible now. She has never been in such a delicate situation, and doesn't have a chance in a million of giving us the slip."

Beffort, who had been scrutinizing the lake for some time, straightened up. "What's happening in Dallas?" he asked the pilot.

The latter took off his earphones. "Take these," he said. "The base at Fort Hood's passing on information continually."

Beffort started listening, and heard the clear voice of the military operator.

"....that hundreds of men are driving back the Pooley. Fifty airplanes normally used for spraying insecticide are also spreading the anti-Pooley perfected by Dr. Alan Soblen and Professor Nelson Manning. A message from George Cooper, Deputy Director of the FBI, tells us that the Pooley will soon be no more than a bad memory. The inhabitants of Dallas are returning o the city in droves. The authorities have requested that everyone wait until the end of the day before returning to their homes. The roads need to be kept clear. The anti-Pooley is being transported around Dallas in trucks, and nothing must get in the way of these vehicles...."

There was a brief interruption, and the speaker continued: "The temporary bureau of information set up in Dallas has just released its latest bulletin. I quote: Two areas of the city are being cleared as a matter of priority, because it's known that people, including two children, were trapped there. Unfortunately, the rescuers have only found dead bodies. In the first place, there is the matter of two young boys, Jack and Gregory Maxwell, and soldiers of the fifth armored division, whose tanks were covered by the Pooley. Here is the list of confirmed victims: Robert Murphy, of Charleston; Richard Lyons, of...."

Smith Beffort, distressed, took off the earphones, informed Akamatsu that Dallas as being liberated, and the three men fell silent again.

Suddenly, the pilot swerved sharply, went into a steep dive, and leveled off just above the surface. At the same time, Akamatsu and Beffort saw the thin stalk of a periscope. Then the apparatus climbed steeply again.

"It was a miracle that I saw it!" cried the pilot, excitedly. "What shall we do, Boss?"

"Inform the navy," said Beffort, immediately.

"What do you want them to do?" Akamatsu asked.

"We need to end this," the G-man said. "I'm afraid that woman will succeed in getting away. By surfacing briefly from time to time she can renew her oxygen-supplies and hold out until nightfall. When it gets dark, surveillance of the lake will become difficult, if not impossible."

Akamatsu frowned. "You want the launches to drop grenades?"

Beffort looked him straight in the eye. "I know what you're thinking, Yosho, but I'd rather see Madame Atomos dead than in flight! Besides, she'll never let us take her alive. We have to seize our chance now, for that she-devil will take advantage of any hesitation."

Impassively, Akamatsu made a fatalistic gesture. "Go ahead," he said, "We do, indeed, need to end this...."

The pilot consulted Beffort with the gaze, and seized his mike in response to a gesture of acceptance. "BX 310 here," he said, "calling the navy."

"Receiving you. Speak."

"I'm directly above the submarine right now. Smith Beffort orders you to fire grenades immediately."

"Received and understood. Will follow orders. Over and out."

"Over and out."

The pilot gained altitude but remained directly above the periscope, which was still visible. The submersible remained immobile while the interception launches approached, sending up sprays of foam.

Beffort and Akamatsu were glued to their seats. Death was hurtling down on Madame Atomos and, for the first time, the sinister woman seemed unaware of the danger. The two men could not believe it, and their tension mounted as the launches drew closer.

Suddenly, the periscope sank—but it was obvious that the maneuver had been carried out too late. The leading launch passed over the exact spot designated by the helicopter and drew away again; then the water trembled and six geysers erupted, while waves rolled away toward the tranquil shores.

The other vessels each made a pass, without respite, and the lake was transformed into a witch's cauldron.

Beffort leaned over, staring at the water stirred up by the explosions. As if to convince himself, he murmured: "She can't get out of that. It's physically impossible."

There was an awkward moment of delay, and then a large patch of oil emerged and spread out over the seething surface.

"Go down," Beffort said to the pilot, and land on the shore. For you, it's over. You can go back to Dallas."

It was four o'clock in the afternoon when the floating dock slowly hoisted the wreck to the surface. The rain had started falling again, and the lake was lugubrious.

An enormous crowd had gathered on the shore. TV and radio networks were transmitting and commenting on the spectacle. It was known that the Pooley had been almost completely destroyed and that Madame Atomos was dead. The sellers of ice creams and hot dogs were making a fortune, and a fairground atmosphere was sweeping the United States.

Akamatsu, Beffort and the Boss, however, standing on the edge of the floating dock, were still stony-faced. The Boss's teeth were planted gum-deep in his cigar, and his was so preoccupied that he had let it go out. He had landed in Waco a short while before, had rushed out of his jet, and had been on the rainswept floating dock ever since, as mute and motionless as a statue.

The chains grated one last time, and a somber mass emerged from the water. Men assembled to its right, hauling on the cable. The pocket submarine swayed after coming entirely free of the liquid element, and its damaged prow scraped the deck. As the crane released the cable it leaned sideways.

They knew that the submarine had taken on water, and that it had been ten fathoms down on the lake bed while the floating dock was brought to the lake. They also knew that no bodies had risen to the surface—that Madame Atomos was still a prisoner in that steel coffin....

It only remained to verify the last point.

The navy men detached the lines, and they waited for the submersible to vomit up all its water. When that was done, a specialist went into the wreck via the breach, remained invisible for a few moments, and reappeared on the conning-tower.

In the poor light, everyone could see that he was pale, as tense as a coiled spring, and that his hands were trembling.

The Boss leapt forward. "Have you seen her?" he spat.

The man shook his head negatively. "The submarine is empty," he said. That produced a profound silence. Then he added: "It was never piloted by Madame Atomos or anyone else."

"What?" said the Boss, in a strangled manner.

The man jabbed a thumb at the conning-tower. "Go see for yourself," he said. "The machine was remote controlled, and stuffed with explosives. If the electrical circuitry hadn't been destroyed when it was sunk, who knows what might have happened? It would have dealt the launches a nasty blow!"

He continued to explain what he thought, but the Boss was no longer listening. He looked at Beffort and Akamatsu, who were thunderstruck, thinking that there was nothing left to do but hand in their resignations. They would not be at the tiller when Madame Atomos reappeared!

"What if her corpse is at the bottom of the lake?" someone asked.

"Surely she's dead!"

The Boss pricked up his ears. He was almost ready to believe it...

Madame Atomos' Xmas

by Jean-Marc & Randy Lofficier

Winter had come early that year and, with the approach of Thanksgiving, consumers' thoughts had already turned towards Christmas.

Dallas had hung its traditional season's decorations
across its boulevards and avenues, and the department
stores on Market Street had begun to decorate their windows accordingly.

There was enough of a chill in the air to easily con-
jure up images of turkey and roasted chestnuts.

Madame Atomos was dejectedly watching the efforts of a clumsy department store employee, promoted
to decorator for the occasion, to hang a red plastic Santa
Claus above an impressive pile of newly-arrived color
televisions.

It was the hour of the local news broadcast.

Only a few months before, her first attack against
the country she hated so much had failed miserably.
However, she had succeeded in inflicting thousands of
deaths upon her sworn enemy: the United States of
America. Still, all that had happened on the East Coast
and the few Texans who knew the truth, despite the
news blackout arranged by the FBI, were used to their
Eastern colleagues' exaggerations. In fact, the good citizens of the Lone Star State took the whole thing with a
hefty grain of salt. Wasn't New York where a giant ape
had allegedly once climbed the Empire State Building?
Hadn't they been told about a flying saucer and a giant

silver robot paralyzing Washington DC? And what about that bronze fella and all his gimmicks? No, really, a good Texan couldn't very well believe in all the tall tales that one read in Eastern papers.

The store employee had just failed to hook the Santa Claus for the third time. Madame Atomos sighed. She had stopped there to look at the local news to see if they reported any suspicious troop movements or special security measures being taken locally. Her next plan would start with the destruction of Texas and her latest discovery, a virtually indestructible plasmoid substance, was slowly maturing at her secret base, located not far away, near the property of a trusting rancher named Calvin Pooley.

Despite her scientific knowledge, Madame Atomos had a poor understanding of American society, much of which left her perplexed. Yet, she realized that, in order to destroy America, she had to gain a better understanding of it. That's why she forced herself, whenever she could, to watch the news–she favored CBS–and, especially, the local news which was often full of revealing details.

But today, this stupid, clumsy man was disturbing her concentration.

Madame Atomos turned the stone of her ring, which looked like a large ruby in a gold setting. It emitted a thin red beam, no thicker than a human hair, which went through the glass and pierced the employee's skull. The man's brain, suddenly subjected to incredibly high temperatures, exploded. He dropped to the floor, where he remained still. A few rivulets of bloodied brain matter began to seep from his nose and ears.

Madame Atomos sighed again and walked off into the night. As she crossed Elm Street, she realized she was bored.

Suddenly, a bit of news she had just watched on television gave her an idea. A magnificent idea. A smile appeared fleetingly on her razor-thin lips. A diabolical plan was already forming inside her prodigious mind. It wouldn't take much more than ten days to execute it, she thought. And her plasmoid wouldn't be ready, in any event, before the new year.

Ten days... Why not twelve days? As in that insipid song, *The Twelve Days of Christmas* that some stores had already begun to play.

The Twelve Days of Christmas, indeed! Why, it would be her own Christmas gift to herself!

Twelve days later exactly–Madame Atomos prided herself on punctuality!–the guinea pig whom she had personally selected and who had just been subjected to an intensive nuclear treatment, was, for the last time, sitting attached to a metal chair in an underground base located near Calvin Pooley's ranch.

Everything was ready. But Madame Atomos left nothing to chance. She had to have the man repeat her instructions one last time.

"Tell me again what you're supposed to do, Mr. Lee Harvey Oswald," whispered the deadly Madame Atomos.[3]

---

[3] According to several reliable witnesses, Lee Harvey Oswald, during the last months of his life, when some of his whereabouts remain unknown to this day, had changed physically, experiencing unexplained hair loss and premature aging.

SF & FANTASY

Guy d'Armen. *Doc Ardan: The City of Gold and Lepers*
G.-J. Arnaud. *The Ice Company*
Aloysius Bertrand. *Gaspard de la Nuit*
Félix Bodin. *The Novel of the Future*
André Caroff. *The Terror of Madame Atomos*
Didier de Chousy. *Ignis*
C. I. Defontenay. *Star (Psi Cassiopeia)*
Charles Derennes. *The People of the Pole*
Harry Dickson. *The Heir of Dracula*
 Sâr Dubnotal *vs. Jack the Ripper*
Alexandre Dumas. *The Return of Lord Ruthven*
J.-C. Dunyach. *The Night Orchid. The Thieves of Silence*
Paul Féval. *Anne of the Isles. Knightshade. Revenants. Vampire City. The Vampire Countess. The Wandering Jew's Daughter*
Paul Féval, *fils. Felifax, the Tiger-Man*
Arnould Galopin. *Doctor Omega*
V. Hugo, Foucher & Meurice. *The Hunchback of Notre-Dame*
O. Joncquel & Theo Varlet. *The Martian Epic*
Jean de La Hire. *Enter the Nyctalope. The Nyctalope on Mars. The Nyctalope vs. Lucifer*
G. Le Faure & H. de Graffigny. *The Extraordinary Adventures of a Russian Scientist Across the Solar System* (2 vols.)
Gustave Le Rouge. *The Vampires of Mars*
Jules Lermina. *Panic in Paris. To-Ho and the Gold Destroyers. Mysteryville.*
Jean-Marc & Randy Lofficier. *Edgar Allan Poe on Mars. The Katrina Protocol. Pacifica. Robonocchio.* (anthologists) *Tales of the Shadowmen* (6 vols.) (non-fiction) *Shadowmen* (2 vols.)
Xavier Mauméjean. *The League of Heroes*
Marie Nizet. *Captain Vampire*
C. Nodier, Beraud & Toussaint-Merle. *Frankenstein*
Henri de Parville. *An Inhabitant of the Planet Mars*
Polidori, C. Nodier, E. Scribe. *Lord Ruthven the Vampire*
P.-A. Ponson du Terrail. *The Vampire and the Devil's Son*

Maurice Renard. *Doctor Lerne. A Man Among the Microbes. The Blue Peril*

Albert Robida. *The Clock of the Centuries. The Adventures of Saturnin Farandoul*

J.-H. Rosny Aîné. *The Navigators of Space. The World of the Variants*

Brian Stableford. *The Shadow of Frankenstein. Frankenstein and the Vampire Countess. The New Faust at the Tragicomique. Sherlock Holmes & The Vampires of Eternity. The Stones of Camelot. The Wayward Muse.* (anthologist) *The Germans on Venus. News from the Moon*

Kurt Steiner. *Ortog*

Villiers de l'Isle-Adam. *The Scaffold. The Vampire Soul*

Philippe Ward. *Artahe*

MYSTERIES & THRILLERS

M. Allain & P. Souvestre. *The Daughter of Fantômas*

Anicet-Bourgeois, Lucien Dabril. *Rocambole*

A. Bisson & G. Livet. *Nick Carter vs. Fantômas*

V. Darlay & H. de Gorsse. *Lupin vs. Holmes: The Stage Play*

Paul Féval. *The Black Coats: The Companions of the Treasure. Gentlemen of the Night. Heart of Steel. The Invisible Weapon. John Devil. The Parisian Jungle. 'Salem Street*

Emile Gaboriau. *Monsieur Lecoq*

Steve Leadley. *Sherlock Holmes: The Circle of Blood*

Maurice Leblanc. *Arsène Lupin: The Hollow Needle. The Blonde Phantom*

Gaston Leroux. *Chéri-Bibi. The Phantom of the Opera. Rouletabille & the Mystery of the Yellow Room*

G. Marot & L. Pericaud. *Nick Carter vs. Jack the Ripper*

William Patrick Maynard. *The Terror of Fu Manchu*

Frank J. Morlock. *Sherlock Holmes: The Grand Horizontals*

P. de Wattyne & Y. Walter. *Sherlock Holmes vs. Fantômas*

David White. *Fantômas in America*